HEART OF A BEAST

Josephine de Moor

HEART OF A BEAST

Josephine de Moor

DoctorZed
Publishing
www.doctorzed.com

First published 2012 by DoctorZed Publishing.

DoctorZed Publishing books may be ordered through booksellers or by contacting:

DoctorZed Publishing
IDAHO
10 Vista Ave
Skye, South Australia 5072
www.doctorzed.com
61-(0)8 8431-4965

ISBN: 978-0-9872495-9-3 (sc)
ISBN: 978-0-9873452-0-2 (e)

A CIP number for this book is available at the National Library of Australia.

This is a work of fiction. Names, characters, places, events, and dialogues are creations of the author or are used fictitiously. Any resemblance to any individuals, alive or dead, is purely coincidental. The views expressed in this work are solely those of the author and do not necessarily reflect the views of the publisher, and the publisher hereby disclaims any responsibility for them.

Cover image Dreamstime.com stock imagery © Alisa Astrouskaya.

Printed in Australia
DoctorZed Publishing rev. date: 08/08/2012

For my husband and soul mate, Robin, and dearest friend Karen Sessa, for all their continued support and encouragement.

ACKNOWLEDGMENTS

First and foremost I would like to thank my long suffering husband and soul mate, Robin, for believing in me even when I didn't.

A very big thank you must go to my dear friends, Karen Sessa and Christine Smith, my auntie, Margaret Butcher, my daughter, Katrina Dennis, and my sisters, Belinda Morrissey and Leanne Zyner, for proof reading and sharing their many valuable suggestions with me.

And I can't forget Karen's husband Ercole Sessa for his wonderful culinary skills that helped Karen and me through many a rough day.

Thanks also to Louise Cusack, author of romantic fantasy, for mentoring me through the early stages of writing this novel and to the members of The MacLeay Island Writers Group for their fresh perspective on my work.

I really must thank all the tour guides on Norfolk Island, who unbeknown to them, helped me with my background research and to the authors of the many reference books written about the second settlement – too many to name individually. I would also like to acknowledge those convicts who lived through these harrowing times and shared their experiences with us through diaries including Martin Cash, John Knatchbull and John F Mortlock.

Finally, my heartfelt gratitude goes to Dr. Scott Zarcinas for taking a chance with *Heart of a Beast* and editing it so brilliantly.

"Let a man's heart be what it will when he comes here, his Man's heart is taken from him, and he is given the heart of a Beast."

Robert Douglas – convict, Norfolk Island, 1834

Chapter One

October, 1847

"Devil's breath!"

Edmund Thornton swore as the bow of The Governor Phillip crashed through yet another wave, tossing him off balance. Spreading his feet further apart to combat the roll of the ship, he vigorously rubbed his hands and arms, trying to get the blood flowing. "Give me God's solid earth to stand on, instead of this infernal moving water. I joined a Regiment of Foot not the blessed Navy!" He stared at the endless horizon of the grey-blue Pacific, wishing more than ever it was the Atlantic, wishing more than ever that his destination was the fog-draped cliffs of Devon instead of the rocky speck of misery he was headed to.

The sound of heavy boots and the brusque orders of the junior officers broke into his thoughts. As he descended the stairs from the quarterdeck down to the deck below he watched the men of the 11th Regiment of Foot, *his* regiment, convening on the main deck. Although young, most had not even attained his own two and twenty years, to a man they took their duties very seriously. He was proud of them. They looked resplendent in their uniform: red jackets with white webbing crisscrossing their chests and grey trousers, their bayonets glistening in the last rays of the day's sun, a splash of colour on an otherwise drab deck.

"FA-L-L IN!" bellowed the sergeant, then turning he saluted Edmund. "All present and correct lieutenant, sir!"

Clasping his hands behind his back he inspected the rows of assembled troop with a critical eye. "Men, our journey comes near to its end today. We will be disembarking on the morn." A cheer erupted from the men. Raising his hand to silence them, he continued, "I hope you have all enjoyed your brief sojourn aboard this brig, because once we land your duties will truly begin. Be warned. Duty in Her Majesty's Penal colony of Norfolk Island will be no picnic. The convicts sent here are considered to be the most incorrigible in colonies and will certainly test all our mettle before we are finished. When I give the order to disembark I expect all kits packed and ready, all boots blackened, all buttons shone, all leggings and shoulder straps pipe-clayed, and all muskets immaculately clean. Is that clearly understood? I want the men of this guard to come ashore as a credit to our beloved Eleventh.' He paused. "Right then, till the morrow, dismiss the men, sergeant."

Deeply inhaling some last breaths of sea air Edmund climbed down the steps that led from the deck into the bowels of the brig towards his cabin. Without thinking he shoved open the cabin door and stepped in, striking his head hard on the low door lintel.

"Devil's breath! When will I learn?" he cussed himself as he dropped into his hammock holding his now throbbing head. Although a seasoned traveller by ship he still had not learnt that, while below decks, normal daily routines for a man who stood roughly six foot in his stocking feet were severely curtailed. Given the cramped and continually moving conditions that his cabin afforded he undressed with some difficulty. Leisurely he stretched his now bare muscular arms, the fingertips of each broad hand brushing against the walls of his cabin.

Lying back in his hammock, sleep eluding him, he stared at the deck beams only a few feet above him. The sound of the waves beating against the timbers of the brig as it lurched and swayed towards its destination pounded in his head, each wave taking him further away from his beloved Sarah. His thoughts shifted to the past. He might only be the second son and unlikely to inherit, but inherit what? He had no intention of following his father into the law and politics. He would leave that for his studious older brother, James. No, he was the athletic one, the son who loved to ride, hunt, and practice sword fighting, the one who loved to gamble. He knew his father had believed he was doing him a great favour when he purchased a commission into the military for him. It had been a fortuitous escape from his creditors, yet his new life had taken him to the other side of the world, far from Sarah, but then his father didn't understand about Sarah. Would he ever again gaze into her sapphire blue eyes, hear the gentle softness of her voice, or feel the silken touch of her hand? Pushing these thoughts from his mind he turned to happier times, happier times with her. Brilliant colours swirled before him, slowly taking on shape.

He drifted into a light sleep as he pictured Sarah and himself strolling together through the well-manicured grounds of his father's Devon estate. But then dark clouds formed on the horizon pushing the images in front of him into shadow.

Another apparition began to haunt his dream, taking the shape of another man. Sarah screamed as the man stumbled in front of her, desperately reaching out for her. Thick stone walls started to rise out the ground around him. Invisible claws ripped at his clothes, his hair grew long and matted. Exhausted, he fell to the ground, pulling his knees to his chest and rocking backwards and forwards, crying out in misery, *"I didn't tell, I didn't tell!"*

He woke in a cold sweat, momentarily confused by his surroundings. He propped himself up on his elbows. "Damn him. Damn everything about him!"

The walls of the cramped, airless cabin seemed to close in on him and for a moment a suffocating feeling of claustrophobia engulfed him. Then it was gone. He smirked. Ironic, wasn't it? Who was really the prisoner, Edmund Thornton or Michael Hanlan?

The light of the early dawn seeped through the slits in his panelled walls making rainbow patterns throughout the cabin. Sliding his braces over his shoulders he grabbed for his uniform jacket. Shoving open his cabin door he escaped into the corridor and made his way up towards the open deck.

Eerie stillness greeted Edmund as he emerged from the darkness below. The sails of the brig hung limp, no wind blew, the choppy seas of the previous day were now gone. Long tendrils of mist twisted upwards from the glassy waters, wrapping around the hull of the brig like the fingers of some ghostly sea monster.

"Just keep her full and by," the captain ordered the man at the helm. "You there," he grabbed another sailor, "ring the ship's bell." Then he ordered to yet another. "And you there, grab a horn and get to the forecastle. I want to hear a constant sound at both ends of the ship to give warning to any other ships that might be in the vicinity."

A grotesque shape began to materialize on the horizon through the fog, shrouded in deep red clouds. The island loomed up before them. To Edmund, the red dawn staining the heavy mist hanging low over the island gave it the appearance of volcanic fire, indeed the very fires of hell. Unseen sea birds squealed overhead like souls of the damned. Edmund glanced up, tilting his head. It was as the rumours said: this was the island on which Satan never slept.

An old sailor clinging to the rigging above found his voice and began to sing, a haunting sea shanty that sent an icy shiver down Edmund's spine:

> *"Did you ever see the Devil?*
> *With his wooden spade and shovel*
> *A digging of potatoes*
> *With his tail cocked up…*

From out of the mist, other sailors answered him in chorus:

> *No I never saw the Devil*
> *With his wooden spade and shovel*
> *A digging of potatoes*
> *With his tail cocked up."*

The cry of "Land O" shouted from above by the watch in the crow's nest interrupted the shanty.

4

"And none too soon," Edmund muttered.

"I beg your pardon, Lieutenant?"

Edmund turned to acknowledge the presence of the Captain of The Governor Phillip standing close behind him. "Nothing, Captain, just longing to stand on something solid again."

"Indeed it's been a long three weeks from Hobart Town. But I can assure you that your ordeal is almost over. Here." The captain offered Edmund a spyglass. "Take a look at your new home, what you can see of her at least."

Taking the spyglass Edmund focused on the island of felons that was to be his home for the foreseeable future.

"Does she meet you expectations?"

"Not quite sure sir. I have heard such conflicting opinions. Most say it's a place of extreme punishment, yet others wax lyrical about its beauty."

"But beware, lieutenant, beauty on the surface can hide all manner of darker, unspeakable demons beneath its façade." The captain's sarcasm was not lost on Edmund.

Through the spyglass the island appeared dull and unwelcoming. In the now fading colours of the dawn, massive cliffs jutted out of the churning sea. Immense waves smashed against them in huge sprays of foam that spat through the air as though alive. Even from this distance Edmund could taste the salt that the waves were tossing into the air. Above the foaming waves, on the peaks of the cliffs, he spied a forest of dark, sombre trees.

"The pines, captain, are truly magnificent."

"Yes indeed and in most places quite impregnable. A formidable prison from whence there can be no hope of escape don't you think?"

As Edmund watched, the scene before him changed. The mists lifted and bright sunlight now bathed the landscape. As the sun rose higher, colours became more vivid, the naked grandeur of the cliffs became more apparent, the pines less foreboding, now with areas of open space around them. The waves still crashed against the cliffs but with less ferocity than they had just moments before;

the plumes of sprays becoming more translucent. Now, for the first time he recognised signs of human habitation. He could just make out a ramshackle collection of dirty, grey buildings set against a background of deep greens and browns on the only piece of low lying land he could so far discern, not at all the fearful sight that he had half expected to see.

Edmund's attention was momentarily averted from his new home to the striking peak of another island jutting at least one thousand feet out of the sea to his right, just before Norfolk Island itself. It, too, was clouded in red mists.

The captain noticed the puzzled frown on Edmund's face and turned to look in the direction of Edmund's spyglass. "I think you'll find you are looking at Phillip Island. Damn fine hunting on that island. Bit of a hefty climb though."

"I didn't realise that there were two islands, sir."

"Actually there are three, lieutenant. The other is known as Nepean Island, really just a rocky outcrop, of no use to man or beast."

The wind was kind to The Governor Phillip for the last part of her journey to Norfolk Island. By mid-afternoon the crew was making preparations to drop anchor in Sydney Bay. An unfortunate name, thought Edmund, the bay now in front of him paled in comparison with the beautiful Sydney Harbour he had anchored in New South Wales.

The first mate arrived at the captain's side. "The landing place is in sight, sir."

"Very well. Give the order to shorten sail."

"Aye-aye, sir. Shorten Sail," hollered the first mate.

"We seem a long way from the shore, captain. Can we not get closer?" Edmund enquired.

The captain pointed at the line of breaking waves over a submerged reef Edmund had not noticed before.... "Send this message to shore if you please." The captain instructed the midshipman in charge of the Marryat signal flags. "The Governor Phillip from Hobart with troops, convicts and supplies." Then he turned to Edmund. "And now we wait, lieutenant. We have shown them that we have not been taken by pirates and we need to be sure that the convicts have not mutinied and taken possession of the island."

"They are signalling back, sir."

"Is it the current secret password?"

The first mate confirmed that it was. The captain's and Edmund's attention was then directed to a signal flag flying close to the landing place.

"What say they now?" enquired the captain.

"Heave to. Will send a boat aboard, sir."

Edmund let out a sigh of relief. The captain said, "It seems, lieutenant, our brief acquaintance is coming to an end. Umm… wait a minute our acquaintance may yet be extended." He checked the shore once more with his spy glass. "Look, can you see Lieutenant? The watch on the island has raised the blue flag meaning that the bar is too dangerous to cross." He checked out the reef. "That's very odd. To me it seems quiet today, especially compared to other crossings I have witnessed. Ah, wait," he focused his glass. "That's better. They have realised their mistake. They have lowered the blue flag and now hoisted the red one." He scanned the shore for any sign of movement. "Yes, look," he lowered the glass and handed it to Edmund. "They are sending a boat. You will be pleased to know that your ordeal will be over in about a half hour."

As Edmund watched, a large barge propelled by about a dozen rowers, presumably convict, judging by their dull grey garb, was making its way steadily towards The Governor Phillip. Once it had been firmly roped to the side the Clerk of the Commissariat boarded.

"Lieutenant Thornton? Captain Travers has requested that you come across in the first barge if you please sir."

Edmund readily agreed, eager to get back onto dry land. Transferring command to the sergeant, he made ready to take his leave.

The clerk looked at Edmund outfitted in full dress uniform, his regimental jacket trimmed in the gold and green of the Eleventh, sabre strapped to his waist, shako on his head. "Lieutenant, may I respectfully suggest that you remove your dress jacket, sabre and shako and stow them safely in your kit as I cannot guarantee you will remain dry."

Bemused, Edmund did as he was instructed and packed them into his kit bag. Then tossing it to the men in the barge he started to climb down the rope ladder.

"Watch your step, sir... stop!" The coxswain on the barge called as Edmund lost his footing and hung on by only one hand as a large wave drenched him from head to foot. He tried desperately to regain his foothold on the ladder, thankful when he felt a firm hand around his ankle, manoeuvring his foot back to the safety of the ladder rung. After a few more steps he seated himself on a bench in the middle of the barge.

The coxswain removed a dry blanket from under the bench, kept there for just such an event, and handed it to Edmund. "Here, sir, wrap this around you," he said. "Very few arrive on the island dry."

Grateful, Edmund wrapped the blanket around his shoulders. Trying to stop himself from shivering he grabbed the edge of the narrow wooden bench and watched dubiously as Norfolk Island drew closer. He noticed with some trepidation that the swell was getting rougher. White caps now began to break over the reef and he began to wonder just how on earth the barge was going to negotiate the reef.

The coxswain pointed to a beacon that he was steering towards. "See that beacon? It has been placed on the reef where there's safe passage," he explained. "Have only capsized once. We'll easily get through today." The man watched the water and waited for the perfect wave to propel them safely through.

Less than half an hour later the barge was being secured to the stone pier at Sydney Bay.

As Edmund prepared to take his first unsteady step onto dry land, a voice that seemed to be of a cultured English gentleman addressed him. It was a voice that sounded oddly familiar.

"Welcome to our island, sir. You were lucky today, the reef was kind. I have seen many a boat capsize out there, some are even forced to swim, if they can, that is."

Looking back at the waves crashing on the nearby cliffs, Edmund was quite relieved that his boat had made it safely to shore. He turned to speak to his informant, expecting to see someone of rank or perhaps one of the civilian staff. Instead, the blasted fellow was dressed in a long, yellow, cutaway, loose fitting frock-coat and trousers, with holes evident in its fraying edges. His face was shaded by a large cabbage-tree hat, his calloused hands helping to steady the barge as its occupants clambered onto the pier.

A convict, a bloody convict. What gave him the right to address an officer, and to speak before being spoken to?

Astounded, Edmund turned away with disdain.

The convict stood back to let Edmund pass, giving a low bow, not uttering another word.

Still infuriated, Edmund picked up his kit. The land beneath his feet felt solid and reassuring, but the voice was as troubling as the waves crashing against the cliffs. Where had he heard it before? Or was it just a trick of the mind? He reassured himself, realising that it was the tone of voice that was familiar, not the actual voice itself. Hadn't he heard that tone many times in the drawing rooms of London, the Officers' Club, indeed in countless of other places? But still the doubt persisted, still niggling him, teasing him to remember.

He stopped in his tracks. Surely not. He spun around, scanning the pier and the men coming to and fro.

"O'Leary, over here now! Pick up those boxes," ordered a heavily built man.

The very same cultured voice that had earlier greeted his arrival acknowledged the command and set to fulfilling it. Edmund exhaled a sigh of relief. Of course it wasn't him, it couldn't possibly be, too much of a coincidence. Australia was a big place. Chances of meeting Michael Hanlan were slim, slim indeed.

Yet still the doubts lingered.

9

Chapter Two

Trying to think of anything other than Michael Hanlan, Edmund found a dry spot on the pier and rummaged through his kit bag to find his jacket, indebted to the clerk for his timely suggestion that he stow it away.

"Lieutenant Thornton, I presume?"

"Yes, sir," Edmund jumped up and saluted his new commanding officer, Captain Travers, a stocky gentleman with greying, mutton-chop sideburns.

"Stand easy, lieutenant. Welcome to Kings Town. I see you have been christened by our Sydney Bay. It happens to us all!" He laughed. "We have not had the pleasure of serving together before, have we? I met your father once, me lad, a fine man, a close friend of Colonel Johnston, I believe. I have been reliably informed, by that same esteemed gentleman, that the son is cut from the same cloth as the father. It will be an honour to serve with you, Thornton. Tell me, has the Regiment met your expectations?"

"To be truthful, sir, it is not exactly the life I had envisaged for myself. When my father told me he had purchased a commission in the Eleventh, I was less than pleased at first."

"And now?" but Captain Travers did not give him time to answer and surmised for himself. "Well, you evidently decided to take up the commission and the Regiment is pleased that you did."

"Thank you, sir. Though I must admit that when I did accept, I had envisioned making my mark on the battlefields, not as a gaoler in Her Majesty's colonies."

Captain Travers chuckled as Edmund followed him through the gathered crowd, struggling to regain his land legs and put his thoughts in order. Of course he'd been reluctant at first to join the regiment. He was angry, damned angry that he had to give up Sarah, just when the opportunity had finally come to win her heart. Yet, surprisingly quickly, he had been able to adapt to and enjoy his new life. True, his father's letters of introduction had granted him access into the finest homes in Sydney and Hobart Town. Although he had done an obligatory tour of some penal settlements in his role as lieutenant, until now he had been able to avoid any real responsibility. His commission to Norfolk Island, he reckoned, was about to change all that.

Putting his hand to his nose Edmund tried to block the vile smells that wafted from the piles of rubbish that seemed to be everywhere he looked. But he could not block out the cries of anguish, of men yelling to be heard, the vulgar coarse language, the boorish laughter that filled the air. Worse, from what he could see of the settlement, all seemed desolate and dreary. Clustered near the pier were groups of dilapidated older buildings, in stark contrast with new construction that he could make out to his right. He observed a group of hunched men chained together digging a trench, no singing accompanied their toil, only forlorn looks and slumped shoulders; very different to the sailors on The Governor Phillip.

"I see you're admiring our new pentagonal prison. The original prison that was built just after the settlement reopened in Eighteen Twenty-Five is becoming quite unusable now," the captain's voice trailed off for a moment. "But to business. I understand you have been with our mighty Elevens about eighteen months?"

"Yes, sir, about that."

"You will find your duties here far more demanding than at any other penal settlement where you have served, lieutenant. The convicts, here, are more rebellious and far more callous. They require much closer scrutiny of their activities and far more severe punishments. We have about sixteen-hundred of 'em with us at present. Both old and new hands"

"Old and new hands sir?"

11

"New hands have come direct from England, they are in the grey uniforms while the old hands are second time offenders from the mainland dressed in yellow."

The sound of clanking chains behind him caught his attention, causing bile to rise in his throat. The sight of convicts still turned his stomach. While on his previous short tours of Penal Settlements he had for the most part been able to avoid any contact with them. On board The Governor Phillip it had been no different. He had made a conscious effort to have nothing to do with the human cargo below decks. He looked on with vague curiosity as the convicts, who had unwillingly shared his passage from Hobart Town, were herded past, the cut of the whip or the stab of a bayonet encouraging them on their way.

As Edmund watched, the convicts were lined up along the shore and each man was loosened from his shackles and then forced to disrobe. In full view of all, the constables then began to perform a total body search of each man. Edmund overheard one of the guards, who was obviously enjoying his charges' discomfort, yell to his fellow guard, "Ne'er know where t' bastards will hide tobacciheh?" His laugh was cruel.

"There but for the grace of God go I," Edmund murmured to himself.

Captain Travers interrupted Edmund's thoughts. "There's a man you should meet, Thornton. George Vessey, our Superintendent of Convicts. Many a young lady has swooned under his stare, I can assure you. But," he lowered his voice, pointing at the now naked throng of men. "He is that lots' worst enemy. Those poor bastards have no idea of what's in store for them. At least you are rid of your floating prison, eh, lieutenant?"

"Yes, sir. But by all accounts I am exchanging it for one a far worse." He stared long and hard at the settlement in front of him. Complete isolation, surrounded by an unyielding sea. No hope of escape. He shuddered at the thought.

"Here, let me introduce you." Captain Travers waved toward the man under discussion, trying to gain his attention. "Mr. Vessey, sir, have you a moment?"

George Vessey displayed an air of arrogance as he walked over to the officers.

"Mr. George Vessey." Captain Travers greeted the superintendent. "May I present to you Lieutenant Edmund Thornton, Her Majesty's Eleventh Regiment."

"Pleased to make your acquaintance, sir."

Edmund shook the extended hand, noting with interest that the man's well-groomed appearance seemed incongruous with the other men in his work party. For reasons unclear to him, Edmund took an instant dislike to the man. Agreed, his looks were striking and would surely flutter a few feminine hearts, but there was something very cruel about his demeanour.

"So I can blame you for this new bunch of rogues." Vessey laughed; a harsh, disdainful sound. "If you want to keep your head on this island, lieutenant, you can't be too lenient with that lot. Mark my words, these scum are no better than animals. They only respond to harsh, decisive discipline. Remember sir, we are the ones in authority and we hold their destinies in our hands."

"I will keep that in mind, Mr. Vessey."

"Please excuse me gentleman, duty calls." Vessey bowed. "I am sure we will be seeing much more of each other, lieutenant. Kings Town is a very small place. But for now I had best get to and process this lot."

"We might as well begin your induction to our island now, Thornton. Mr. Vessey is very thorough in his interrogation of newly arrived convicts. You might learn something of your new charges. Shall we watch?" Captain Travers moved to follow the superintendent and Edmund followed.

Still naked the convicts were then pushed toward a table that had been set up in the shade of a large pine only a short distance from the pier. Many seemed unperturbed by their nakedness showing a defiance that was not lost on Edmund as they walked over to the table, while others stumbled across, trying to hide their manhood with their hands. Behind the table sat two clerks, pencil stubs in hand and large leather ledgers opened in front of them. Mr. Vessey grilled each convict individually and the clerks scribbled in the ledgers, trying to keep up.

"Name?"

"Caleb Peters."

"Caleb Peters, what?" demanded the superintendent.

"Um…Caleb Peters, sir."

"Age?"

"Sixteen, sir"

"From where do you hail?"

"Buxted, Sussex, sir."

"What crime?"

"Pick pocketing, sir."

"Height?" Mr. Vessey assessed the man and then answered his own question, "about five feet two inches, stocky build, ruddy complexion. Did you get all that?" he said, directing his disdain to the clerk who wasn't keeping up. The clerk continued to scribble in the ledger and Vessey addressed the constable who had searched the convict. "Any distinguishing marks on this one?"

"A red birthmark on his left buttock and a tattoo of an anchor on his right shoulder, sir."

"Right then, give him his new uniform."

Watching the man dress, Edmund saw that the "uniform" was nothing more than a striped shirt, a yellow duck frock coat, a pair of trousers, a straw hat, stout boots and a coarse woollen jacket.

The clerks continued to record in the ledgers as each convict was interrogated.

"Name?" There was a long pause. "Name?" Vessey questioned, harsher this time.

A constable hit the convict standing in front of the superintendent with the truncheon he was holding. "Speak up when you're spoken to by the super!"

Without warning the man bolted.

"Stop him!" Vessey yelled.

The convict's bid for freedom was short lived. With well-practiced athleticism, Edmund raced after the man and tackled him before he had run very far. After a short struggle he dragged the convict back in front of Vessey.

George Vessey nodded his appreciation toward Edmund. "Well done lieutenant, you have quite a burst of speed about you." Pushing the convict to his knees he said. "That will be all now, lieutenant, I can take it from here."

"As you wish." Edmund stepped back.

Vessey turned his attention to the convict, his lips twisting into a cynical smile, relishing the chance to put on a show for his new audience. "Perhaps six hours, hanging by your arms, facing a cold stone wall, will curb your need to run."

A young constable standing nearby looked horrified. "But sir, he's naked."

Vessey turned on him. "So? Perhaps that will teach the sod I mean business! Now take him away!"

The constable still hesitated.

"If you want to join him, I can arrange for you to be hung spread eagled also. Now get him out of my sight!"

When the last man was processed, George Vessey ordered the convicts into line and recited the standing regulations of the settlement, giving implicit descriptions of the punishments they would incur if any of the rules were breached. "The rest you will learn as you go along, I am sure. There are many here who are very willing to keep you on the straight and narrow." Then he ordered his constables to march them to the barracks.

Sauntering back to Edmund and Captain Travers as though nothing untoward or unusual had happened, Vessey said, "So captain, have you told the lieutenant of our principal means of keeping these felons at bay?"

"No, Mr. Vessey, I thought I would leave that privilege to you."

"Fear, lieutenant, fear, our most trusted friend. Fear of the ever watchful spy. Fear of the informer. Fear of punishment. Fear of me. All wonderful tools. My office door is always open to anyone, be he official or convict, who wishes to report to me any breach of discipline no matter how trivial. It could be as slight as being late for muster because a man stops to tie his bootlaces. I then deal with each case as I see fit. This, Lieutenant, is how we keep order on this island. The informer could be anyone in their acquaintance, even the man chained next to him in his work gang. Keep it in mind, Lieutenant. You never know when it might come in handy." He sniggered and strode away.

"Strange man," Captain Travers remarked. "I think you would agree."

Edmund nodded.

"Be on your toes around him, Thornton. His network of spies works well. He is vicious in his punishments and expects all to be. But, saying that, do not hesitate to call on him if you need help in controlling your charges, you will find him a useful ally, although many find his ways distasteful. Come, Lieutenant." Captain Travers put his hand on Edmund's shoulder. "I am sure you have had enough of convicts for today. We must be getting on, the Commandant is expecting us."

Unkempt convicts jumped out of the way of the oncoming officers, knuckling their foreheads as they grabbed off their caps. Ignoring them, the captain gave a running commentary of the buildings they were passing. "Just over there you will see the crank mill, a wonderful deterrent to convicts." Edmund was quite disturbed by the inhumane cries emanating from the building and wondered at what type of punishment was taking place inside. But he didn't have time to ask. Captain Travers was warming to his task as tour master and quickly went on. "That three-storied building, the one behind that high stone wall on your left, is the prisoners' barracks. Our last Commandant saw a need for both a Protestant chapel and one for those of the... Romanish faith." Captain Travers almost spat the word. "Although, personally, I see no need for that one," he said under his breath. "Strangely, he chose to build them on opposite outer walls of the barracks. To me they seem to mock each other, don't you think?" Almost as an afterthought, he quickly added, "The prisoners' dormitories and the court house are also housed within that area."

Edmund noticed that the prisoners' barracks seemed to be deserted, though the foul smells that emanated from the prisoners' mess in the lumberyard turned his stomach. All the while the sea roared just below them. Edmund trudged on, every now and then nodding and making appropriate sounds of approval.

Captain Travers nudged Edmund in the ribs. "Wake up, Lieutenant. I was saying that Flagstaff Hill over there lords over it all. You get quite a good view of the settlement from up there, Thornton. You should climb it as soon as you get the chance." Without taking a breath he continued, "You will find that everything here in Kings Town is within walking distance. Quite convenient, really."

"Yes, quite, sir...umm... I haven't seen any shops or ale houses, Captain. Where do the soldiers and civilian staff purchase provisions?"

"Purchase provisions?" the captain laughed. "I'm afraid there is nowhere here for you to spend your well-earned pay. Just see it as enforced savings and dream of how you will spend it back on the mainland. I tell you, Thornton, planning how to spend my pay has got me through many a restless night." Captain Travers went on. "We are just about self-sufficient here on the island. Many of the soldiers have their own vegetable gardens, we can hunt and fish when we are not on duty, and lemons, guava and other fruits grow abundantly in the wild. The Commissariat Store, that three-story building just over there, stores our grain and distributes all other necessities according to need. We have bakeries and butchers and also blacksmiths, tin smiths and even shoe makers, more often than not convict managed. We are dependent on some stores coming from the mainland and if these arrive on time you should want for nothing during your stay here."

After a good ten-minute's walk along dirt roads inland, Edmund followed Captain Travers up a slight incline and found himself looking at Government House.

"It's quite a fortified establishment isn't it sir. I can see a sentry, and is that a couple of cannons standing at the entrance?"

17

"Yes indeed, and if you look closely all the windows are barred. But think about it, Thornton. The threat of a convict uprising is ever present here and so one needs to be vigilant at all times and take no chances. You will have noticed when we passed the military barracks just across the road, Military Road by the way, it is surrounded by high defensive walls for the very same reason."

"But when I looked at the row of cottages that neighbour the barracks they seemed to have no defences. Are they all empty, sir?"

"Indeed not. They are the civilian officers' residences. They have been built with hidden cellars so that the occupants can at least hide in the event of an uprising."

Neither said another word as they strode over the paved veranda. Captain Travers lifted the heavy brass doorknob and rapped three times on the whitewashed pine door.

The Commandant's man led them down a dark hallway, lit only by one small lamp on the hallway table. Their shadows threw long ghostly forms on papered walls.

Opening the door to a room in front of them he announced, "Captain William Travers and Lieutenant Edmund Thornton of Her Majesty's Eleventh Regiment of Foot newly arrived from Hobart Town per The Governor Phillip now at anchor in the bay, Sir, Madame."

Major Henry Boyce, commandant of Norfolk Island, tapped his pipe into the ornate grating of the fireplace where a blazing flame glowed before striding across the deep-red carpet towards his guests. "Ah Travers, so your re-enforcements have finally arrived? You are most welcome on our island, Lieutenant. You know my wife of course Travers. Lieutenant, may I present to you my wife, Mrs. Catherine Boyce."

Standing, Mrs. Boyce came over to greet them. Both men gave a rigid bow.

"Welcome to Kings Town and to our home, gentleman. Now that you are here I will take my leave. I am sure you have much business to discuss." With a rustle of silk she left the room.

The Commandant indicated three straight backed wooden chairs around a small table neatly piled with papers. "Would either of you gentleman care for a pipe before we begin?" Without looking up he handed each of the officers a clay pipe and tobacco. "I understand Lieutenant Thornton that you have had previous experience in penal settlements?"

"Only some, sir, mostly as an observer, I'm afraid."

Major Boyce looked for confirmation from Captain Travers. Lighting a taper from one of the candles illuminating the room, the captain proceeded to light Major Boyce's and Edmund's pipes before answering, "Sir, I have been informed by very reliable sources that Lieutenant Thornton is well suited to taking charge of guard duties in a settlement such as this." He then lit his own pipe before extinguishing the taper.

Major Boyce murmured, "We'll see, we'll see. Your duties, Lieutenant, will for the most part entail guard duty, and being on hand at all times to quell any disturbances. We have civilian staff to supervise the convicts at work and in the barracks. But every time a work detail leaves the confines of the settlement I expect a garrison of fully armed soldiers to be with them. Is that understood?"

Edmund nodded and the commandant continued. "However, if you witness any breach of regulations, whether it be convict, civilian or even the men of your own regiment, it must be immediately reported and appropriate action taken. We do not spare the lash on this island Lieutenant and I expect your full support in this matter, is that understood? "

"Yes sir."

"Right then, I am sure that you must want to settle into your quarters. I bid you both good day."

A short walk directly back across Military Road bought Edmund and his captain to the impressive three-storey military barracks.

"Here we are then, Lieutenant, your new home. But before we go in, may I suggest we climb the guard tower. It affords an excellent view of King's Town."

Reaching the top, Captain Travers pointed to the row of cottages, in varying stages of completion, which neighboured the barracks.

"As you can see the civilian cottages are well guarded by their close proximity to the military barracks and of course we have a full view of the prisoner barracks. At least that's not too close. The stench would be unbearable. But we should be getting in; even springtime in the subtropics it can still get quite cool."

Climbing back down from the tower, Captain Travers summoned a nearby soldier. "I have taken the liberty of assigning Corporal Evans, here, to you as your batman, Thornton. He has proved a very dependable soldier and I am sure he will be able to answer any further questions you might have."

Edmund saluted. "Thank you, sir."

"Take the lieutenant to his quarters, Evans."

"Immediately, sir." Corporal Evans picked up Edmund's kit.

"The rest of your luggage should be landed by the morrow, Lieutenant, till then." Captain Travers returned Edmund's salute.

Edmund could not help but take notice of the young soldier he was now following. His flawless uniform, his erect stature, his long decisive stride, all spoke of a man proud to serve Her Majesty. It made him even more self-conscious of his own dusty boots after his hike from the pier and tried to walk with a heavier step to dislodge some of the offending dirt. He was so engrossed in what he doing that he almost walked right past the corporal when he came to an abrupt stop in front of a door.

Pushing open the door, Edmund was pleased to find two rooms opening into each other, one a bedroom and the other a sitting room with a large open fireplace, facing which were two well-padded chairs. In a corner, by the only window, there was a small dining table with four mismatched chairs. In the smaller room Edmund noted two bunks. He looked with curiosity towards his escort.

The corporal answered his officer's unspoken question. "You will be sharing your quarters with Lieutenant Saunders, sir. You will no doubt meet him in the officers' mess this evening."

"It seems that he loves to hunt," Edmund said, stroking one of the many animal pelts that hung on the walls, at the same time admiring the colourful display of stuffed parrots. "I do not recognise many of these species but they certainly make a fine show. I look forward to meeting him. I have been known to be quite adept at hunting too, so we will at least have that in common."

At that moment, Edmund was startled by the arrival of his new roommate. "Here, clean these, Evans," the man said, sauntering past and throwing a brace of pigeons onto the table in front of Edmund, giving him only a cursory nod. "Pigeon pie for dinner." He slumped onto the nearest chair. "And bring a bottle of rum!"

"It looks to me as though you have supplied dinner for at least a week." Edmund held out his hand and introduced himself.

"Been expecting you. Lieutenant Richard Saunders," his roommate said, shaking Edmund's hand with vigour. "Hunt, do you? Mind you, there is not much to hunt for here on the island, mainly rabbits and feral cats I'm afraid."

Evans brought over two mugs and a bottle of rum. Saunders snatched the bottle and poured two generous serves, handing one to Edmund.

"I've been known to win the brush," replied Edmund.

"The brush! God save us from gentlemen hunters! Can't kill the quarry yourself, let the hounds do it for you and then you claim the prize of the fox's tail. Have you ever actually killed anything yourself?"

"I have been on a couple of duck hunts, of course. But thinking about it, there were always so many shooters that I can't, with any confidence, tell you I killed any myself."

"Well, you have come to the master. I will just have to blood you."

Edmund drained his mug. Wiping his lips, he asked, "So it's only hunting and duty on this island?"

"No." Saunders said. "There is a social side, much scarier than hunting, in fact. Beware Mrs. Boyce, the commandant's wife. She enjoys organising social events with the other women in the settlement and expects all to attend, no matter the circumstance. Mind you, the Miss Boyce is quite a beauty." Saunders refilled his mug. "So if you don't enjoy social engagements, Lieutenant, you had best start thinking up excuses now!" He sauntered over to the mantle, chose a clay pipe from his collection and packed it with tobacco. He offered another to Edmund, breaking off the end to give him a fresh mouthpiece. Lighting a taper in the fireplace, he lit both pipes. He drew deeply on his, and then blew smoke rings into the air. "Do you have a sweetheart waiting for you?"

"No, no." Edmund caught himself. "Not really. There is a young lady with whom I correspond back in England but I haven't had the pleasure of receiving a letter from her yet."

"Well, I wouldn't hold your breath, Thornton. It will be nigh on a year before you would see any sort of reply. Well, that's settled then. A hunting expedition to Phillip Island is definitely in order. No people, just rabbits and goats. There's a small cabin that is usually kept well stocked so we will only have to take our guns. I understand a couple of fellows are due to come back from their hunting expedition on the morrow. We can go over in the barge in the morning, if you like. Nothing like a good hunt to soothe a broken heart." Saunders refilled Edmund's mug. "We need to drink a toast to my new friend's first hunt!"

Unpacking his kit that evening Edmund took out a small leather pouch. Untying the strap he removed his most treasured possession. Sarah's likeness stared up at him from the small painted portrait in its gilded frame. Memories, unbidden and unwanted invaded his thoughts. Memories of the day she had entrusted it to him. Her words still rang in his ears, stabbed at his heart.

"Find him, please find him for me. Keep him safe and please… give him this small trinket of my love."

He had promised her, hadn't he? His own words of agreement choked him. *Yes, Sarah, we were three great friends till you chose to give your love to him and not me!*

Frustrated, he climbed into bed; the luxury of a soft mattress and the fresh smell of new sheets soon lulled him into a dreamless sleep.

Edmund eagerly jumped into the barge the next morning, stowing his gun beneath the bench. It began to wallow under the movement of the waves as he sat. Surveying the surging surf across the reef, Edmund braced himself for the crossing to Phillip Island.

Saunders laughed at his stiffness. "Loosen up old man, you look at though you are about to mount the gibbet… and not as the executioner!"

Edmund managed a smile. With apprehension he loosened his grip on the thwart and watched as Philip Island loomed closer. Within three quarters of an hour, they had reached the shore. Grabbing his gun and looping it over his shoulder Edmund climbed out of the barge onto a flat bed of rock, surrounded by seemingly sheer cliffs.

Saunders pointed towards a wide fissure in the cliff. "That's the way up, I'm afraid. Bit tricky at first, but you'll get the hang of it, I'm sure."

Edmund looked up at the almost perpendicular climb. "I'm glad I only have my gun to be concerned with. I would hate to try climbing this with a full kit."

Edmund lagged behind the sure-footed Saunders, stopping every yard or so to regain his footing as parts of the path crumbled away beneath him. The sound of the stones as they cascaded down the cliff was disconcerting. Gaining the top, Edmund looked back down, for the first time realising he had climbed seven hundred feet or so. "Not bad, eh, Saunders, for a country gentleman?" The words caught in his throat. In front of him was an almost impenetrable bramble of vines, creepers and small bushes, some almost waist high.

"Seems impassable at first sight, doesn't it?" Saunders said. "Just follow me, I'll see you right." Hoisting his gun onto his shoulder, Saunders started to hack through the brush with a hatchet that he had carried in his belt. Edmund followed his example.

"Damm!" Edmund untangled his jacket from the brambles, receiving a deep scratch for his trouble.

Finally they reached the cabin and after introductions, the hunters already there advised them on the best places to hunt.

Saunders' enthusiasm was contagious, taking shots at anything that moved, pointing out easy shots to Edmund. Rabbits of all sizes and colours were plentiful and proved to be easy sport. They had soon bagged themselves more than they could carry.

"You're a good shot for a gentleman," Saunders mocked, "but now for the real test of a true hunter."

Edmund slumped exhausted onto a rocky outcrop. "True test?"

"I'll set a snare over there." Saunders pointed to a clump of bushes. "Should be simple enough to catch a live one."

Edmund was too tired to comprehend his companion's meaning.

With well-practiced hands Saunders set up the snare he had brought with him from the cabin. "Might as well eat while we're waiting," he said.

Both men were soon engrossed in eating a meal of bacon, bread and pickles they had bought in a sack. Draining his mug of tea Saunders jumped up. "Better go and check on the snare. Are you coming, Thornton?"

Edmund jumped up and strode after his friend.

"There! Got one!" Saunders walked over to the snare and grabbed the squirming rabbit. He handed it to Edmund.

Edmund shot a look of puzzlement toward his companion.

"Well, gentleman," Saunders teased. "He's no good to us alive, is he?" he said, mimicking the action of wringing the rabbit's neck.

Edmund stood in shock for a moment, feeling the warmth of the animal's body, feeling its frightened struggles.

"Surely you do not mean?"

"Surely I do mean." Again Saunders mimicked the action. "Come on man, it's easy."

"Easy for you… I don't think I can…"

Saunders stood there, his arms folded, staring at Edmund. Edmund knew this was the moment that would define the future of their friendship.

Gritting his teeth, holding his breath, Edmund grabbed the rabbit's head in one hand and the base of its neck in the other, then jerked them in a sudden, twisting motion. He heard a *snap!* like the breaking of a twig. The rabbit went limp.

He stared in disbelief at the lifeless animal in his hands. His initial impulse was to drop it, but on seeing Saunders expression of approval, the immensity of what he had just done dawned on him. The sense of ultimate power, of life and death, in his own hands, his own two hands, consumed and aroused him. He held the rabbit high above his head in victory. A mass of seabirds screeched into the sky as a primal cry of triumph ripped through the air.

Chapter Three

Sarah Henshall stared out of her family's library window to the glow of smouldering autumn leaves. The burning mounds of the year's first fall thickened the air outside with smoke. The air inside the library was just as thick. They had been arguing most of the afternoon.

"Winter will be upon us soon. I can already feel the chill of its winds and the damp of its rain." Elizabeth Adams sighed at her niece, who was thumbing through a large volume of botanical drawings pretending to ignore her.

Sarah tried to concentrate on the book, but her thoughts were in turmoil. What had happened to the carefree girl of two days ago? Only two days ago, all had been different. She and her father had raked together those same autumn leaves now burning in the yard, throwing them at each other, laughing and joking together. But that was two days ago, and father was now gone.

Just like my Michael. She slammed shut her book and stared out of the window, wiping the tears running down her cheeks with the back of her hand. *But,* she corrected herself. *Father was not like Michael. Michael still lived.*

She wiped away more tears, sure in her heart that one day Michael would return, that they would be together again, never to be parted. She fingered the gold locket hanging around her neck on a thin, black, velvet ribbon. He had given it to her just before...

She blocked the thought, holding her locket tighter, forcing herself to remember happier times. He had asked for a lock of her hair and then cut one of his own ginger curls, twisting them together so that neither the beginning nor the end of each was distinct in itself, entwined forever, never to be separated. Placing the hair in the delicate locket she now held, he had then tied it around her slim white neck in a neat, small bow. "Now we belong to each other forever," he had promised. "No one can break the bond that holds us together."

Never had Sarah imagined such a romantic token of love. He had asked for her hand then, and she had promised to remain faithful forever. She trembled even now with the memory. She could still see the love that shone in his eyes, feel the tender stroke of his fingers. She touched her lips, the warmth of their first kiss still lingering there. A secret betrothal, she smiled to herself. She intended to keep her promise at all costs.

She was certain that she would see Michael again but at the same time she was beginning to understand that she would never see her father; never read with him; never play chess with him. Never again would he stroke her brow and kiss her goodnight.

Sarah could not force the memory of her father's last day out of her mind. It had tormented her time and time again over the past two days, just as it did now.

Strong winds had blown that night. Branches had moaned and creaked under its onslaught. In the morning she had woken to beautiful carpet of multi-coloured autumn leaves. She had just thrown a handful of the yellow, orange and red leaves at her father, when she heard the crack above her, heard the rustling sound, a sound that became a tremendous roar with no warning. She rubbed her bruised arm at the memory of her father shoving her out of the way of the falling branch. She had screamed. Then, all became silent. In that one moment in time, her whole world collapsed.

Now she tried to concentrate on the muffled voices of her aunt and Judge Forsyth. She tried to understand what was happening. Sarah knew they were discussing her, discussing her future, making decisions that would affect the rest of her life.

She turned the pages of the book, biting her lip, trying to stop herself from speaking. *Who are these people? I have never even met Mrs. Forsyth before, and the judge... I think I remember visiting him with my father in his office once. And now they have complete control of my life... Why?*

"It is all in the will, Mrs. Adams. You must understand that your brother, William, believed he was doing the right thing for his daughter." Judge Forsyth waved the offending document at Sarah's aunt.

"I understand, my dear Judge, that Sarah is now an independently wealthy young lady. But to stipulate that she not benefit from her father's wealth until the day she marries, that I do not understand."

Margaret Forsyth, who had been sitting quietly in the corner of the room with her embroidery, could no longer keep her own counsel. "My dear Elizabeth, I am sure the judge and your brother know what is best for Sarah."

"But why can she not continue to live with me?" Elizabeth Adams demanded.

Aunt Elizabeth need not worry, Sarah thought. *I will marry as soon as my Michael comes home. Until then, I will continue to live with her. I am sure Michael will see her well provided for after our marriage.*

"The will is very clear in that regard, Mrs. Adams." Judge Forsyth continued. "You have been bequeathed the small cottage for your sole use and a very generous annuity for a widowed sister which should see you very comfortable. But Sarah has been made my ward until she marries and, as such, I suggest that she lives with Mrs. Forsyth and me."

Sarah panicked. The volume she had been concentrating on fell to the floor with a thud. *Leave her father's home? No! They do not understand. I have to stay here! Michael needs to know where I am when he returns. If I am not here, he will not know where to find me!*

Aunt Elizabeth picked up the volume and replaced it back onto the bookshelf.

Sarah grabbed her aunt's hand. "Dearest Aunt, I do not want to leave you. Please aunt," she begged, her eyes pleading with her aunt for understanding.

Freeing her hand from Sarah's, Aunt Elizabeth put her finger to her niece's lips. "Hush now my darling. It will all be for the best,

I am sure." She turned toward the judge again. "What do you propose, sir?"

"It is truly exciting, Elizabeth." Margaret Forsyth answered for her husband. "The judge has been asked to go to the colonies. Would you believe it, the Australian colonies?"

Sarah eyes widened with sudden delight. Were her ears deceiving her? Did Mrs. Forsyth say the Australian Colonies? She was sure that was where Edmund told her Michael had been sent. Here was her chance. Maybe she did not need to stay with her aunt after all, maybe she could go to Michael, be with him, look after him in Australia.

Then, as if in answer to Sarah's unspoken question, Elizabeth Adams said in disbelief. "The Australian colonies? You propose that the child should accompany you? Do you know what you are asking of me, Margaret? You are asking me to accept that I allow my only niece, my brother's only child, may the Lord rest his soul, to travel across the seven seas to a strange land on the other side of the world!"

"She is not a child any more, Elizabeth. She is seventeen years-old, quite the young lady in fact." Margaret Forsyth paused. "And there is another reason I believe the journey may be in Miss Henshall's best interest."

"And what pray, Margaret, might that be?"

"Have you given any thought to the girl's future? Think of it, my dear Elizabeth. We do not want her to become a lonely spinster, dependent upon the generosity of relatives, do we?"

"And how do you propose to change that situation?"

"The judge and I have not been blessed with children of our own and I can assure you we will treat Miss Henshall as if she was our own child. I enjoy wide and varied social contacts. We see this journey as one in which Miss Henshall's horizons may be broadened, where we can introduce her to the right people. Perhaps even find her an eligible beau. I would revel in such a responsible task, if you would allow me?"

"I need time to think, Margaret. Certainly I can see the sense in your generous proposal, but I need time to ponder on the consequences of what you are suggesting." Elizabeth Adams picked up her embroidery to signify, that in her opinion, the conversation was over.

Sarah realised she had to speak now or her aunt might convince the judge not to take her, not to take her to her Michael. She tried to temper her enthusiasm before she spoke. Her eagerness might raise suspicion and difficult questions might be asked. Still, the sound of her own voice startled her.

"What an adventure, Aunt! You know I have always wanted to travel. Papa had promised me a season on the continent next year." Her voice wavered. *That was not to be, there was nothing here for her now,* she admitted to herself. *Her father was dead, and her Michael was gone. No, her world was no longer in this place, but it could be in the new world.* She smiled sweetly at her aunt.

"I would like to speak to my niece alone," Elizabeth said.

Mrs. Forsyth and her husband nodded as Elizabeth Adams motioned to her niece to follow her into the next room.

Once they were out of earshot Elizabeth turned to Sarah. "Do not think that I do not understand your sudden eagerness to accompany the Forsyths, my dear."

Sarah tried to look innocent, as though she had no idea of what her aunt might be intimating.

"What on earth can you hope to achieve, Sarah?" Elizabeth Adams took her niece's hand in her own. "The chance that you may find him must be very slim indeed." She looked straight into Sarah's clear, blue eyes, tears forming in her own. "Would you not consider another from the many suitors who have called? What about that other gentleman? The one who used to call with Mr. Hanlan, a fine looking man, I seem to recall. What was his name?"

"I presume you mean Lieutenant Thornton, Aunt." Sarah tried to stop her aunt's trembling hands. "I am sorry to disappoint you, but he, too, has left our shores, and is now on Her Majesty's service somewhere in the colonies. I have received a couple of missives from him since he left, nigh on a year ago now, but the return address is never the same." She turned and stared out into the garden, trying not to meet her aunt's pleading eyes. "The lieutenant was a good friend, Aunt, a good friend to both Michael... I mean Mr. Hanlan, and me."

"Oh, I see. At least he is on the right side of the law," she mumbled to herself. "But why him? Why leave all you know and care about, for him? Why follow this felon to the other side of the earth? I know that is why you are so keen to accompany the Forsyths."

"He is not a felon," Sarah retorted. "It was so out of character for him. I believe that someone must have coerced him to do it."

"Yes, I must admit that it did seem to be out of character with the young man your father and I have known for so many years. The young man we happily agreed to court you. It seems we couldn't have been more wrong."

"You were not wrong, Aunt. We have been friends since childhood. You knew him well, how could you even think he could..." She left the words unspoken. "Dearest Aunt?" She squeezed her aunt's hand. "I cannot possibly miss this opportunity to find out what has happened to him. Please understand, it will not be offered to me again." She stood there twirling one of her long auburn ringlets around her finger. The endearing pout she had perfected over the years, showed clearly on her face.

"Very well, I know it is useless to continue to argue. Your father always gave into you, Sarah dear, why should I be any different. But, please do me this one favour. The Forsyths may not be quite so understanding, especially considering Mr. Forsyth is a judge, so please do not breathe a word of your true intentions to them."

Sarah leaned over towards her aunt and rained kisses on her wrinkled, tearstained cheeks.

"Come, come now child, there will be time for that later." Aunt Elizabeth rose from her chair. "We have much to do now."

Chapter Four

Michael Hanlan always found it difficult to enter the convicts' mess, the place known as the lumberyard. The area was filthy, and the din of six hundred men sitting at crudely carved wooden tables was deafening. The putrid stench coming from the cooking pots did not make eating their contents a palatable expectation. But, as nothing else was forthcoming, ever, he waited in line for his share of the lumpy hominy to be slapped into his bowl. Taking a hunk of bread and holding his bowl at arm's length, to keep from smelling its contents, he walked toward the eating tables.

"Hey, you there, o'er here!" It was a pleasant, if not jovial, Irish voice addressing him from across at the far table. The man was beaming from ear to ear. "Here join us, we can make room." He squashed his neighbour further up the bench so that Michael could sit.

"You're the one they call the Bard, ain't ya?"

"That's what they call me."

The man looked at Michael. "So, if we don't be callin' you the Bard, what *do* we be callin' you?"

Michael contemplated the Irishman's request as he sat down. He had to admit he liked being known as the Bard; it gave him a sense of anonymity. It was as though he was two separate men. Michael Hanlan, the man who loves Sarah Henshall, who dreams of lying in her arms and exchanging vows at the pulpit of St. Mary's. Michael Hanlan, untainted and worthy to return to her side when this nightmare was over. Then there was the Bard, the man who had to endure all the harshness of this life, the man who had to take the beatings and suffer, the man who could be left behind when this nightmare was over.

An answer not forthcoming, the man continued, "Not givin' your christened name, eh? I can respect that, keep our past to ourselves, I say. I'm O'Malley, just plain O'Malley and to be sure I am very pleased to make your acquaintance, Bard."

His handshake was firm and genuine. It gave Michael confidence that he had found a new friend, one whom he could rely on even in this desolate place.

Studying the insipid hominy on his spoon Michael sighed. "Rather like lumpy rice pudding, don't you think?"

"In appearance only, heh? Takes a while to get used to it, don't it?"

"Sure does." Michael put the spoon down and picked up his hunk of bread hoping to find it a little more palatable.

"And beware o' the bread." O'Malley waved his spoon in Michael's face. "There's a lot o' talk 'bout grinding both the corn cobs and the husks to make our bread. Makes it go further."

Another man sitting at the table piped up. "Aye, we calls it our 'scrubbing brush'."

"Scrubbing brush?" Michael broke off a chunk and put it in his mouth and tried to chew it. It stuck to the top of his mouth, almost choking him as he tried to dislodge it with his tongue.

O'Malley grabbed up his hunk of bread and picked at it. "Yeah. It's so rough that it scrubs out your innards and brings on dysent'ry." He started to laugh nervously, before becoming more sombre.

"Well, it looks as though I have but two choices. Risk dying of dysentery or starve to death!" Michael forced a laugh as he tried to swallow another chunk.

On the clang of the settlement bell calling early morning muster, the convict dormitory of over one hundred souls became a hive of activity. Oaths, curses and obscenities met the most innocent of ears. The foul stench of the night buckets filled the air.

Scratching the newly acquired bites from the bedbugs with which he shared his bunk, Michael bent over and picked up his filthy blanket from the floor where he had discarded it during the night, still damp from his night sweats. He rubbed his stomach, reminded of the sharp cramps that had broken his sleep.

After dressing Michael shuffled over to where O'Malley and his group were huddled, hands in pockets, deep in conversation.

"Hey mate you don't look too good." O'Malley offered his arm to Michael for support.

"I'll be all right." Michael mumbled. *I have to be.*

"Fire in your belly? The scrubbing brush got you, eh?"

"Yeah, but it's not that bad."

"Still, better report sick this mornin'. There've been deaths, you know. Shouldn't take chances, eh?"

Michael nodded.

"You lot get ov'r here now or I swear you'll feel the cut of the cat before this day's out!" yelled a burly guard.

"Yeah, yeah." One of O'Malley's cronies answered under his breath as the group sauntered over to where the muster guards were calling the names for the day's assignments.

Michael struggled to stay upright, leaning heavily on O'Malley.

O'Malley's number was called early in the roll call.

"Sorry, mate that's me. Now you report sick." O'Malley walked over to his gang leaving Michael to fend for himself.

Upon hearing his number, Michael struggled forward and knuckled his forehead in respect.

Marking off his roll, the muster-master yelled, "Quarries for you today."

With much discomfort, he shuffled over to his assigned gang.

"Break...fast!"

The gangs ambled over to the lumberyard and settled down to eat.

The smell of the hominy as it was slopped into his bowl brought Michael to his knees. He grabbed at his cramping stomach. With a fiery pain gnawing at his innards, he tried to claw his way over to the closest stone wall for privacy, retching violently.

"Devil's teeth, not another one! Get that man to the hospital now!" the superintendent yelled. "He's no damned use to me in this condition. Can't afford another one dead."

Two constables dragged Michael up from his knees. He could feel their torn fingernails digging through his threadbare shirt. He flinched, yet in his weakened state he was grateful for their support, letting his body hang limp between them.

Michael stumbled up the steep, stoned hospital steps, all energy drained, exhausted.

The surgeon's assistant clutched Michael's mop of ginger curls and jerked up his drooping head. "Who is it this time?"

"This be the Bard," said one of the guards.

"Heard about him. Not one of our usual malingerers, is he?" He poked and prodded Michael's stomach. "Probably a gentleman in his past life," he said with contempt. "Think they're better than the rest of us. Great leveller, this place, eh? Can't handle the food, stomach's too sensitive. Most likely won't last out the night."

His stomach lurching again, Michael whimpered, "Please sir, need a privy."

"Well, this one's obviously not faking." The assistant surgeon jumped out of the way to miss the splatter. "Get him out of my dispensing room, now! And send an orderly to clean up this mess!"

With relief, Michael lay down on the pallet he was led to. The pungent odours of sickness permeated the stonewalls and the foul smells from the privy wafted through the ward so thick he could taste it with every breath he took.

"First time I seen ya in here, ain't it?"

With difficulty, Michael rolled over to find a wizened older convict lying on the pallet next to him. He could only nod his recognition.

Raising himself on one elbow, the old man studied Michael. "Simmons is the name. By the looks of you it be dysentery, ain't it?"

Michael looked at him through watery eyes.

"No need to speak, seen it all before. They will be round soon and force some vile concoction down your throat, made from the bark of a medicinal tree so I'm told. Haven't seen it do much good though. Least we get fed better in here, wheaten flour bread, real meat and fruit," he said with a dreamy glean in his eyes. "So no need to gain your feet too quickly, eh?" He winked.

At the mention of food Michael's stomach lurched once more. He retched over the side of his pallet into his chamber pot. "Why now, why now?" he moaned, too exhausted to even wipe the dribble from his mouth. He felt in fear for his very soul.

The surgeon, a kindly old man, took pity on Michael. He paid daily visits to his bedside, trying to coax him to swallow the concoction he had prepared to relieve Michael's discomfort. It made Michael choke and splutter so little reached his stomach. The surgeon would often sit by Michael placing cooling cloths on his forehead in an effort to reduce his fever, listening to him call for one named Sarah in his delirium.

With time Michael woke and began to gain strength. The surgeon encouraged him to take a little bread and then tempted him with meat and fruit.

"Who is Sarah?" the surgeon ventured to ask one day.

Michael groaned. He felt ashamed at the tears blinding his eyes. He rolled away from the old man so that he could not see him cry. He watched mesmerised, as two droplets water raced each other down the moist stone wall. Even the walls seemed to be crying for his lost Sarah. It felt almost sacrilege to speak her name in a place such as this, so he remained silent.

The surgeon put a reassuring hand on Michael's shoulder and quietly left his bedside.

A familiar voice, a well-loved voice from the past broke through Michael's tears. *"Come on Mick, me lad. Be strong. This is no time to feel sorry for yourself, young man. Now, pull yourself together and get on with it,"* his father's voice said.

"I will try father, but it is so very hard."

Thoughts of his father brought many memories of him flooding back, both happy and sad. Michael realised, then, that it had been seven years since his father had passed to his reward. *I was twelve years old, too young to become head of the household.* It seemed an eternity ago now, but yes, he recalculated in his mind, it was only seven years ago. *My God, it's the same length of time I'm condemned to spend in this unearthly place. Can I really expect Sarah to wait seven years for me?* He seethed with anger at himself, anger at his stupidity, anger at his loss. He took a deep breath and tried to relax.

Sarah's beautiful face materialised on the stone wall in front of him, her eyes filled with love, as they were in all his dreams. *Sarah was safe,* he assured himself, *safe with her father and with Edmund. Yes, Sarah is safe at home in England. She will wait for me, I am certain of it.* His mood became optimistic. *And for my part, I must make sure I return to her.*

The surgeon was surprised to find Michael up the next morning, begging to be discharged.

Michael was sitting cross-legged in the dirt near the sea wall, immersed in plaiting a strand of flax he had found by the side of the path, when O'Malley's shadow passed over him.

"Haven't seen you in about three weeks, heh Bard? Heard you had the dysent'ry real bad. Not expected to live, they said. You right now? Still don't look too good to me."

Michael wiped the beading sweat from his brow. "Well, as you can see, here I am, alive and well. Although for how much longer I do not know. The food in the hospital is far better than what we're expected to eat out here. How's a man supposed to work on such meagre rations? My belly is always rumbling with hunger. But at least I'm not messing myself as often now."

"To be sure, frustratin' ain't it? All this fresh fruit and vegetable everywhere, growin' wild and we can't touch it for fear of feeling the cut of the cat." He kicked a wild lemon that had fallen to the ground in frustration.

Michael only grunted.

O'Malley sat down and watched as Michael braided the pieces of flax into a delicate pattern. "You got a flair for that ain't ya?

Ever made bonnets or hats from it? Women love bonnets. Would prob'bly pay a high price, too, for such a luxury." He rubbed his bristled chin thoughtfully.

Michael looked up this time. He stopped plaiting and looked straight out in front of him, a wistful, lonely look. "I have not thought about that in a long time. It seems like another lifetime, now." Looking at the long plait he had made, he continued in a quiet voice. "I have made hats before. My mother's friend was a celebrated milliner. She enjoyed teaching my young sister to make straw bonnets and I, in turn, could not help but pick up the skill. Not that it will do me much good here, I suppose."

"As it happens, it might just do ya some real good," his companion said. "See those fellas over there?" He nodded toward a group of four men sitting twenty yards away. "They're me mess mates. We be lookin' for one to join us."

Michael looked over at the group. "Why me?"

"We be lookin' for one with such skills, skills to make things that ain't read'ly available, so we can barter them for extra food, like fruit and veggies."

Michael cocked his eyebrows.

"Ain't you heard all the scramblin' in the barracks after we're locked in for the night? Not all are looking for companionship, if you know what I mean." He tapped the side of his nose. "Most are workin' at a trade in secret. Johnson o'er there is an accomplished tailor and Peters can mend any boot a treat. It's easy to find soldiers, free overseers and even their wives who be willin' to pay for such work if you know who to speak to. That's where I come in. I trade the goods for tea, sugar and sometimes even tobacci. We share the proceeds fair 'n square like amongst ourselves. Look at them, don't they look well fed, strong? They'll live out their sentences. Not like some poor blighters around here. What da' ya say? Will ya join us?"

O'Malley had definitely roused his interest, he had no intention finishing up like the old second timer who was limping passed at that moment, back hunched, covered in sores.

Michael lifted the plait of straw from his lap and examined it. Could something as simple as this be the answer he was looking for? The decision was easy. He shook O'Malley's extended hand with enthusiasm. "Maybe Johnson can help me sew the straw plaits into bonnets."

Chapter Five

That night, Edmund was woken from his slumber by a pair of rough hands. He rubbed the sleep from his eyes, trying to focus on what his fellow officer was yelling in his ear.

"Thornton, come on man, wake up! The superintendent of convicts has ordered a surprise inspection of the convicts' barracks. Our presence is required. Should be a bit of sport, eh?"

"What? What?" spluttered Edmund.

Saunders repeated, "The constables are going into the convicts' barracks tonight, a surprise raid. Come on, I don't want to miss it. Your first time, eh, now you'll see how we treat the swine here on the island." He laughed raucously. "No more than they deserve. Incorrigible felons, one and all."

Not sure if he agreed with his companion's opinion of the convicts, Edmund dressed, contemplating what the raid might uncover. He checked his musket.

"Hurry up! That musket is much too cumbersome, Thornton. Here, use this pistol instead and let's be off." Lieutenant Saunders handed Edmund the partner to his own pistol. Shoving it into his belt he rushed out of the door, trying to catch up to his companion who was already mounting one of the horses being held by a convict stable hand.

It was a tranquil, early summer's night. The only sound that interrupted its peace was the incessant buzzing of night insects. A full moon spread light over the rough stone walls of the convicts' barracks, presenting a calm facade, belying what lay behind them.

The two officers rode towards the group of men gathering at about two-hundred yards from the heavy wooden gates of the barracks.

George Vessey was pacing back and forth. When the officers arrived he growled at them through pursed thin lips. "About time! By God, get off those horses. Want to wake up the whole settlement? This is supposed to be a surprise inspection, not an invitation to dinner!"

Lieutenant Saunders wasn't so cock-sure anymore. "With respect sir, it's Lieutenant Thornton's first raid and he's not used to being woken in the middle of the night. He will be quicker next time, I assure you, sir."

Edmund glared at his companion. Already surprised at the change in his companion in the presence of the superintendent, Edmund was even more surprised when, as soon as Mr. Vessey was out of earshot, Saunders easily changed back to his arrogant self.

"What you waiting for Thornton? Hurry up, man. I don't want to miss any of the fun."

Edmund followed at Saunders' heels towards the largest of the three convict dormitories. As the heavy wooden doors were thrown open and the constables rushed in, a shrill warning whistle echoed through the barracks. "R-A-I-D!" was bellowed from unseen lips. The dormitory became a confused frenzy of men scrambling for their own hammocks and the blowing out of contraband candles.

Saunders nodded to Edmund to guard the other side of the entrance, whispering with obvious pleasure, "Get your pistol ready Thornton, our task is to stop any of the blighters trying to escape!"

Edmund stood braced with his feet set apart, pistol in his hand. He could just make out in the dim moonlight through the window at the other end of the dormitory two long lines of canvas hammocks in two tiers with a stone aisle of about four feet in width between them.

Not too wide to stop any attempted bolt, surmised Edmund.

The occasional "shshsh" and blasphemous utterances could be heard in the dark depths of the dormitory.

Then came an uneasy quiet, far worse to Edmund's ears, than the mutterings of hardened voices.

Saunders looked at Edmund and winked. "Wait for it. We're in for it now!"

The constables fanned out, their smoky lamps mingling with the dank smells of the ward. Edmund could see at least one-hundred pairs of eyes glaring back in the yellow glow of the lamps. Randomly choosing their victims, the constables dragged the protesting men from their hammocks into the narrow aisle. The convicts exploded in a mighty roar, jeering at the constables, screaming obscenities and yelling encouragement to those being hauled past them.

To Edmund it was a scene of absolute chaos but even in the chaos there seemed order. Edmund watched as one-by-one, convicts, accused of sodomy, or of having contraband in their possession, or some other minor misdemeanour, were shoved past him by the constables toward the soldiers waiting in the corridor.

A thunderous shout reverberated through the barracks. "Bolter!"

Edmund stood steadfast in the doorway, pistol steady in his hand. Before he could catch his breath, he was face-to-face with a convict who could have been his twin. It was like looking into a mirror. He could see himself in the man's desperate eyes, a man denied his freedom, denied his dignity. For a fleeting moment he toyed with the idea of letting him pass, letting him gain his freedom. He began to loosen his grip. Only Saunders saw him faltering and stepped in, restraining the struggling convict before anyone else reached them.

Edmund took a step backwards, stunned. Then he came to his senses, took control of his emotions and helped Saunders with his captive.

"Well done, Lieutenants, very commendable," Mr. Vessey said when he reached them, puffing. "I knew... if it came to it... I could rely on the two of you. So who do we have here? Edward Lawton, I believe."

Edmund's jaw dropped. *Edward Lawton, Edmund Thornton, Edward Lawton.* He played with the words, both names falling easily off his tongue, the similarity unnerving. A cold sweat broke out on his forehead. "My worst nightmare," he murmured. "Oh my God, I am witnessing my own worst nightmare."

Pushing the convict to his knees, George Vessey seized him by the throat, forced his head back with his truncheon and shoved his dirty forefinger into the convict's mouth to open it wide. "Ah, so what have we here?" He dug around the man's mouth. "Tobacci, if I am not mistaken, and I am never mistaken, am I?" He glanced at the milling constables and soldiers, who nodded in agreement, then turned his attention back to the convict. "Tobacci, as if you did not know, is forbidden to convicts." He shoved his finger further down the convict's throat. The big man choked and tried to bite down on the superintendent's finger. Vessey slapped him across his face with his free hand. Regaining his balance, Edward spat towards Edmund. Saunders jumped forward and struck him with the butt of his pistol.

"Take this man, Lieutenant, and put him in irons. The Commandant will deal with him and the others in the morning. A productive night, if I do say so myself."

Edmund and Saunders dragged Edward Lawton between them to the blacksmith's forge. They pounded on the door. The bleary-eyed blacksmith who answered reluctantly found his tools and fastened a set of heavy irons around the ankles of the convict. Once they had incarcerated their charge in one of the lockups with other accused convicts captured in the night raid, the two lieutenants made their way back to their quarters in silence.

Saunders was the first to reach home. Bursting through the door, he demanded Evans find them both a drink. Edmund slumped in one of the armchairs facing the fireplace.

Draining his glass, Edmund indicated the need for another. He was still cursing himself at his show of weakness in the night's events. Until now he had always been able to distance himself from the treatment of the convicts. He had never felt the need to be so involved before. It unnerved him.

"What on earth happened out there, Thornton?"

Edmund jumped. "Didn't you see his face?" he said, "It's... it's like looking in a mirror... and his name, *our* names, they sound so very much alike. A reminder..."

"A reminder of what? What on earth are you babbling about?"

"Nothing, forget it. I'm going back to bed." With that said, Edmund stormed into the other room.

"Thornton, we are required at the police court this morning. Come on man, we can't be late for this one too," Saunders said.

Edmund gulped down the last morsels of his breakfast of fresh fruit and hot scones while pulling on his jacket.

Both men rushed into the darkened Police Courtroom just as the Commandant, Major Boyce, and Mr. Vessey were taking their seats behind a large wooden desk. Edmund watched as his *doppelganger*, Edward Lawton, was brought before the assembled magistrates. Their amazing likeness still staggered him.

Both Edmund and Saunders were asked to give details of the events of the night before. Edmund could not look the convict in the eye and mumbled his testimony. Saunders, on the other hand, proudly stated his version of what had transpired. Lawton was given no chance to defend himself.

Without further ado, Major Boyce readied himself to give sentence.

"Having heard the testimony of Lieutenants Thornton and Saunders regarding the events of this past night we are ready to render our decision," said Major Boyce in a booming voice. "Convict Edward Lawton, you have been found guilty of having traces of tobacco on your person. The standard punishment for this offence is twenty-five lashes. But," he paused to give significance to his next words, "we also find you guilty of attempting to escape and spitting at an officer. For this you shall be sentenced..."

Major Boyce's voice trailed away from Edmund as another voice took its place. It was another voice, in another court, in another time. "Prisoner at the bar, having being found guilty of the crime of theft, you are hereby sentenced to be transported beyond the seas to such place as Her Majesty shall direct." In his mind's eye, Edmund jumped to catch Sarah as she fainted next to him.

The reverie was short-lived. Lieutenant Saunders was nudging him in the ribs with his elbow and smiling. "You're a strange one, Thornton. I never know what you're going to do. Next time you try to push me over, give me a little warning!" Saunders laughed as they walked out of the Police court and then along the coastline. "You know, though, you're right, you could easily be mistaken for that convict and he for you. The likeness is truly remarkable. You're very lucky man that God in his wisdom put you on your path and he on his, and not the other way 'round."

Edmund felt uncomfortable but to change the subject he enquired, "What happened last night, Saunders? Is the possession of tobacco banned totally amongst the convicts here? It wasn't at my last station in Hobart Town, although I was there such a short time before being transferred here. It seems such a minor offence to have caused so much trouble."

"Ah, the good ol' tobacco tracks. You know the superintendent probably found nothing, just something that could have been tobacco stuck in the rogue's teeth." Saunders laughed callously. "Serves him right for trying to bolt, that'll teach him to mind his place." Shoving a wad of his own chewing tobacco into his mouth, he continued, "Yeah, I have heard that the authorities in Van Diemen's Land have become soft and allowed some convicts tobacco as a reward. But not here, by Jove." He chewed his tobacco with relish, baring browned stained teeth. "The rogues here don't deserve such luxuries."

"But twenty-five lashes? It seems such a heavy sentence for a little piece of tobacco."

Edmund collapsed onto his bed that night not even bothering to remove his clothes. He tossed and turned. For some reason his bedding felt more uncomfortable than ever. Lumps seemed to appear where no lumps had been before, each one prodding his back and then his side. Visions of the numerous floggings of the many faceless and nameless persons he had witnessed in the past haunted his dreams. One of the faceless men took on flesh and became Edward Lawton tied to the whipping-triangle, writhing under the lash. But then Edmund felt the twine fixing his own wrists to the triangle and then the sudden, sharp cut of the lash stung his back. One...two...three... he writhed in pain.

He woke with a start and sat bolt upright, his breath coming in short sharp gasps. His bedding was drenched with perspiration. He felt his back to make sure it was not scared or bleeding. It wasn't. He sat for a long while staring into the darkness of the other room. He could hear the call of the night birds and the wind through the trees, now familiar sounds, comforting sounds. Feeling more at ease he undressed and once again lay on his bed, hands behind his head and gazed at the ceiling. He was all right, he assured himself. Nothing was going to happen.

No-one here knows. No-one here needs to know, he told himself. *If I keep my nerve, no-one will ever guess the truth.*

Chapter Six

Blinking in the bright sunlight after many hours below decks writing in her journal, Sarah opened her parasol to shade out the sun. The cool sea air was a pleasant change from the stale, clammy conditions of her cabin. The deck was bustling with activity. Sailors were carrying out their daily routines; some swabbing the decks, some coiling rope, some mending sails, and others aloft in the rigging.

"Ah, there you are, Miss Henshall. Here come sit by me." Margaret Forsyth patted the folding chair next to her with her gloved hand. "It is good to see you that you were thoughtful enough to bring up a parasol and gloves. We would not want that fine porcelain skin of yours to freckle now, would we?"

Sarah's black taffeta mourning-gown rustled as she negotiated her way across the deck to where Mrs. Forsyth was reading in the shade of a canvas awning.

Margaret Forsyth continued, "I was wondering when you might grace us with your presence on deck. Personally, I find our drab cabins too much to contend with." She took a breath. "It was very generous of the captain to set up this awning to shade us, was it not?"

"Yes, very generous indeed." Sarah smiled at her guardian's enthusiasm.

"Did you know, Miss Henshall, that when you smile, I do believe your whole face lights up? No wonder every man on this ship including, might I say, the captain himself, is captivated by your very presence. The black of your gown becomes you. It highlights your auburn hair and fine complexion."

"You flatter me, Mrs. Forsyth." Sarah felt a warm flush spreading across her face. "What are you reading ma'am?" she questioned, trying to avoid another session about the worthwhile attributes of every eligible man on board.

"Oh, this?" The older lady turned the book over, "Have you read *The Old Curiosity Shop*, Sarah? I am still quite affected when one of the characters gets framed for robbery and sentenced to transportation. He's quite innocent, you know. I have read it three times so far this voyage and will probably be forced to read it three more times before it is over." She closed it and put it down. "I had such great expectations of this voyage, Miss Henshall. I do not mind telling you. I thought it was to be a great adventure but instead I find it tedious and boring."

Sarah had learned early in her acquaintance with Mrs. Forsyth that the lady enjoyed talking and needed little encouragement to continue. "Perhaps I could read it to you, Mrs. Forsyth? It might give you a different perspective."

"Perhaps, my dear, but not today," she said. Then her face lit up. "I quite forgot. We have been invited to dine again at the captain's table this evening. I believe we can thank your good self for the captain's continual kind ministrations upon us."

"I am sure I do not understand, ma'am."

"The man is very keen on you, Sarah, I am sure. He is very good looking, you must admit, and from a very fine family I am told. Such an eligible gentleman ready for marriage, I'm sure. Would your aunt not be impressed if I found you a husband so soon on our voyage?"

"But Mrs. Forsyth, I am in mourning for my father. It would be truly frivolous of me to entertain the notion of courting at a time such as this. Surely all on board are aware of my loss and should honour my feelings." Sarah stood, upsetting her chair, and walked across to the bulwark, staring out to sea. She held onto the smooth wooden rail to gain her balance, feeling its warmth pulsate through her body. She glanced back at Mrs. Forsyth, who had picked up her book again. *Why must she continually talk to me of marriage? I know she means well, but she does not know my heart belongs to only one man.* She grasped her locket and mouthed a prayer for

Michael's safe return. Then taking a deep breath she returned to her guardian's side.

Margaret Forsyth looked up. "Are you feeling better, my dear? I realise your loss is still raw. But, I believe your father would not have wanted you to stop living now that he is passed, God rest his soul." She held out her hand to Sarah. "Would you help me up? These old bones are not what they were. Perhaps we could take a turn around the deck?"

"That would be most pleasant, ma'am."

Straining with both hands, Sarah assisted Mrs. Forsyth to her feet, grateful that the movement of the ship helped in her task.

"I can see that you care for none of the fine men on this ship, Miss Henshall. No, I think you have only eyes for one man."

Sarah stopped and stared at her companion in stunned disbelief. "I am sure, ma'am, I do not know of whom you speak."

"Of course you do, my dear. Do not be so coy with me. Your Aunt Elizabeth told me all about your young man."

Oh, my God, she knows!

"He must be a very special man, Miss Henshall. A very special man indeed, for you to travel half way around the world in the small hope of finding him."

Sarah tried to speak, to deny the woman's speculation, but the words caught in her throat.

"Your Aunt Elizabeth and I have no secrets, my dear."

Sarah found her voice. "But Aunt Elizabeth told me not to speak of him." She was shivering now, not sure whether to be relieved that her secret was known or panicked that she would not be allowed to continue her quest.

"This Lieutenant Edmund Thornton must indeed be a fine man to deserve such loyalty from you."

Surprise and relief raced through Sarah. She forced a smile, "Lieutenant Thornton," she repeated.

"You sound surprised, Sarah. Of course, Lieutenant Thornton! Who else did you think I was speaking of? Your aunt spoke of your high regard for him before we sailed. She said you hoped that you might meet him in the colonies."

Sarah began to walk on, weighing up her options. *What harm would there be in letting Mrs. Forsyth believe that it is Edmund I am seeking? There were certain advantages in doing so. Firstly, if I agree that it is Edmund who fills all my waking thoughts, she will stop pestering me about meeting other men. And best of all, if I find Edmund, perhaps he will have already found Michael!*

"I do so love a secret, Miss Henshall, and you have kept this one so very well. I have been waiting for nearly five months for you to speak of it. So, I thought I would put it upon myself to bring it up. Tell me, my secretive young lady, just who is this young man? I must know more. I insist you tell me all about him."

Sarah found it easy to speak of Edmund. They had been such close friends for so long. She was able to answer all her guardian's idle questions, all the while feeling as though a heavy burden was being lifted from her shoulders. Often she would speak of her attachment to Michael as though it was to Edmund and Margaret Forsyth was none the wiser of the deception.

"With your permission, Miss Henshall, I might speak to the judge of your quest. *Your quest,*" Margaret Forsyth smiled, "that does sound exciting, does it not? Excitement, just what this tedious journey needs."

"The judge, ma'am?" Sarah tried to curb the panic in her voice. "Why do we need to trouble such an important man?"

"Because he is the judge, my dear, and because he is a very important man. He will be able to open doors that will be closed to us."

"Open doors ma'am?"

"Find where your lieutenant is, of course, my dear. I understand the colonies are vast. We might never find him. I am sure though, with the judge's contacts, the task will become easier. And when he is found we could perhaps organise an excursion and surprise him. Now, that would be a treat… to see his face when he sees you again for the first time. That would be truly wonderful."

Sarah returned to the ship's rail. The daunting task she had given herself, she realised, would become insurmountable for her to tackle on her own. She would need help if she was to succeed.

Trying to contain her eagerness, Sarah casually turned back toward her guardian and accepted her suggestion.

Chapter Seven

The morning bell clanged, summoning the convicts to muster. Edmund had already been up most of the night, the oppressive heat of February affecting his sleep, so he arrived early to the prisoner barracks to take charge of the guard. His hair was still wet from his morning bathe in the bay, but the welcome cool of the water had not stayed long and he now stood sweating profusely in his heavy uniform. The convicts shuffled into the yard from their dormitories in answer to the bell, some only in their trousers, many ignoring the directives being shouted by the guards. It was obvious, Edmund thought as he surveyed the wretched, unkempt throng of men, to recognise those that had been sent direct from England and those who were second-time colonial offenders. The English prisoners were relatively well behaved, lining up in silence as the regulations ordered, whilst the second-timers jeered and cajoled them into disorder. Edmund and his constables pushed and shoved the offending men into line, and when the reverend finally arrived to conduct the morning prayers all was in order.

As one of the officers in charge, Edmund took part in the roll-call and selection of the gangs for the day's work. He marked their names on the grubby, well-used roll and, as usual, found some were missing from muster, still lingering in the dormitories hoping to avoid detection or complaining of some or other ailment they hoped would excuse them from duty. As on previous occasions, he sent a detachment of guards into the dormitories to hunt out the malingerers and to march to the hospital those who considered themselves too sick for duty. He knew from experience many were feigning illness and would soon re-join their companions in the lumberyard.

After twenty minutes all men were accounted for. Edmund then joined the guard of his assigned gang and guided them into the mess. As they were one of the last gangs to enter, there were neither seats nor tables for them and they were forced to find space on the rough dirt floor to sit.

Watching the men stuffing the gluggy meal into their mouths bought bile to Edmund's throat. Looking away he noticed that his batman, Corporal Evans, was looking just as uneasy.

"It's unbearably hot isn't it, Evans...?" Edmund stopped in mid-sentence. That voice, that same refined voice he'd heard on the pier the day he first arrived, was clearly audible over the rabble. At least on first inspection it seemed to be the same voice. Looking around to find its source, his attention was drawn to a group of men sitting nearby. They were listening intently to that voice, but the man himself had his back to Edmund. He caught snatches of what seemed to be a story about England. He heard references to shady country lanes, dense London fogs, but not wanting to reveal his eavesdropping he could not be sure.

Moving closer to his batman, Edmund pointed. "Evans, see that prisoner over there? Do you know his name?"

"Which one sir?" he said, looking in the direction Edmund was gesturing.

"That one. The man with his back to us. He seems to be telling a story."

"Oh him, he's harmless enough, sir. I believe he's been known as the Bard since he arrived here." He coughed to clear his throat. "Probably no-one knows his real name now. Seems he has a gift for telling stories, especially ones about good ol' England. His stories are always so vivid, sir. You can picture yourself safe back home. I have witnessed some of the most hardened criminals cry like babies when listening to one of his tales." He stopped and listened to the Bard speak. "Cultured voice hasn't he, sir, probably well-educated don't you think? He seems to be learned on so many subjects. Wonder what he did to end up here?"

Evans's astute assumptions bothered Edmund even more. Images of Michael Hanlan again intruded into his thoughts but he ignored them, shutting out even the slightest possibility that his ex-friend might indeed be on this island. No, there had to be another explanation, he assured himself, trying in vain to catch a glimpse of the Bard's face.

Determined to put all his fears to rest, Edmund started to make his way to the front of the group. Suddenly, a ruckus broke out near the entrance of the lumberyard. Reacting in haste, Edmund directed Evans to take charge of the work gang and, cocking his pistol in readiness, pushed his way through the wall of convicts that had amassed before him. The din was incredible as pannikins were noisily thumped on tables and the convicts started to cheer, some even jumping on tables to get a better look. Soldiers drew their pistols and jostled the men into control. Yet even though Edmund stood nearly a head taller than most in lumberyard he could not get a clear view of the disturbance.

Then he saw Saunders. By the look of the broad grin on his face it seemed he was enjoying himself as he struggled to contain a man. The other men who had been cheering were quiet now, waiting to see the outcome of the altercation.

"Heh, Saunders, it seems I am always getting you out of trouble." Edmund did not look at his fellow officer, but kept his eyes and his pistol trained on the men in front of him.

"On the contrary, my dear Thornton, it is I who always invite you to join in the fun."

"We believe what we believe." Edmund smiled. "Now what have we here?"

"I think those three might belong to you, Thornton? I believe they're from your detachment." Saunders twisted his head in the direction of three bedraggled looking soldiers. "Think they've been in for a swim instead of reporting for duty! Isn't that right, soldiers?"

Edmund looked at the three sorry excuses for soldiers, their clothes and hair dripping wet, their faces turned to the ground.

"Salute when you are spoken to by a superior," Edmund yelled. Immediately all three stood to attention and saluted. The convicts cheered, but soon became quiet when they saw Saunders staring at them, still holding his captive, who had by now stopped struggling to watch. "It seems you did not feel it necessary to appear for the change of the guard this morning. This is inexcusable." Edmund glared at the soldiers. They sunk their chins to their chest in shame. "And now, it seems that you've incited this group to mayhem."

"Just this one," Saunders interrupted, still holding the convict securely in his grasp. "He saw it as a chance to bolt. But I was too quick for him!"

Edmund looked across at the convict Saunders was restraining and the colour drained from his face.

"I see you recognise him. May I present Edward Lawton, known throughout the settlement as a man with an ungovernable temper and the strength of two?"

Edmund regained his senses. "Well, what happens to him is up to you, Saunders. But these three are mine. The honour of the regiment is at stake here." Not taking his gaze away from the soldiers, he said, "Look at me when I speak to you. I will be recommending at least three dozen lashes for each of you and that, gentlemen, is being lenient in my opinion." He shoved them forward toward some nearby soldiers of the Eleventh. "I am ashamed of you." Then, to the other soldiers: "Lock these three up and let them sweat on what their punishment might be."

Saunders, too, shoved his prisoner towards the soldiers. "Lock 'em up together. They might enjoy each other's company!" He watched as the group marched away. "You know, Thornton, I don't think I will ever understand you. You're here to guard the convicts and keep them in order but rarely have I seen you put one on report. You know the other officers are beginning to talk, don't you? Your men are more afraid of you than the convicts are. I say again, you're a strange one, Thornton. You see many of the punishments ordered for the convicts too harsh for the offence, but when it comes to your own men, no punishment seems harsh enough, no matter the crime."

"But they nearly caused a riot. You said so yourself," Edmund said, shocked at the accusations.

"And your convict from the raid the other night would have killed you given half a chance."

"I have to make an example of them. The honour of the Regiment is at stake, Saunders, don't you see? The honour of the Regiment..." Edmund's voice trailed off.

Edmund strode confidently into the prisoners' barrack compound the next morning in full uniform. Nothing could deter him from his single minded determination to epitomise the perfect officer under any circumstance. Yet the sight of the wooden frame that had been erected in the centre of the open space onto which a flogging triangle had been affixed made him catch his breathe. Steeling himself to show an air of calm and self-confidence to his assembled men, Edmund stepped forward.

The sergeant saluted Edmund. "All present and correct, sir."

Edmund returned the salute and then remained motionless for a moment, collecting his thoughts before addressing his assembled men. "Bring forth the prisoners," he commanded.

The three young soldiers who had caused the convict mayhem the day before were led out between two armed soldiers, wearing only their trousers.

Edmund addressed his men in a loud voice, mustering as much authority as he could. "Men, in the absence of our Captain Travers who has been taken poorly this morning, it has become my duty to direct today's punishments." His voice hardened. "We are seen as the upholders of the law in the penal settlements of the Australian Colonies. To break these laws brings dishonour to our uniform and to our young Queen. It brings disgrace on our very own regiment." Edmund paused to let the importance of his words sink in, he then continued, "These three men standing here before you now are accused of breaking one of those laws – being absent from duty. They will therefore be punished according to the laws and customs of Her Majesty's Regiments of Foot, unless someone will speak for them."

There was an agonising silence. Taking a deep breath Edmund pronounced sentence. "So be it, seize up the first. Three dozen if you please. Flog well man and do your duty."

Edmund did not flinch as each lash found its mark. "Ni-ne... T-en...El-even..." Strong and clear, the sergeant's voice echoed throughout the compound. Edmund could clearly see the face of the soldier lashed to the flogging triangle. With a ghoulish sense of self-interest, he watched the man's face contort in agony as each lash found its mark.

"Thirty-four...Thirty-five...Thirty-six," droned the deep voice of the sergeant "Three dozen, sir."

"Very good." Edmund admired the soldier's strength of character. He had suffered his punishment well, not uttering a sound, upholding the honour of the regiment. "Take the prisoner down," he ordered. "Next!"

The bloody spectacle continued till all three had received the total of their sentence.

Disgusted and disappointed by the morning's events, Edmund threw off his boots and flopped into his favourite chair by the fireplace, glad his duty was finished. He mulled over what had happened earlier for perhaps the hundredth time since the event. Was Saunders right? Was he too harsh with his own men?

"No, by God!" He thumped the arm of his chair. "The honour of the Regiment is of highest importance, no matter the circumstance."

Chapter Eight

Edmund identified himself to the sentry on duty at Government House.

The soldier saluted. "Good morning Lieutenant, the Commandant is expecting you." He indicated to a wooden bench in the corridor. "Please be seated. I will inform him that you're here."

Edmund sat and waited, but he was not kept long. Soon he recognised a familiar figure coming towards him, hand out held. Edmund tried to salute but the Commandant gripped his hand in a firm handshake.

"It's good to see you Thornton, what's it been? Eight weeks now since we have had the pleasure of your company?" Not waiting for an answer he continued, "I have summoned you today to charge you with a special duty. The barque, The Lady Franklin, out of Sydney, should make anchor in the bay sometime on the morrow, all being well. She is late. It will hold up proceedings but our new judge and his wife are expected to be on board."

"A judge, sir?"

"Yes, the powers that be have finally decided to send us a resident judge. I have never understood why they decided to place this prison in the middle of nowhere but in their great wisdom forget to give us the power to deal with capital crimes. It's been damnable inconvenient if you ask me."

"I quite agree, sir."

"Right then, I charge you to meet the ship's master and carry out the required inspections before allowing any person aboard her to land. Is that understood? I will leave that in your capable hands. Dismissed!"

Standing on the pier the next morning, in full dress uniform, Edmund watched as the fine barque made her way gracefully into the bay under full sail. Surveying the high swell crashing over the reef he questioned the coxswain who was preparing the long boat in readiness to unload the ship once it had anchored. "Do you think they will be able to make land today?"

"I have seen it worse, sir. Though, I understand we are expecting a lady this time." Edmund nodded in acknowledgement and the coxswain continued. "She might find it a little uncomfortable, sir. But we should be quite safe."

A small crowd was beginning to form around him as news of the ship's arrival filtered through the settlement. The ladies were all dressed in their Sunday finery and the men too had dressed for the occasion. Kings Town had been ripe with speculation and rumour about the judge and his wife since news of their imminent arrival had spread and none were going to miss their first appearance.

"They have anchored, sir. Should I hoist the flag to let them know it's safe to land?"

Edmund surveyed the surf one last time and looked at the coxswain. "I will trust your judgment, my man. You know more of the sea and her temperamental moods than I ever will."

"Very good, sir. Thank you, sir."

Another watched the barque, dressed neither in finery nor his Sunday best. The Bard's ragged clothes hung loosely on his body, his ginger hair matted in the wind. He had forgotten that he was supposed to be digging a drain and stood with his pick halfway in the air, mesmerised by the sight of the ship entering the bay. Lowering his pick, he leant on its handle and gazed at the barque, sails billowing, looking like the majestic white swans he had once seen gliding freely on the River Thames. One day soon, he prayed, a ship such as this will deliver him to freedom; deliver him back into the arms of his Sarah. He watched as the swan slowly lost its beautiful white plumage as the sails were furled and the anchor dropped. Then, grotesquely, the swan transformed into a stark skeleton disgorging itself of its human cargo. No longer a key to freedom, it now brought home to him just how imprisoned on this god-forsaken island he really was.

Michael felt a firm warning tug on his ragged shirt. "Heh mate, watch it. The guard's a comin'."

He looked up to see the convict working next to him pointing, but too late. A dark shadow fell over him. "Well, what have we here?"

Michael felt the sharp point of the guard's bayonet in his ribs. "You day dreamin' Bard? That's not like you."

Edmund balanced in the centre of the long-boat and grabbed hold of the bottom rung of the ladder that had been thrown down to him.

"Permission to come aboard?" he called as he reached the top and heaved himself onto the barque's deck.

"Permission granted," replied the ship's bos'n. "Your name, sir?"

Edmund turned to salute the quarterdeck as protocol demanded. "Whoa!" he grabbed the wooden rail of the deck to stop himself from falling as the waves pitched the barque to starboard. "Begging your pardon sir, I had forgotten how unsteady I am on the deck of a ship. It has been nigh on nine months since I have had the pleasure. Please excuse me. I am Lieutenant Edmund Thornton of Her Majesty's Eleventh Regiment of Foot, at your service, sir." He saluted, now steadier on his feet.

"I understand exactly how you feel, Lieutenant. I have the same problem when I am on dry land," said the man standing in front of him, chuckling. "If you will kindly follow me I will inform the captain of your arrival."

Edmund followed the bos'n to the captain's cabin.

The captain met them at the top of the stairs. "Captain William Snelling at your service sir, captain of Her Majesty's barque, The

Lady Franklin, newly arrived from Sydney with dispatches and personnel for Norfolk Island."

"Lieutenant Edmund Thornton. Pleased to make your acquaintance, sir. I understand you have our new judge and his wife on board, captain," Edmund said, scanning the deck.

"That would be me, Lieutenant." A stocky, balding gentleman with a curling grey moustache and monocle stepped forward. "I am Judge John Forsyth. My wife and her companion are still below decks readying our belongings for landing and will join us directly."

Edmund saluted. "On behalf of Commandant Boyce, I welcome you, sir, to Her Majesty's penal settlement, Norfolk Island."

"I am not a military man, sir, and as such do not expect your salute, but I welcome your kindness. My wife and I are looking forward to our posting on your island."

Captain Snelling interjected. "Would both you gentlemen care to join me in my cabin for a tot of rum? I can hand over the dispatches and letters to you then, Lieutenant."

"Very good captain, lead the way." Edmund stepped back to let the captain pass.

"Please excuse me, gentleman, I might take my leave of you both and help my wife with her last minute preparations." The judge turned and disappeared below decks.

"That reminds me, sir." Edmund pulled a letter he had written to Sarah from his jacket inside pocket and handed it to the captain. "Would you be so kind as to see to the safe delivery of this, captain?"

"Ah, a sweetheart, Lieutenant?" the captain inquired, taking the letter from Edmund's outstretched hand.

"Not exactly, sir, but someone I hold in very high regard and will probably never have the good fortune to meet again."

"You can depend that I will deliver it myself to the captain of an England bound transport."

"Thank you, sir. I will be very much indebted."

The captain directed Edmund towards his cabin to complete the necessary formalities.

The inspections and paperwork were completed in good time and the captain and Edmund soon joined the judge and his wife on the deck.

"May I present my wife, Lieutenant?" asked the judge.

A plump, little woman smiled up at Edmund as he bowed. "Welcome to our island, Mrs. Forsyth. I hope your stay with us will be a pleasant one."

"I am looking forward to it, lieutenant." Then, looking behind and to the side, she said, "Now, where is that girl?"

"She said she had forgotten something or other and so has just gone below to collect it, my dear," Judge Forsyth answered her. "She should be up directly."

"Oh, bother!" a female voice said.

All turned to face the young lady in a sensible grey travelling dress and a large bonnet, struggling with the hem of her skirt that had apparently caught on some unseen snag. Edmund was the first to react and strode toward her offering assistance. The faint smell of lavender tickled his nose as he moved closer.

"Good morning, miss. You seem to be in some discomfort. Would it be too forward of me to offer my assistance?"

"Why, thank you, kind sir. My skirt seems to be caught on a nail or some such," she answered without looking up as she tried to untangle herself, brushing away a wisp of auburn hair that had escaped from beneath her bonnet.

Edmund's heart leapt into his throat, the smell of lavender, the voice, the auburn hair... "Sarah!" he breathed.

"I beg your pardon?" She looked up from her dress. "How do you know...? Edmund! I mean, Lieutenant Thornton. What on earth...?"

Their eyes met and they were both momentarily speechless.

"Of all the people... I had hoped, but never expected...." Sarah regarded him with a speculative gaze. "You do cut a fine figure in your uniform, sir. I had quite forgotten. Oh, it is so good to see you." She lowered her eyes as Edmund's heart lurched, but he merely stared, tongue-tied.

61

"Well, do not just stand there. Were you not taught, sir, that it is rude to stare!" She laughed. "Now, Lieutenant Thornton, do something to save this damsel in distress."

Recovering, Edmund said, "Miss H-Henshall, h-how wonderful to m-meet you again." He was ashamed at the sound of his own voice. It sounded so stifled, so unnatural. It was all wrong. It was not at all the reunion he had repeatedly created in his mind. He chastised himself for his clumsiness. It was supposed to be wonderful, both professing their undying love for each other, not him stammering like a bumbling oaf. At last he worked up enough courage to look directly at Sarah, thankful she was no longer looking at him, counting his blessings that she had not seemed to notice his shortcomings. She was once again concentrating on trying to release her skirt from its snag.

"H-Here, let me," Edmund said as he bent down to detach her underskirt from the spike on which it had caught. Trembling fingers made his attempts awkward and futile.

Sarah lifted her top skirts ever so slightly, just enough to expose her slender ankle in its pink coloured hose and her dainty, black leather boot. "There, that may help. Does it?" She placed her other hand on his shoulder to help keep her balance.

Following his gaze to her ankle she laughed. "Why, Lieutenant Thornton. You are so very bold. I do not remember you as such."

Edmund swallowed hard, the intensity of his own desire shocking him. The imprint of her hand seemed to burn into his shoulder. It was all he could do not to reach up and take her hand in his.

"What on earth is taking so long? What...Lieutenant? Miss Henshall, are you all right?" Judge Forsyth asked.

Sarah dropped her skirt hem just as her under-skirt became free. Edmund nearly fell backwards down the hatchway stairs in his haste to stand and acknowledge the judge's presence.

Sarah exclaimed, "Oh, Judge Forsyth, is it not wonderful? The lieutenant and I are old friends. We spent many hours together back home with our mutual friend, Mr. Hanlan." Obvious joy bubbled in her voice and her eyes glistened with excitement.

The judge's eyebrows rose inquiringly. "Umm, well, I suppose introductions are superfluous," he said, looking at both of them.

Awkwardly, Edmund cleared his throat and stood to attention. "Begging your pardon, sir, Miss Henshall's skirt had become caught and I offered her my assistance."

"Good, good," the judge murmured, looking at them with uncertainty.

Clasping Edmund's hand in her excitement Sarah cried, "Mrs. Forsyth was so worried, sir, that I would miss the company of people my own age. She need not worry now." She felt Edmund's hand tighten around hers. Her cheeks burnt with embarrassment and she withdrew her hand, too late becoming conscious of how forward she must appear.

"I am sure Mrs. Forsyth will be most happy for you Sarah, my dear," said the judge, "but for the moment we need to concentrate on disembarking. Lieutenant, will you please lead the way."

Chapter Nine

Margaret Forsyth watched as her husband, Sarah and the lieutenant walked toward her, all compensating for the pitch of the barque. "Oh, my dear child, are you sick?" She touched Sarah's forehead with the back of her hand. "Look how flushed you are. She looks quite ill. Do you not think so, Mr. Forsyth? We must find her somewhere to sit. Fancy you becoming sick just before we are about to disembark. You always seemed the healthiest of us all on the long, tiring voyage from England, and now the voyage from Sydney. She needs a drink of port. Can you fetch a glass of port for her please, Captain Snelling."

"Mrs. Forsyth, please take a breath," ordered her husband. "Sarah is quite well."

Edmund's mouth twitched with amusement. He felt drawn to this friendly woman. She talked a great deal, but her infectious smile matched Sarah's. Both these women were going to be a welcome distraction on such a dull and deadly island.

"She is far from sick, my dear. In fact, I believe she is quite well. Would you believe it, we have travelled half way around the world to places unknown to us, and now our young companion immediately renews a friendship with an old acquaintance."

"How wonderful, Mr. Forsyth," responded his wife, looking approvingly at the two young people in front of her. "Of course, Lieutenant Thornton," she said. "You are Lieutenant Edmund Thornton, are you not?"

"Yes, ma'am," answered Edmund, confused. "Have we met before?"

"Oh no, Lieutenant. But I certainly feel as though I know you. Sarah spoke of you often on the voyage. I believe she holds you in very high regard, sir."

Sarah blushed. "Please, Mrs. Forsyth."

Edmund stared, wordlessly, from Mrs. Forsyth to Sarah, his heart pounding.

"Sarah spoke of me?" he found his voice.

"All the time."

"You exaggerate so, Mrs. Forsyth." Sarah turned to Edmund. "I only told her that we were close acquaintances."

Edmund was not listening – the thought of her speaking of him to anyone sent his spirits soaring.

"I am sorry to interrupt such pleasantries." Captain Snelling came over to the group. "But you should make haste now to disembark before it becomes impossible for you to land today."

Margaret Forsyth looked toward the shore. "Captain... Lieutenant?" she implored. "Surely, we must sail in closer to the pier so that we can step ashore safely." She looked from one to the other for an answer.

The captain chose to respond. "See that line of waves breaking just ahead, Mrs. Forsyth. It covers a submerged reef that blocks the entrance to the bay."

"Then how...?" Margaret Forsyth interrupted, her gloved hands beginning to shake.

"The long-boat on which the lieutenant arrived this morning is the only way to safely cross that reef, Mrs. Forsyth."

She edged over to the barque's side and stared down into the small boat that was pitching with the waves. "In that? How on earth... I'll drown." She breathed in short nervous gasps.

"Never fear, ma'am. We will get you to the settlement without mishap."

She turned to her husband and implored, "Mr. Forsyth, I cannot swim. I do not want to drown! John, help me. Please help me!"

"Could someone please bring my wife a stool, and perhaps a glass of port to settle her nerves? She is not one to usually submit to the vapours."

Sarah took the glass of port handed to her by a young steward and offered it to her distressed guardian. "We will be fine, Mrs. Forsyth. I cannot swim either, but I know for a fact that Lieutenant Thornton is a strong swimmer."

Margaret Forsyth did not look up, but the occasional gentle sob escaped from her throat.

Sarah went on. "It was about two and a half years ago now, was it not, Lieutenant?"

Edmund shrugged, but Sarah was not deterred. "We were picnicking near a river. There were four of us, the lieutenant, myself, our friend Mr. Hanlan and his young sister, Jane. Jane's puppy, the cutest thing you ever saw, ran away and slipped into the river. Without thinking, Jane ran to the edge and also lost her balance and fell in. It was so frightening. Mr. Hanlan could not swim. In fact I believe he is frightened of water. I was sure Jane was going to drown. We were all screaming, the poor little dog was yelping. But Lieutenant Thornton kept his wits about him and jumped in. He not only saved Jane but also the puppy."

Mrs. Forsyth looked up from examining her hands, which she was nervously wringing in her lap, and stared up at Edmund as Sarah continued. "The lieutenant was magnificent! Michael, Mr. Hanlan I mean, swore then and there that he was indebted to the lieutenant for life. I remember he said that no matter how difficult the request, he would do anything to repay his debt. So you see, Mrs. Forsyth, we could not be in safer hands."

"And you saved the puppy?" Margaret Forsyth looked at Edmund.

"Yes, ma'am, the puppy too. And you, ma'am, are far more important to us all than a puppy. I promise to swim extra well, if called upon!"

A huge smile broke across Mrs. Forsyth's face. "Well, I suppose we had better get it over with, had we not?"

Judge Forsyth took his wife's hand and squeezed it gently. "That's my girl, everything will be all right," he whispered and then he acknowledged Edmund. "See, my dear, we are in good hands. We will certainly be safe under the lieutenant's watchful eye."

Mrs. Forsyth shuffled with trepidation to peer again at the long-boat bobbing on the water near the barque's hull. "But how, pray tell, do we get onto that boat, captain? You cannot be expecting Miss Henshall and me to climb down that rickety old ladder? Our skirts alone would prohibit this."

"Oh no, ma'am, of course not, but we do not often have the pleasure of having two such lovely ladies as passengers. If you would be so kind as to look behind you ma'am, you will find the means of your descent."

All turned to look in the direction Captain Snelling was indicating. There before them stood a large wooden frame, rigged with ropes and pulleys.

"It is not very elegant. I am sorry, Mrs. Forsyth, but it is the best I can offer."

The judge looked incredulously at the contraption. "If memory serves me correctly captain, is this not the way you land cattle and horses? I am sure I witnessed just such a landing when we arrived in Sydney Town." The captain nodded in answer. "Clearly then, sir, you cannot expect my wife and Miss Henshall to be treated in such an undignified manner."

"You are correct sir, but I have taken the liberty of getting a couple of the sailors to stitch up this harness especially for the ladies. I can guarantee that no livestock has ever been near it. It is most definitely the safest way for the ladies to gain access to the long-boat below."

Mrs. Forsyth eyed it doubtfully.

"I will go first, Mrs. Forsyth, if you would like." Sarah tried to sound brave, although her stomach was churning.

"No, you certainly will not, my dear," said her guardian. "You certainly will not. I will. How on earth could I look your aunt in the face and tell her that I looked after you to the best of my ability and then tell her that you drowned." She held up a hand to silence Sarah's protests. "No, it is settled. I will not hear any arguments. Then, if it is safe for me, you can follow."

Squeezing both Mrs. Forsyth and her voluminous petticoats and skirts into the chair proved quite an exercise for the ship's crew.

When she was strapped in, she motioned to her husband to join her. She kissed him on the cheek whispering, "I love you John, I have not told you that often enough, have I? If I drown, write to my sister and tell her I died bravely, won't you?"

Just the hint of a smile curved the corners of the judge's mouth. "You will be quite safe, my dear. After all, we have a hero in our midst, remember?"

"Right, all is well then," the captain said. "Ah, by the way, Lieutenant, I take it then that you will now deliver this letter yourself." He handed back the letter Edmund had entrusted to him earlier.

"Th-thank you sir, I will," Edmund stammered in embarrassment, stuffing it back into his jacket pocket.

The captain indicated to Edmund that he descend the ladder first. "That way, if there are any mishaps, which I am sure there will not be, you will be on hand to play hero again."

Once Edmund had scrambled down the ladder, Mrs. Forsyth was raised high above the barque's bulwark. For a moment it seemed that she was suspended in mid-air as the sailors on board the barque and those on the long-boat below worked the ropes. She screamed as a gust of wind seemed to take control of her descent.

Edmund threw off his jacket and tried to regulate the wayward ropes himself, at the same time yelling, so as to be heard over the wind, comforting words to the anxious woman. "You can open your eyes Mrs. Forsyth. You are safe now." Edmund untied the strapping fastening the lady in the chair and offered his hand.

Slowly she opened one eye, then the other and looked toward Edmund. "Well, you definitely are a hero, are you not, Lieutenant? Thank you sir, I owe you my life."

"Not at all ma'am, you have been very brave today."

Mrs. Forsyth glanced up toward Sarah who was staring down from the rail above. She pulled Edmund down onto the seat beside her, whispering, "We must not frighten Miss Henshall, must we? Might I entreat you, Lieutenant, to look up at her and smile? I believe that should put the child at ease."

That was one of the easiest requests Edmund had ever had to fulfil. Just knowing Sarah was so near kept the smile on his face.

"It was quite easy, my dear, nothing to it, really," Margaret Forsyth called.

Sarah was excited at the prospect of her ride in the harness and positioned herself to best advantage in the sacking chair. At first she squeezed her eyes closed as she felt the sensation of her feet leaving the deck, but soon she could not resist opening them.

"Oh, my goodness!" She laughed with glee. "The landing in boring old Sydney Town was nothing like this!" She could taste the salt spray on her lips. Giggling, she held onto her bonnet as the wind tried to claim it. It was over too soon. She was almost disappointed to feel her feet touch the deck of the long-boat.

"Are we ready Judge Forsyth? Ladies?" Edmund enquired. "Let me assure you, we have the most experienced coxswain on the island in charge of this boat." The coxswain nodded "And," continued Edmund, "his crew cannot be surpassed. But still we need to be prepared, so please hold tight and stay completely still." Checking the height of the waves that were now breaking over the submerged reef he turned to the man at the helm. "It looks as if the sea is in one of her more cantankerous moods. What do you think coxswain? Can we cross the reef?"

"I believe so, sir. I have been watching the waves closely while our passengers have been boarding. Although we will need to shove off immediately, are you ready?"

"But what about our belongings?" wailed Mrs. Forsyth.

"Do not fret, ma'am. Your belongings will be landed over the next few days. The captain took the liberty of asking Miss Henshall to pack a small bag for you. See, there it is behind you. Tonight you are to be the guests of the Commandant and Mrs. Boyce."

Margaret Forsyth began to smooth her dress and adjust her bonnet. She enjoyed being fussed over and being the guest of such important personage.

"We will see you on shore tomorrow, Captain Snelling," Edmund yelled up to the captain, who returned his salute with a relieved smile.

Mrs. Forsyth shuffled closer to her husband. He put a comforting arm around her shoulders. Sarah on the other hand, could not contain her excitement and fidgeted non-stop.

"Please Miss Henshall!" Edmund admonished. "I must implore you to sit very still. We do not want the boat to tip over do we?" Her nearness was overwhelming and he had to look away so as to avoid drawing attention to his feelings.

Sarah took Edmund's gentle reprimand to heart and sat very straight and very still next to him but her face was flush with excitement. She watched as the dozen or so rowers pulled the long-boat closer and closer to the reef. The waves looked very threatening and she became concerned that the boat might indeed capsize.

Mrs. Forsyth again became distressed. "We are going to drown. We are all going to drown. Oh, look at me I am drenched." she wailed. "How on earth can I be presented to the commandant, looking like this?"

Her husband tried to reassure her, still holding her as he had.

Edmund told her of other crossings he had experienced, "... so you can see Mrs. Forsyth, very few people land on Norfolk completely dry, including myself."

Sarah scanned the waves breaking over it trying to find just where the long-boat could cross. The coxswain and crew waited until just the right moment to attempt the crossing. Catching the crest of a perfect wave they plummeted through the unseen passage to the smoother waters on the other side. Sarah squealed with delight.

The last part of the journey was uneventful, by comparison, and the party were soon being helped out of the long-boat onto dry land. Mrs. Forsyth looked back down at the unsteady boat bobbing in the waves. Turning to her husband, she said, "Mr. Forsyth you are now officially marooned on this island because even God himself could not convince me to undertake that journey ever again."

Chapter Ten

Burning with curiosity about her new acquaintances, but at the same time dismally aware of her bedraggled appearance, Mrs. Forsyth pushed Sarah forward so that she would encounter any person of rank or social standing first. First impressions were of great importance, and here she was the wife of a newly arrived dignitary, looking, she was sure, like a scullery maid. She tried in vain to straighten her dishevelled costume. Concentrating on climbing the slippery stone stairs of the pier she bumped straight into Sarah as the girl paused to curtsey to the welcoming party.

"Sarah... oh!" Margaret Forsyth looked up and saw an elegant woman standing at the top of the steps. "Please excuse me, ma'am. I am afraid that I lost my balance."

"Mrs. Forsyth?" the lady on the pier asked.

"I beg your pardon ma'am. I am sorry but I cannot hear you above the din of the waves. Oh dear, here comes another. Sarah, we must leave this place in great haste before we are washed out to sea!"

The lady laughed a most genteel, quiet laugh. "I know how you feel Mrs. Forsyth. I felt the same way when I arrived." She held out her hand in welcome. "I am Mrs. Catherine Boyce, wife of the Commandant. How wonderful to meet you. I do hope that your sea voyage agreed with you."

"It was an experience to say the least, Mrs. Boyce. One I would not like to have again in the near future." Margaret Forsyth looked back at the long-boat she had just left and shuddered. Then remembering how she must look, she said, "Oh dear, look at me. Please forgive my appearance, Mrs. Boyce. I do declare I must look a sight."

"No matter, Mrs. Forsyth, we all arrived in the same condition. It is the curse of our island. That is why I thought to meet you first before the crowd up there surrounds you and inundates you with questions. I will warn you now that we are all starved for news from home. Here." She reached for the cloak and bonnet held by her ladies' maid. "Take these and cover your wet clothes. You will at least feel a little more presentable."

Margaret Forsyth allowed Sarah to remove her wet bonnet and replace it with the new one. She wrapped the long cloak around her, covering her damp, limp skirts.

Mrs. Boyce assessed the effect. "There, no-one will know."

"You look very well now, my dear." Judge Forsyth smiled at his wife. Then, turning to Mrs. Boyce, he removed his top hat and gave a low, exaggerated bow. "How can I thank you for your kind consideration of my wife, Mrs. Boyce?"

"Speak no more of it, Judge Forsyth," she said. "My husband is looking forward to meeting you. Please excuse him for not being down here to greet you personally. He has been detained by some urgent official business. Now, who is this pretty young thing who has been standing so quietly all this while?"

"Oh, my goodness, just where are my manners?" Margaret Forsyth fussed. "This landing has me all in a tither." Pulling Sarah forward, she said, "Mrs. Boyce, may I present my companion, Miss Sarah Henshall. She is the niece of a very close acquaintance of mine. She is now Judge Forsyth's ward, since her father's untimely passing. God rest his soul. This is her first time away from home. Such a joy, so very helpful, I do not know how I would have survived the voyage without her."

Before she could continue her husband interrupted. "I am sure, my dear, there will be plenty of time to exchange family histories. After all we will be here for some time."

"Welcome to Kings Town, Miss Henshall." Mrs. Boyce smiled at Sarah. "We are looking forward to having you all stay with us at Government House until all your furniture and belongings are landed. A lovely house has been prepared for you on Military Road, directly across from Government House and next to what we call the old military barracks, so you will be quite safe."

Mrs. Forsyth shuddered.

Mrs. Boyce continued, "Sarah, would you mind sharing a room my daughter, Annie? She is about your age."

"Thank you ma'am, I will look forward to meeting her."

"I am sure you will not be lacking in company whilst on our island. There is a marked shortage of young ladies here. Is that not so, Lieutenant?" Mrs. Boyce looked at Edmund.

"Yes, Mrs. Boyce." Edmund forced a smile. Strong feelings of jealousy surged through him. No-one else was going to have his Sarah if he had anything to do with it, he promised himself.

"Ahem," Mrs. Boyce cleared her throat. "Lieutenant, are you not forgetting that my husband has charged you to bring the judge to him the moment he arrives."

Edmund reluctantly turned his gaze from Sarah to the Commandant's wife and stood to attention. "Yes, ma'am, of course." Edmund faced the judge. "Unfortunately sir, your ship anchored a couple of days later than was expected. There is some pressing official business that requires your immediate attention. I can assure you that Mrs. Forsyth and Miss Henshall will be in very good hands." He bowed to the women and then addressed the judge again. "Follow me if you would be so kind, sir. Mrs. Boyce is right. The Commandant will be becoming anxious for your attendance at today's proceedings."

Mrs. Boyce nodded in agreement. "I am sure I can cope, Lieutenant."

The men strode away.

"Come now, Mrs. Forsyth, we too should be getting on our way. So many of the town's folk want to meet you." Catherine Boyce gently guided her away.

"Yes, of course, Mrs. Boyce, of course. I was quite forgetting myself."

The two elder ladies walked arm in arm up the stone pier, chatting all the while as though they had known each other for many years. Sarah followed close behind, still staring after Edmund as he strode away. It was very clear to her that he now carried himself with a commanding air of self-assurance that was not there back in Devon.

Military life obviously agrees with him, she thought with a smile. *But still, he will never hold a candle to my Michael. He is as dark as my Michael is fair with his ginger hair, freckles, cheeky grin, and mischievous blue eyes.* She felt for the gold locket hidden under the lace at her breast, her heart aching for the man who had gifted it to her.

But what luck to have met Edmund so soon upon arrival. She was sure that between the two of them they would be able to find Michael without delay, wherever he was. Kissing the locket tenderly she tucked it back into its hiding place.

As the ladies approached the waiting carriage at the top of the path, Mrs. Forsyth was surrounded by the other women of the settlement, all eager to hear news from the outside world. She was in her element. She loved being the centre of attention. Sarah's absence was not noticed.

Lifting her skirts, Sarah stepped nimbly around the rotting mounds of rubbish piled high against the grey stone walls of the unkempt buildings. Screwing up her nose at the foul smells, she inhaled the lavender water on her handkerchief, trying to block out the stench that seemed to emanate from the very ground itself. She had heard stories of the slums of London, but no image came close to what she now witnessed.

Yet even in such a horrid place, she managed to find some beauty. She looked beyond the dark silhouettes of the distorted buildings towards the vibrant colour of the majestic pines on the hill behind the settlement, and marvelled at the stark contrast.

"Excuse me, ma'am!" A brusque, deep voice interrupted her thoughts.

Startled, Sarah jumped back against a wall as a gang of men in chains shuffled past, guarded by escorts with fixed bayonets. One of the chained men smiled at her but the other four men walked on with heads drooped. Curiosity made her follow. She tried to keep hidden in the shadows as the men disappeared into a large crowd. It was then that she saw Judge Forsyth speaking to another man in uniform. Edmund was standing nearby. She stared as the judge scrutinised some papers. He signed them and handed them to Edmund.

The group of five men that she had been following reappeared, now loosened from their chains, climbing up a set of wooden stairs to a high platform. They were followed by two others who, by the mode of their dress, Sarah concluded, must have been religious ministers. Upon reaching the platform the men knelt before the ministers and in loud but faltering voices began to recite prayers and bow their heads to receive blessings.

A loud voice from the crowd yelled, "You're a lucky bugger, Smith. You're making your escape from this hell hole."

One of the men on the platform yelled back, grinning broadly, "Yeah, but not quite the freedom I was looking for, heh?"

With a sharp stab of recognition, Sarah saw it was the convict who had smiled at her.

It was not until ropes were being adjusted around the necks of the five men and hoods being pulled over their faces that Sarah understood what was happening.

Mrs. Boyce grabbed Sarah's attention just before the trap door opened. "Not something for a young lady to witness, my dear," she said, and gently led Sarah away by the arm. "Come, Mrs. Forsyth is already in the carriage waiting for you."

Sarah shuddered as she heard, rather than saw, the clanking of the trapdoor giving way beneath the unfortunate men. She clutched her breast, feeling for the locket, willing Michael to be safe. Then leaning on the older woman's arm, Sarah made her way to where Margaret Forsyth waited, already seated in the waiting carriage.

"Finally, Sarah. Where on earth have you been, child?"

"I am sorry Mrs. Forsyth."

"Do not be too harsh with her, Mrs. Forsyth. The poor child has just witnessed a most distressing incident." Then changing the subject, she continued, "Mrs. Forsyth has just informed me that Lieutenant Thornton is an old friend of yours, Sarah. I will arrange to invite him to join us for a meal this evening. That should help you feel at home."

"Thank you for your kindness ma'am."

"Now we must get on, by the look of the dark clouds a storm is coming."

His duties completed, Edmund excused himself from the judge and the Commandant. He walked away with long strides. As though of one mind, the gathered crowd stepped back to let him through. He noticed none of them, his thoughts about Sarah in turmoil. He reported to the Commandant's office, left the dispatches from the barque, made his excuses to the Commandant's aides, and stumbled out into the sunshine, not sure exactly what to do next.

He was anxious to leave the settlement far behind. He ordered one of the convict grooms in charge of the government stables to saddle him a horse. He fiddled with a rope as the groom struggled with a large black steed. Grabbing the reins from the convict, he flung himself into the saddle and dug his heels deep into the animal's sides. The horse raced off in a startled gallop and it took all of Edmund's considerable horsemanship to keep his seat. Even so, he let the animal have its head.

The stench of the prison settlement was left far behind as familiar scenery flashed past. Edmund sat low in the saddle whispering encouraging yet unintelligible words into the stallion's ear, urging him on, urging him faster. A thick screen of choking dust rose around them. Dry grass and leaves, thrown into the air by the horse's hooves, became entangled in its mane and tail. Edmund's eyes began to smart from the dust, which filled his mouth, his nose, his ears, but still he continued riding.

Only when a large flock of birds rose into the sky, flapping and squawking before them, did Edmund become conscious of his surroundings. He struggled to pull up his horse before both went over the cliff that had appeared in front of them. The horse skidded to a halt, snorting as it tried to clear its throat and nose of the heavy dust. Edmund's heart was hammering, his breathing ragged.

Ceaseless, endless questions swirled through his brain. *Sarah, here on the island! Can she know how I feel? She spoke of me to Mrs. Forsyth. Could she possibly feel the same?*

As he sat astride his horse above the cliff, staring out to sea, the sky became darker, the clouds thicker, the sea rougher. The front of the storm had arrived quicker than he'd anticipated. Lace-like sprays of water rose high into the air as the waves crashed against the rocks below. Lightning flashed out to sea. Seconds later, the sound of thunder reverberated across the island. Startled seabirds took to the sky, then circled enmasse and sought the safety of their nests on the cliffs. The stallion pawed at the ground in frustration at having to stay put. Edmund looked up, disoriented, as another clap of thunder broke through the air. Taking hold of the reins, just as the rain began to fall in large, heavy drops, he encouraged his steed back to the settlement. They went at a trot this time, the ground becoming soggy, muddy, harder for the horse to retain its footing, but the welcome downpour washed away the thick layer of dust from both man and beast. Eventually horse and master reached the summit of Flagstaff Hill, the settlement of Kings Town spread out before them.

"Sarah… She's actually here." He let the comforting thoughts wash over him. With great satisfaction, he said with a smirk, "No-one will stand in my way now, no-one!" But then a cynical, inner voice cut through his thoughts. *What if the Bard is Michael? What if Michael really is here? Does Sarah know this?*

"Oh God!" he said aloud. "Is that why she's here? Will the judge find out and tell her?"

He knew then that he could not take that chance. Filled with newfound fortitude, he dug his heels into the sides of his mount and raced down the hill.

Chapter Eleven

"Welcome Lieutenant Thornton." Catherine Boyce collapsed her fan and held out her hand as Edmund climbed the stairs to the veranda of Government House. "I am so pleased you could accept our dinner invitation at such short notice."

"Thank you for your kind invitation, Mrs. Boyce." Edmund bowed low. "It was a most welcome surprise."

"Good evening, sir." Edmund saluted her husband, who was standing behind her cleaning his pipe.

"Good evening, lieutenant." The Major returned the salute.

Edmund stood to attention, unsure of what was expected of him.

The Major looked up. "Stand easy, Thornton, you are my guest tonight. I think we can forgo formalities for one night."

"Yes, sir," Edmund answered, although he could not let the formalities go so easily.

"The truth be told, Lieutenant." Major Boyce moved forward and stood next to his wife. "My wife is worried you are lonely here in the settlement. She believes that you spend too much of your time at your duties."

His wife playfully hit him with her fan as he continued. "She has also made me promise I will not give you full duty on the day of the upcoming picnic so that you can join us in welcoming our guests." The commandant put an arm around his wife, smiling. "Very persuasive woman, my wife, Lieutenant. So I have given you the afternoon free but charge you with another special duty."

"Sir?" Edmund questioned, confused.

"Your duty, Lieutenant, will be to attend the picnic and sit at our table. I know I can depend on you, Thornton. We must all enjoy some free time, so you will join us. That is an order, Lieutenant." Major Boyce laughed.

"If you gentleman will excuse me." Mrs. Boyce began to descend the veranda steps. "I might go and fetch the judge, Mrs. Forsyth and Miss Henshall. They are taking a turn around the garden with our daughter."

Feeling uncomfortable in his superior's presence, Edmund stood by the veranda railing and scanned the extensive grounds of Government House, hoping for a glimpse of Sarah.

Disappointed, he turned back toward the Commandant as the man asked, "Would you care for a tot of rum, lieutenant?"

"Very kind, sir." Edmund accepted the mug and drained half of it, looking for courage. "It was good of you and your wife to invite me to dine this evening, sir. It was quite unexpected."

"Unexpected, by Jove. If you had heard Mrs. Boyce and Mrs. Forsyth talking this afternoon, you would not think it so unexpected. Once my dear wife found out that you and Miss Henshall were acquainted… I warn you, Lieutenant, they are already planning the nuptials!" He laughed. "Fine joke, do you not think?"

"A fine joke, sir, but I am sure you are mistaken. Miss Henshall and I are just very good friends."

"Perhaps you had better let the ladies know your intentions, then."

"Intentions, sir?" Edmund answered, now flustered. "I assure you, sir, we are just good friends."

"Do not panic so, Lieutenant. Let us just allow the ladies to have their fun, matchmaking. There is so little to occupy them on this dratted island. You and Miss Henshall are free to make of it what you will. Perhaps you might care to join them in the garden."

"It would be a pleasure, sir," Edmund answered, almost too eagerly.

The Major shrugged, but said no more as he led the way down the veranda steps and out onto the manicured gardens of Government

House. Mrs. Forsyth and Annie Boyce, arms linked, came gliding across the grounds.

The elder lady held out her hand in greeting. "Ah, Lieutenant Thornton, it is a pleasure to meet you again."

"The pleasure is all mine, I assure you, Mrs. Forsyth." Edmund kissed her hand.

"Oohh, Lieutenant, you are forward, sir." She twittered as she removed her hand. "I presume you are already acquainted with Miss Boyce. She has been a most excellent guide this afternoon." She patted Annie's hand affectionately.

"Good afternoon, Miss Boyce."

Edmund considered the shy girl. Her mousy brown hair and large brown eyes were not to his liking. In truth, he could not see why Saunders spoke so highly of her. But then, he had eyes for only one, and all paled in comparison to her.

"Good afternoon, Lieutenant," she said, almost whispering.

"Now where is that girl?" Margaret Forsyth fussed. "Dawdling behind as usual."

Sarah strolled around the side of the house. Edmund's breath caught in his throat. She looked even more delicate and ethereal than she did in his most treasured miniature. His heart pounding, Edmund stood staring longer than was considered polite and Judge Forsyth cleared his throat in warning.

"Miss Henshall." To his dismay his voice broke. "How delightful to see you again." Edmund bowed low.

Sarah smiled and bobbed politely back. "Welcome Lieutenant. Are not the gardens magnificent? And see, over there," she pointed. "You can just catch a glimpse of the bay. Can you not almost taste the salt of the sea?"

"Maybe, the young people might like to take a turn about the garden before we retire inside for our meal," Catherine Boyce suggested. "It is such a beautiful evening after yesterday's storm. It seems such a shame to waste it. All too soon those pesky, biting mosquitoes will take over the night and spoil it for walking."

"Yes, yes, you must," Margaret Forsyth was quick to agree.

Annie Boyce began to rise from her seat.

Margaret Forsyth motioned for her to sit again. "There is no need for you to accompany the lieutenant and Miss Henshall, Miss Boyce." She smiled knowingly at Mrs. Boyce. "We will watch them from the veranda. Just to assure that Miss Henshall's virtues are protected."

Sarah took the proffered arm of Edmund. At her touch he felt his heart jolt and his pulse race. In silence, Sarah guided him across the freshly cut English turf, past the herbaceous borders now filled with flowers. Sadly, to Sarah, they were almost at the end of their bloom.

Overcoming his nerves, Edmund enquired, "I trust your father is well, Miss Henshall."

A dark shadow passed across Sarah's face. "He passed nigh on a year ago now, just as the leaves were beginning to turn. He is with mother, Lieutenant. I am still in mourning but Mrs. Forsyth suggested I no longer wear black here on the island. She felt the island would be gloomy enough. I am sure father would understand."

"I am sorry," was all he could say.

"I know." She took his hand and squeezed it. "Lieutenant, 'Miss Henshall' sounds so formal. Are we not almost as brother and sister? Perhaps you might consider calling me Sarah when we are among friends."

Edmund froze and unconsciously gripped her hand tighter. *Brother and sister, be damned.*

"Lieutenant, you think me forward," said Sarah.

Edmund took a deep breath and considered his answer. He knew he could never say her name without giving away his true feelings toward her. "No, no, I do not think you forward. But let us settle on 'Miss Sarah'."

"'Miss Sarah' it is then. And your parents, Lieutenant? Are they well?"

"Quite well, I am led to believe, Miss Henshall, I mean Miss Sarah, in fact I received an extensive missive from my dear mother on the same ship that brought your unexpected but very welcome arrival. Mother wrote that my brother James is to take his bar examination."

"A lawyer in the family. How fortuitous in today's torrid society."

Edmund was taken aback. He searched Sarah's face for the meaning behind those words. *Did she know? No. Her eyes gave no indication that she knew.*

"Maybe your brother…" she stopped in mid-sentence. Edmund gave her a strange, unexplained look.

The sound of a bell summoned the couple back to the house, just as the first hint of a sunset tinged the horizon with soft yellowing orange.

Jefferies, the Boyce's assigned servant, announced that dinner was ready. Major Boyce offered his arm to Margaret Forsyth while the judge escorted Catherine Boyce into the house. Edmund offered his arms to both Sarah and Annie.

As the door of the dining room opened, the dozen or so candles lighting the room flickered in the draft, sending eerie shadows across the pale pink walls. The Major decanted the wine while Jefferies placed large plates heaped with steaming meat and vegetables on the table. The aroma of lamb and rosemary soon filled the room.

"That will be all for the moment, Jefferies." Mrs. Boyce waved her servant away. "We have been very fortunate that we found Jefferies on this island, Mrs. Forsyth."

"Indeed. He is a convict then, Mrs. Boyce?"

"Yes, Mrs. Forsyth he is, but he was a butler back home. That is, until he was convicted of stealing a candelabra from his master's house. Mind you, he says he is innocent. I have been told that they all say that. It seems our gaols must be filled with innocent men."

Edmund shifted uncomfortably in his seat but joined the others in polite laughter as he accepted a glass of red wine from the Major. "A nice drop straight from the vineyards of the new free town of Adelaide," whispered the Major in his ear. "Can you believe they make wine in Australia? Damn fine stuff, too, if you ask me."

Mrs. Boyce continued. "Jeffries says that he took it to the silversmith as instructed by his master and he, of course, accuses the silversmith of stealing it. I would like to believe him. It helps me to feel safe in my bed at night. But, no matter, he has proved to be a touch of class on this godforsaken island."

"Perhaps, Lieutenant Thornton, you might do us the honour of carving?" Major Boyce interrupted.

"It would be a pleasure, sir." Edmund hesitated as he picked up the carving set from the table and stared at the succulent leg of lamb on a silver salver, surrounded by steaming potatoes, pumpkin and carrots. He froze, holding the knife and fork in the air. Disturbing memories of a silver salver discarded in haste had momentarily returned to haunt him.

"Are you all right, Lieutenant Thornton? Is the lamb not to your liking?" enquired Mrs. Boyce. "I am sure I can get Jefferies to organise something more to your taste."

Edmund regained his composure. "No, no, ma'am. The meal is very much to my liking." Doing some quick thinking in order to cover up his lapse, he added, "It is... just that I have not had the privilege to sit at such a fine table for many months now."

Soon, the room was filled with friendly chatter and the clinking of glassware and crockery. As the night wore on, the candles began to smoke and splutter, but the vigilant Jefferies never allowed the room to fall into complete darkness, discreetly replacing them as the need arose.

Chapter Twelve

The next morning Commandant Boyce was seated with his family and guests at breakfast on the veranda when his man servant, politely interrupted.

"Excuse me, sir, there is a messenger from The Lady Franklin at the gate."

The Commandant swallowed and wiped his mouth with a linen napkin. "Show him up."

The messenger shuffled onto the front veranda scrunching his cap in his hands. "Captain Snelling sends his compliments and requests that the judge and his wife meet him at their house this afternoon," he rattled off like a puppet. "He assures them that all is in readiness for their immediate occupation."

Although Margaret Forsyth had been looking forward to such an announcement, it still caught her unawares. "Oh dear, so much to do, so very much to do, so little time. Come Sarah no time to tarry," she said, as flustered and rattled as the messenger. "You must go to the house, Mr. Forsyth and oversee the unpacking."

"As you wish, my dear."

The morning was spent trying to find one thing, pack another and layout yet another. But by luncheon all was in readiness for the Forsyth's departure. Judge Forsyth returned to Government House just as the carriage arrived.

"How can we ever thank you and your family for making our first few days on Norfolk Island so pleasurable, Mrs. Boyce?" Margaret

Forsyth said as she tied her bonnet tightly under her chin and started to make her way towards the waiting carriage.

"Let me assure you Mrs. Forsyth it has been a pleasure for us all. I am sure we will be seeing much of each other, after all we will be close neighbours."

"Yes, of course you are right, Mrs. Boyce. If it was not for this stifling heat we could probably walk. When this dratted hot spell is over it will surely make a pleasant excursion to walk between our homes."

Mrs. Boyce laughed. "It is indeed unusually mild for the month of April but if you find this uncomfortable Mrs. Forsyth you will find the humidity our summer months round Christmas most stifling."

"Oh dear, how will I cope? I will most certainly expire."

"Come along, my dear." The judge interrupted. "We do not want to keep the good captain waiting. Thank you once again Major, Mrs. Boyce, for your hospitality." He helped Sarah and then his wife into the waiting carriage.

Margaret Forsyth waved a white handkerchief out of the carriage window as it jerked down the long drive of Government House's extensive grounds. Just as Mrs. Boyce had predicted, the journey was finished almost as soon as it had begun.

Mrs. Forsyth had admired the neat row of quaint houses just across from Government house the day before. She was most pleased when the carriage halted at the gate of her new home, a charming stone residence with wide verandas on three sides and well laid out gardens. She noted with satisfaction that the one chosen for the judge was quite large in comparison to the others. "Just as it should be," she murmured with approval. "Have you seen how close we are to the barracks, Sarah? We will definitely be able to sleep peacefully at night knowing the military is close."

Her husband pushed open the gate and Mrs. Forsyth, followed by Sarah, made her way up the flagstone pathway leading to the house, muttering to herself all the while, making mental notes of tasks that would have to be undertaken.

Captain Snelling was standing on the extensive veranda orchestrating the placement of the last of the Forsyth's copious belongings. "Welcome to your new home, Mrs. Forsyth, Miss Henshall." He greeted them with a deep bow. "I hope all meets with your approval, ma'am?"

"Thank you, captain. Your thoughtfulness is much appreciated." She bowed back in recognition of the captain and then turned back to her husband. "There is a welcoming cool breeze up here on the veranda. I believe we will be most comfortable here. Yes very comfortable indeed."

"Now, my dear, do not expect too much," Judge Forsyth warned as he followed his wife inside, "There is still much to be done."

Stopping just inside the door, Margaret Forsyth surveyed the jumble of baggage, furniture and packing cases all precariously balanced in the hallway. "Never have you spoken a truer word, Mr. Forsyth."

"We thought it best, my dear, for you to decide where you would like all the knick-knacks placed. But as you will see," gestured the judge as he opened the door of one of the front rooms, "I have taken the liberty of setting up the front room as our bedroom so at least we will have somewhere to sleep tonight, unless of course you would find it more comfortable to spend another night at Government House?"

"No," she said, "we shall sleep in our own bed tonight. Have you also set up Sarah's sleeping quarters?"

"There is a fine little room at the end of the veranda, that I think she will find most comfortable."

"Thank you, sir." Sarah bobbed.

"Right, now Sarah, there is much to be done and I see no reason why we cannot do it ourselves. Put on an apron and roll up those sleeves, girl, we have much unpacking, scouring and dusting to complete before nightfall."

"My dear, we have been fortunate enough to have two convict servants assigned to us to attend to such chores."

"I know, I know, Mr. Forsyth, but they are men. Why on earth the Governor of New South Wales saw fit to determine that no female convicts were to be incarcerated on this blessed island I will never understand. How on earth do the authorities expect those large clumsy men's hands to be able to clean and polish such delicate china and crystal such as these?" She held up her favourite vase, minutely checking it for cracks or any other sign of damage. "No, there is nothing to it, but to do it ourselves."

Sarah looked up from winding the skein of wool which Edmund was holding for her. "I do so wish it would stop raining so heavily," she said.

They were sitting in the front room of the Forsyth home with the judge and his wife, surrounded by shelves displaying the judge's books and Mrs. Forsyth's valued ornaments. The Forsyths had been in residence for two weeks now. To Edmund, the best part of all was its location, right in the shadow of the Military Barracks. When he could not be with Sarah, he spent many hours in the guard tower of the barracks, just watching her in the garden, reminiscing, hoping.

"It is a blessing that it is raining at all, Miss Sarah." Edmund moved his hands further apart so as to hold the wool taut. "The island is in dire need of a good drenching."

"I know, but I am so bored." Sarah sighed. "I do so miss reading and sketching in the garden. Have you noticed the two green parrots that have been my companions out there? I hope they have found suitable shelter from all this rain."

"I'm sure they will be all right," said Edmund, smiling.

"They are called Norfolk Parakeets," said Judge Forsyth, looking up from his reading material next to his wife, "and they're endemic to the island. I have also heard others call them the Tasman Parakeet. Their scientific name is *Cyanoramphuscookii.*" He cleared his throat. "Anyway, perhaps we could pass the time by telling stories. I heard a fine one yesterday. The story involved you, Lieutenant."

Edmund stared at the judge. The familiar feeling of panic surged through his veins once more.

"I hear, sir, you recently had an adventure."

Edmund gulped. "An adventure, sir?"

"Perhaps I should restate that as a misadventure." He chuckled as he continued making sure he had everyone's complete attention. "Only a few days ago, was it not, Lieutenant?"

Edmund realised the story the judge was about to tell and smiled in relief. "Pray continue sir. It will be interesting to see how the story is now told."

Making sure his audience was listening Judge Forsyth began with a flourish. "After court yesterday, I was enjoying a brandy with some other officers and they told a story of some interest that is spreading through the settlement. It seems, Lieutenant, that you and Lieutenant Saunders embarked on a hunting expedition…" He started to laugh.

Edmund interrupted, "Sir, if I am to be the laughing stock of the settlement, at least allow me to tell my version of the incident to the ladies."

The judge smiled. "The floor is yours!"

"On the day in question," Edmund said, clearing his throat and putting down the wool he was holding, taking care not to tangle it, "Lieutenant Saunders and I decided to undertake an expedition to see if we could find a more direct route to Mount Pitt."

"Mount Pitt?" interrupted his hostess.

"Begging your pardon, ma'am, I forget you are so newly arrived. Mount Pitt is the highest point on Norfolk Island. It is some distance inland from Kings Town."

"Oh… Pray continue."

"At first it proved to be easy to plot a course along our chosen route, but as we drew closer to the peak we found ourselves entangled in some very high ferns. No matter which way we turned, we could not find a way out. As it was coming on dusk, and losing all hope of rescue that night, I suggested we remain where we were and wait till morning. Saunders, however, was a little more impatient to return to the settlement than I."

"I have heard that he is an impatient man in many facets of his life," said the judge.

"So impatient this day, sir, that he chose to climb a nearby tree so that he could assess our situation. I sat at the bottom of the tree, drinking the last of our rum. Next minute he was clamouring down the tree pointing excitedly in the direction he believed we should take. Jokingly, I suggested that each of us in turn, try to make a path by throwing ourselves on the ferns to flatten them. Saunders actually thought this a good idea!"

"He did, by Jove!" The judge could not help but interrupt once again.

Edmund smiled at the memory. "My idea proved an impossible task, just as I had presumed it to be, but never the less we made a little headway and found ourselves on a slight rise. We agreed it would be futile to keep trying in the dark so we endeavoured to make ourselves comfortable. It was then that the sound of voices drifted toward us."

Here the judge could not help but take over the rest of the story. "Can you picture this? Two officers waving madly, yelling at the top of their lungs, jumping up and down, doing anything to gain attention." He stood up and waved his hands in the air for emphasis. "It must have been quite a sight, I am sure. And who do you suppose the rescuing team was? A group of convicts, no less, on their way home from road works in the area. Very fortuitous for you, do you not think, Thornton, my man."

"Very fortuitous indeed, sir." Edmund finished lamely. "But now it seems I am to be the laughing stock of the settlement for some time yet." Edmund looked at the smiling faces around the room, all with their eyes fixed on him. He could see they were trying to withhold their mirth. He could not help it, and burst into raucous laughter at the thought of how ridiculous it must have looked to others. As if his laugh was a sign, the others joined in.

The judge then sat back down, adding, "I must admit though, the Bard's version is much more embellished. But still you tell a good story, Thornton."

Edmund became serious. "The Bard, sir?" he asked, a little more indignantly than he would have wished. Everyone in the room became more sombre at the sound of Edmund's voice.

"I understand, Thornton, that he was one of your intrepid rescuers!"

"Who is this Bard?" asked Sarah.

"He is a convict, my dear, one who has a remarkable ability to tell stories with much feeling. Both convict and officer alike enjoy his tales," Judge Forsyth said.

"But he is still a convict, sir! In no way is he a man to be admired, no matter his talent," Edmund said.

"It is funny, though," the judge continued. "I can find no record of the Bard's true name or the nature of his crime. He is apparently such a well behaved convict that no-one has bothered to find out his true identity."

Edmund's face reddened, but the dim lighting in the room concealed his anger from the others. "Just as it should be, sir. These scoundrels do not warrant identities…"

Margaret Forsyth hastily interjected. "Please gentleman I would appreciate if you would refrain from discussing any aspects of convicts or this settlement this evening." Then changing the subject she asked, "Do you play cards, Lieutenant?"

Edmund politely declined. It had been the consequence of his addiction to cards and gambling that had forced his father to purchase his commission in the first place. Then seeing another of his favourite games set up in the corner, he asked, "Judge Forsyth, would you do me the honour of challenging me to a game of chess?"

"I am afraid I have never quite mastered the game, Lieutenant, but I believe young Miss Henshall is quite a formidable player. Maybe she would not mind accepting your challenge."

"I would love to, Lieutenant," Sarah exclaimed, and she brushed past the two men towards the small square table where the chessmen were waiting in regimental lines. In her enthusiasm her full skirts knocked the edge of the board, knocking down some of the pieces.

"Whoa, little lady!" Edmund smiled, as he righted the fallen pieces. "You do not want to destroy the whole regiment before even a single shot is fired."

"The regiment?" enquired Sarah.

"Do you not see, Miss Sarah? Chess is very like a well-planned campaign. All are prepared to sacrifice themselves for protection of Queen and country. All in a regiment must be prepared to give their all for the honour of the regiment. No one person is more important than the regiment as a whole."

Sarah made sure she held her skirts close as she sat down. "I see, Lieutenant. So you see me as your adversary this day. I will endeavour to make your campaign worthwhile."

Edmund sat in the opposite straight-backed wooden chair and started to determine his tactics.

Sarah fingered a pawn as if to make a move, and looked towards the others in the room. Relieved, she noticed that the judge and Mrs. Forsyth both seemed to be engrossed in their own game of cards, taking no notice of the chess players.

She hesitated, taking Edmund's measure. *Was this the right time? When would be the right time?*

Taking a deep breath she stared straight into Edmund's eyes. "Edmund," she whispered. "I have been waiting for a time that I might speak with you privately." Once again she looked towards her guardians to make sure she was not being overheard. "You have been in the colonies for a while now. I was wondering if by chance you may have heard any news about... about Michael."

A shadow of anger swept across Edmund's face.

Startled at such a response, Sarah could only stare, waiting for an answer.

"This is probably not the best time to discuss such a topic, Miss Henshall."

To Sarah Edmund's reply sounded forced, indeed angry.

Edmund moved his knight forcibly to its new position and then invited Sarah to make her next move.

"What are you two whispering about over there?" mocked Mrs. Forsyth. "You know it is very rude to whisper in company!"

Both Sarah and Edmund remained silent.

Adding insult to injury, as the game progressed Edmund found he was continually defending his position from Sarah's skilful attacks. With every move he became more and more frustrated, defending both Sarah on the board and Michael in the forefront of his thoughts. Exasperated, Edmund broke. "You know, every man is expendable in the protection of the regiment, even a well-respected and well liked man." His voice grated as he flicked another pawn off the board.

Sarah looked up, a look of shock pasted on her face, but she continued her campaign undeterred. "Checkmate!" she said triumphantly. "Now who is going to protect your precious regiment, Lieutenant?"

Chapter Thirteen

"Your orders?" barked the constable at the police checkpoint on the outskirts of the settlement.

The gang overseer shoved his crumpled papers into the man's hand, as though it was an affront to be asked.

"Righto' then," the constable said, scanning the papers. "It says ten men with five push carts – one, two, three, umm." He pointed his finger at each man. "Right, all seems in order. Clearin' land, collectin' rocks, eh? Don't look as if some of 'em will even make it to the field."

As each of the convicts passed, they doffed their caps at the constable, but he ignored them.

"I think he could be right about not reaching the field," moaned old Sinclair, stumbling along next to Michael, trying to keep his balance on the rocky path. "We still have that steep climb ahead of us."

"Do not fret so, Sinclair." Michael looked with pity at the man next to him. A stooped, greyed man, he looked old beyond his years. A good gust of wind could blow him over and send him tumbling into the thickets by the path. "You are not strong enough, Sinclair. I can push for both of us. Just make a show of pushing, so no questions will be asked. Let me take the brunt of the load."

"You are sent from God, that be sure, Bard." Sinclair put his free, callused hand on Michael's shoulder. "I am sure I would be six feet under by now, if it wasn't for your kindness."

Michael smiled and braced himself to take the full weight of the cart.

A tall convict ahead of them, turned around to have his say. "It's these damned overseers, getting privileges for the amount of work done by their gang, so they push the weak to do as much as the strong. It ain't fair, it just ain't fair!"

"Perhaps this might make it fairer?" The convict felt the jab of a constable's bayonet in his side. "Now shut your mouth and keep walkin'."

"Well at least it's down 'ill all the way back." The convict laughed in the constable's face and received another jab for his trouble.

"Mind me words, O'Brien. It'll be the bridle next time you op'n your mouth."

O'Brien slammed his mouth shut in an exaggerated mannerism designed to infuriate the constable, who had walked ahead to admonish another unfortunate man.

After much heaving, pushing and even pulling, the carts were finally in place to receive their load of boulders. Shackles removed, the men went to work.

"Struth, they actually expect to farm this plot?" said Michael, wiping the sweat from his forehead. "It's more stone than dirt." Muscles straining, he lifted another boulder onto the cart. He glanced over at Sinclair, who was struggling under a much lighter load. He was still doing a fair share of the work in Michael's eyes, but not so in the eyes of the overseer. Michael watched in horror as the whip struck the old man's bent back. It came down with such force that Sinclair toppled to the ground in an agonised, writhing heap.

"Meal time!" echoed across the field.

Michael tried to help Sinclair to his feet and half carried him over to the shade. "Here drink this," he said, handing Sinclair a mug of water and a hunk of hard, dry bread.

"Wish it was ale, truly I do." Sinclair moaned. "Fortify me for the rest of the day, it would." The old man looked around and motioned Michael to follow him. "Too cold in the shade, let's sit o'r there on those large boulders."

The constables were too engrossed in their rations of ale and meat to give but a passing glance to the two men moving into the sun.

"This will do. Nobody else can hear us. Come closer. Don't want any constables or flashmen to hear, they speak fair to your face and then sell you out to the authorities behind your back." Sinclair glanced around. Speaking in low, husky tones, he continued. "I be too old for this, Bard. I want to see England just one more time before I die."

"I, too, look forward to going home," Michael answered. "It's just a matter of working hard, keeping low, doing as you're ordered and not making any disturbances. The time will soon go. Life is hard I agree, but it can be endured." *Has to be endured*, Michael added in his head.

"No, I can't, not anymore." Sinclair started to raise his voice, but caught himself as the constables looked over at them. He waited until they had returned to their meal and then whispered in Michael's ear. "I've been told of an escape plan."

Michael pulled away in shock, but remembered to keep his voice low. "You must be mad. I have not heard of one successful escape. Lives are always lost."

"Ahh, but none have been as well organised, nor as well planned as this one, to be sure."

"But failure." Michael creased his brow in concern. "The price of failure is high. You'll hang."

"Won't fail, can't fail." Sinclair said. Cautiously looking around once more, he pulled Michael closer. "There's a boat, you see. Well, at least it's nearly a boat. They be building it bit by bit, hidden down in a cave near the beach. Many be scavenging for provisions, equipment. They've promised to take all those who help them. They would welcome a good strong man like you, I'm sure."

"What? Leave all this?" Michael gestured in a sweeping motion, taking in all around him. Then, more seriously, so that Sinclair would not take offence, he continued. "Kind offer, but I value my neck," he said. "I have too much to live for to take any chances now. I have a sweetheart, the prettiest young lady you could ever set your eyes upon. I promised I would come back to her and I have never broken my word to her yet. I am determined to do all I can to survive this hell, and truly, I would suggest you do the same."

Sinclair gulped his remaining water. "So be it, but I must take me chance. I don't see another coming soon. Better to hang than continue to live as a beast of burden."

Michael mulled over the old man's words as he dug his toes into the dirt, straining his legs and arms, trying to keep the over-loaded cart from hurtling down the steep slope. A vision of Sarah waiting for him to return grew strong in his mind. Perhaps old Sinclair was right. Perhaps he should take a chance. *Never know, it could succeed,* he told himself. *I could return to Sarah sooner.* Visions of the noose breaking his neck brought him back to the moment. The load in his cart suddenly felt heavier and began sliding, ever so dangerously, backwards.

Struggling, he gained control of the cart, as his thoughts returned to his day in court back in England. He had watched Sarah's face when the judge had pronounced him guilty. He could still see the brave little smile that broke through her tears as their eyes met. She had blown him a kiss. A kiss now planted in his memory, one that, even now nearly two years on, he still held close to his heart. It was at that moment, in that dark, dingy courtroom, that he had vowed to do nothing to jeopardize his return to her. His heavy load now seemed lighter, as he felt Sarah willing him back into her arms.

Chapter Fourteen

It was Saturday morning, the one morning each week that the Commandant had declared a "free" day for the convicts. Although they could not do as they pleased, the convicts could spend their time under guard in more relaxing endeavours. The men who Edmund and Richard Saunders were charged with that morning sat in groups on the rocky outcrops, mending or washing their clothes. Even though it was early May, the day was still quite mild, and some braved the cool water of the protected bay to relieve their tortured bodies from the heat. Pulling at his own tightly fitting collar, and feeling the perspiration running down his back, Edmund watched with envy as the men splashed and caroused in the refreshing water.

Most of the convicts were naked, free of inhibitions. He was amused at their pie-bald appearance. For all intents and purpose, it looked as though some had removed the bottom half of their clothing but had forgotten to remove the top garment. For such was the deep tan many had gained from the burning sun, with only their trousers on for comfort. Few did not show shiny white scars, the result of the cat-o-nine-tails and its tragic work.

It was an easy duty. Finding a cool, smooth rock upon which to sit, Edmund contemplated his future. As usual, his thoughts turned to Sarah. So close, yet still unattainable. Maybe today, at the picnic, there would be a chance to demonstrate his worth to her.

Staring out into the bay, his attention was drawn to a pale orange crab that was stepping sideways towards the apparent safety of the water. Glad of the diversion, Edmund relaxed, laughing at its clumsiness. Just then, a large gannet swooped down from the sky and scooped up the defenceless crustacean in its beak.

"Ah, now that is the way to abolish Michael Hanlan from my thoughts. Remove all trace of him. Make it as though he never set foot on this earth." He laughed bitterly. "If only". But even as he watched, the crab did not give up its fight for life so easily. The bird did not have it all its own way and had to struggle to win over its prey, trying to swallow the crab whole. The bird took off, the crab writhing in its beak. But the crab made one last enormous attempt at freedom and fell from the gannet's beak into the safety of the sea below. The bird dived into the waves after it, but came to the surface empty.

Edmund took a moment to take in what he had just witnessed, shaken by the crab's ultimate triumph over adversity. Was this an omen?

A small knot of convicts sat on some rocks nearby, pointing and laughing at the bird. Trying to calm his nerves, Edmund listened to their idle chatter. He heard some of the men cajoling one of their group to tell a story.

"It was the beginning of spring as I remember it... the cry of that bird made me think of it."

Edmund gasped. The voice of the Bard rang out clear and loud, only twenty feet from him. He looked up, but the shadows thwarted his view. He started to edge closer, to at last learn the identity of this blasted man.

The Bard continued. "We were walking by a stream that meandered through the woods on the edge of our town. There were three of us. Suddenly, an enormous white goose came hissing and squawking towards us. Its nest must have been nearby, but I did not see it. The goose loomed large in front of us. The young girl that was with us screamed and ran for cover behind me. Not that I was of much help to my poor damsel in distress." A gentle ripple of laughter passed through his small audience. "But our companion, now there's a brave man for you. Taking stock of our dire situation he picked up the nearest stick. Brandishing it like a sword, he made many exaggerated movements towards the goose..."

Edmund's jaw dropped. He stopped edging toward the group, remembering that day well. He had been trying to show Sarah that he was the more deserving of her affection, not that man of little consequence, Michael Hanlan.

Regaining his composure, he inched his way closer to where he could see the speaker's face, all the while still hidden in shadow of the surrounding trees. His heart sank, there was no mistake. He could make out the distinctive cleft chin hidden under the sparse beard growth. The freckles were paler, the skin more sallow, the ginger hair matted, but there was no mistaking those mischievous blue eyes.

Michael Hanlan was sitting in flesh and blood before him.

The warning whistle pierced through the air. Startled seabirds flocked as one into the cloudless sky. Emily Bay became a mass of movement and sound. Soldiers shouted orders, convicts groaned as they realised their momentary freedom was now at an end. The convicts then stood, making pretence of finding missing articles, anything to extend the precious moments of liberty. Red coated soldiers, with bayonets fixed, moved among the ragged crowd, jabbing and prodding the men into compliance.

"Come on then, Thornton. This infernal duty is finally at an end." Lieutenant Saunders meandered over to Edmund. He stood a moment, but Edmund did not acknowledge his presence, just stared in front of him, his face contorted in an uneasy frown.

"Seen a ghost, have we?" Saunders followed Edmund's gaze but could see nothing amiss.

"Um, ah..." Edmund lost sight of Michael in the throng of humanity milling in front of him. He looked around. "Oh, it's you, Saunders. Ghost? No, no." His mouth took on an unpleasant twist. *A ghost, no, this apparition was flesh and blood and could be dealt with.*

"Come on. They'll be waiting for us at the picnic, Thornton. Let's get this lot back to the barracks and off our hands."

Two large oxen, as festively decorated with coloured ribbons as the wagon they pulled, plodded up the dirt road that passed the Forsyth's home. Sarah ran to the gate to meet the occupants. The wagon had been fitted out with planked seats that were now filled with excited passengers, all dressed in their Sunday finery. It came to a stop in front of Sarah.

"Is Mrs. Forsyth to join us?" asked Mrs. Boyce.

As she spoke Margaret Forsyth ambled down the pathway. Although it was not far, she was quite out of breath when she reached the wagon. Both the convict wagon drivers disembarked to help her into her seat, much to the delight of other occupants.

"I believe you will find the Bumboras quite pleasant, Mrs. Forsyth. The picnic grounds are well shaded," Mrs. Boyce informed her friend. "My husband has assured me that he and the judge will meet us there, but I suppose that depends on the hunting."

Before Mrs. Forsyth could answer, two horses and their riders raced towards them in a cloud of dust. The riders slowed as they approached the wagon, touching their hats in polite acknowledgment of the ladies, then gained speed once more and raced passed.

"Well I never. These young upstarts…" Mrs. Boyce dusted the dirt off her skirt. Sarah smiled, recognising Edmund as one of the riders.

The wagon master cracked his whip and his oxen plodded on.

"Race you!" yelled Edmund as he dug his heels into the wide flank of his brown mount.

Saunders followed suit and soon dust was flying in a thick red cloud behind them. The horses raced over Flagstaff Hill and then on towards the Bumboras, their skilled riders guiding them through thick clusters of pines and around large, ragged boulder outcrops, both men yelling with exuberance, urging their horses on. Finally they raced down a steep dirt road that brought them to a halt in wide, open parkland framed by lofty pines.

"I'll beat you next time, Saunders, mark my words," said Edmund, panting, as he reined in his horse and surveyed the scene in front of him.

One large white oak tree dominated the landscape. Long tables laden with food were set up under its spreading branches, while outdoor folding chairs were placed in clusters around smaller tables. Most of the chairs were already occupied by women, dressed in gay colours, deep in conversation while their men stood nearby in groups chatting and drinking.

Saunders looked around for a beer. "Hey, you there, bring us a couple of tankards," he ordered a passing convict, who scuttled off to do the officer's bidding.

"Thornton, here, drink this."

Edmund took the tankard at the same time noting the arrival of the wagon. He strained to catch a glimpse of Sarah. His face lit up. "Over there, can you see her? She is near the wagon with Mrs. Boyce and Mrs. Forsyth."

"Who?" Saunders looked in the direction his friend was pointing.

"Miss Henshall, who do you think?"

"Have you ever seen such beauty?"

At that moment the Commandant and the judge walked toward the wagon followed closely by a couple of convicts carrying guns and a brace of pigeons. Edmund saw his opportunity. "Come on Saunders, grab a couple more tankards and follow me."

He strode forward, sharing a warm-hearted smile with Sarah as he got closer. Then, with much difficulty, he transferred his attention to her guardians, as protocol dictated.

"Good day to you all." Edmund bowed. "I hope the hunting went well?" He looked toward the Commandant.

"Very well," Commandant Boyce said as he took the tankards Sanders held and handed one to the judge. "Ah, just what we needed." He drained his tankard in one gulp.

Edmund pushed Saunders forward. "Judge and Mrs. Forsyth may I present Lieutenant Richard Saunders, I am unsure if you have already met."

Mrs. Forsyth held out her hand in greeting as the lieutenant bowed low.

Edmund then once again, turned his attentions to Sarah. "Lieutenant Saunders, I have the very great pleasure of introducing you to a very dear acquaintance of mine from England, Miss Sarah Henshall."

"It is an honour to make your acquaintance, Miss Henshall."

"It is a pleasure to finally meet you, Lieutenant. I have already heard much about you. Lieutenant Thornton has kept us entertained with some of your hunting exploits."

The loud clanging of the dinner bell sounded throughout the Bumboras. The aroma of spit-roasting pigs, fresh baked bread and boiling potatoes filled the air. Every free family on the island had raided their personal larders in order to contribute to the picnic. When all were full and toasts had been drunk to their young Queen, a lone fiddler struck up a lively dance tune.

Edmund did not join in the merrymaking. Although he had managed to sit close to Sarah during the picnic, she had taken little notice of him throughout the luncheon. He sat dejectedly sipping his beer, his gaze never straying from her. He brooded as she conversed with Annie Boyce. He had hoped for more.

He allowed his thoughts to return to the near encounter with Michael Hanlan on the beach earlier. He could no longer deny his existence on the island. He looked at Sarah. It was a small island. People talked. It would not be long before she found out the truth, the truth that Michael was alive.

"God's breath, you're a lucky man, Thornton. Miss Henshall is a most agreeable looking woman." Saunders slapped his fellow officer across the back.

Edmund did not turn, but continued to look in Sarah's direction.

"By Jove, Thornton, you're completely smitten, man. Does the lady return your affection? Could the mighty Thornton actually be captivated by this young lady's charm?" Saunders said as he sat down beside him.

"She captured my heart long ago, Saunders. I have worshipped her from afar since we were first introduced." Edmund responded in earnest. "But there is no hope. Her heart belongs to another... and I would take it kindly if you would keep your thoughts about her at bay."

"You have no worries there, I can assure you, my attentions are elsewhere engaged. But, my dear Thornton, the other man, he's not here, is he? How could he be on this island of the damned? Here's your chance man, don't you see?"

Edmund deliberated on Saunders' words. Of course! Here was his answer. It was there all the time. No-one but him knew that the Bard was, in fact, Michael Hanlan. It would be easy to keep up the pretence. No-one else need know. The chance of Sarah meeting any convict, let alone the Bard, was remote indeed. He knew the ladies of the settlement were well protected from any contact with them. As one in authority on the island, it would not be difficult to make sure that their paths never crossed. He then remembered Vessey's underground system of convict informants.

A self-satisfied smile spread across his face. *Perhaps I could use them to my advantage.*

At that moment, a shadow fell over the men. They both looked up to see a pretty, pale pink parasol framing the face of an equally pretty young lady.

"Are all the officers on this island as lazy as you two?" Sarah laughed and tried to pull Edmund from his sitting position. "Come, I am feeling energetic. I would be most pleased if you gentleman would escort me on my walk. I am sure I can hear waves breaking on rocks just over that rise and I long to see them."

Edmund was momentarily taken aback, but soon regained his composure and eagerly accepted her lace-gloved hand. "Then, see them you shall, Miss Sarah. Are you coming Saunders?"

Fluttering her eyelashes, Sarah asked, "Perhaps, Lieutenant Saunders, we could also encourage Miss Boyce to accompany us."

"That would be most delightful, I'm sure, Miss Henshall."

"Keep your parasol up and your gloves on, ladies," Mrs. Forsyth called after them. "The sun is fierce today and we would not want you to freckle."

"We will keep to the shade, never you fear, Mrs. Forsyth," Sarah laughed back to her guardian. She took Edmund's arm and followed Annie and Lieutenant Saunders.

Chapter Fifteen

The party strolled towards the rocky bay, Lieutenant Saunders leading the way, stopping the group every few steps so that he could satisfy Annie's curiosity about something or other that had caught her inquisitive eye. Away from her mother's over bearing protectiveness she seemed overwhelmed by her surroundings and eager to explore everything.

"Mr. Hanlan would have loved this place, do you not think, Edmund?" Sarah said wistfully. "Do you remember, Lieutenant? Michael could never walk past an unusual plant without stopping to examine it."

Edmund stood very erect, but only for a moment. He glowered at her and then turned away. Something in Edmund's stance cautioned Sarah not to mention Michael's name again that day, although she still could not understand Edmund's refusal to speak of him. She yearned to speak of her beloved to the only other person on the island that even knew of his existence.

She allowed herself to revel in self-pity for only a short while. Further along the path, she turned her attention to her friend pointing at a bird's nest, noticing that Edmund was showing an excessive amount of interest in it. Sarah had to admit, she was most impressed with Edmund's patience with the Annie's endless questions. He was proving to be an enigma. She did not remember him being such a patient man. He had always seemed so morose and irritable when he had accompanied Michael and her on their frequent walks. She had never been sure if he actually enjoyed walking at all, but here he was smiling and joking, obviously enjoying himself. She watched him closely and then shrugged, no longer trying to figure him out.

As they approached the edge of the grassy green, Edmund began to survey the tangle of climbers, shrubs and trees that blocked their path, looking for a reasonably clear trail. Finding one he thought suitable he started to move toward it.

"Ahem!" Sarah politely coughed, twirling her parasol and swishing her full skirts from side to side as Edmund raised his eyebrows quizzically.

Sarah dusted an imaginary speck of dirt from her pale pink cotton skirt and fluttered her long lashes innocently. "If we are to take that path, Lieutenant Thornton, Miss Boyce and I will certainly become entangled in the undergrowth along its edges. Or, dear Edmund, was that your plan?" She glanced at Edmund, teasing him. She enjoyed watching his discomfort. By no means was she blind to his attraction for her, in fact it was strangely flattering. But… she felt for the locket always near her heart.

"No, no, Miss Sarah… I didn't think…" Edmund said. "I will find another path."

"It seems, ladies that the pleasure of accompanying you both falls to me." Richard Saunders offered an arm to Sarah and Annie and they followed Edmund at a more sedate pace.

Eventually, a well-trodden track was found. Sarah broke away from the trio and joined Edmund. They walked in silence, a little behind the rest of the party.

"Is not this island truly beautiful, Edmund? I can call you Edmund when we are alone, can I not?" Sarah said after a while.

"I would be proud that you consider me to be such a close friend," Edmund said. He pushed away a drooping vine that had dropped onto their path and scanned the area. He considered her observation about their surroundings. He had to admit to himself that he did not much care for the scenery of Norfolk Island. In fact, much detail had completely escaped his notice. He had immersed himself into his duties with little time for anything else. Now, with Sarah on his arm, everything seemed to take on a new brilliance, brighter colours, and sweeter sounds.

He now saw what Sarah saw – great, dull green pines reaching up to the heavens, scrubby trees with luxuriant climbers entangled throughout their branches, gigantic palm fronds. He had not thought so many shades of green possible. Every now and then a clump of wildflowers broke through and added splashes of reds, yellows and pinks to the carpet of greens and browns. He bent down and picked a wild orchid, the palest of yellow in colour, and handed it to Sarah.

"To be truthful, Miss Sarah, I had not noticed the island's true beauty until today." He smiled and was rewarded with a smile brighter than his own. "And now sweet maid, I will never be able to look at it without thinking of you as well."

Sarah kissed the orchid and then placed it in his belt. "There, you shall have a keepsake to remind you of this day always."

Remind him of the day, no, it would always remind him of her.

The chosen path hugged a dry creek bed, scattered here and there with deep puddles. Great black boulders dotted the sandy shore while high cliffs on either side of the bay protected it from the full force of the open sea. Immense waves crashed against the cliffs, sending sprays of water to wet the unexpected visitors, through which a rainbow arched like a multi-coloured bridge of light. Distracted by the moment that had passed between him and Sarah, Edmund had not realised that while Saunders had marched ahead clearing the path, Annie had lagged behind.

Frantically retracing their steps he quickly spied Annie making her way to what appeared to be the upturned hull of a rowing-boat. "That woman needs to learn to control her innate curiosity, Saunders," he said, and turned to his comrade, "or maybe you should be more attentive of the young lady."

At first the screams were drowned out by the screeches of a large flock of sea birds disturbed from their rest and the crashing of waves upon the granite cliffs.

Sarah was the first to sense something was wrong. She could hear a sound that she believed did not belong to the sea. Slowly she turned, and felt the blood freeze in her veins.

Edmund swung around. "Oh my God!" With a practiced eye he took stock of the situation. "Sarah, get down low and stay here."

Without replying, Sarah sank to the ground as Edmund thrust something into her shaking hands. "Here, use this if need be."

But Sarah took no heed of what he was saying or doing. "I will be all right, just go!"

As though in a dream, Sarah watched the unspeakable ordeal that was unfolding on the beach, a nightmare from which she could not awaken. Icy panic twisted around her heart, a cold knot formed in her stomach. Everything was unreal. The atmosphere grew heavy, no wind blew. She struggled to breathe. Her vision became hazy, as though dark clouds had rolled in and blotted out the bright sunlight that had been there only moments before. She watched, her body not answering her need to move. Edmund and Lieutenant Saunders seemed to be running in slow motion. She tried to call after them, to tell them to run faster but the words stuck in her throat. She opened her mouth to yell to Annie that all would be right, that help was on its way, but no sound came.

Without doubt the phantoms before her were from the very depths of hell itself. There was one, no two animal-like beings. Both with wild hair, twigs and leaves entangled within it. Fiercely grinning filthy faces showed yellow broken teeth, and small darting eyes, long angular hair-covered limbs, great groping hands left no doubt: these beasts could not be men. In their midst was a perfect angel, valiantly trying to fight against them, poking and prodding at the phantoms with what looked like an oar, struggling for all she was worth. Then the biggest, hairiest of the two grabbed Annie around the waist and laughed, a vicious, unearthly laugh that echoed throughout the bay.

Sarah watched. Sarah listened. But strain as she might, although she could see Edmund's mouth moving, she could only hear loud muffled, incoherent sounds. Nothing was clear, nothing except that ungodly laugh.

She felt numb. A scene of desperation was playing out before her and she could do nothing but sit and stare, biting her lip to stifle the scream that threatened to escape. The two convicts stood defiant, challenging the two officers to use their swords while they themselves held only broken farm implements as weapons. Sarah could not see Edmund's or Richard's face and could only catch small fragments of what they were saying. But it was plainly obvious the convicts were enraged that their escape plan had been thwarted. She stared at the flimsy, unfinished boat over which the dramatic scene was being played. She had heard of other attempts by the convicts to build boats and escape from the hell they now found themselves, but these men, these monsters, were now so desperate they were willing to take an innocent woman as hostage.

Looking down she spied the pistol on the ground next to her feet. The lieutenant's earlier words hit her with force, *"Use this if you need to."* She picked it up. It felt cold and hard but familiar in her hands. In happier days in Devon, her father had drilled her in the art of pistol shooting, much to the horror of her aunt. Shooting apples on a fence post had been easy, but did she dare use it against another human being? She looked to Annie who was struggling against the brute that held her captive. She fought with her own uncertainty only a moment longer. Seeing Edmund in danger, she saw her Michael. She became resolute in what she must do.

The decision made, she took a deep breath, forbidding herself to tremble. Remembering her father's teachings, she grasped the pistol in both her hands, feeling its weight, checking its cocking pin. She aimed it at the convict closest to her hiding place and cocked it. The clicking of the pin seemed to echo throughout the bay. Startled, she looked towards the convicts but neither seemed to have heard. Just as she was about to fire, the convict in her sights dragged Annie roughly from his mate and held her in front of him. It seemed he was trying to prove some point or other to Edmund and Richard. He kept pointing from the woman to the boat, yelling obscenities. Sarah's eyes misted over. She became unsure of her aim and her confidence in her own ability drained from her.

Swallowing hard, she prayed for the strength to continue. As if in answer to that prayer, a vision of her father appeared before her. *"Be brave my darling. You know you can do anything you put your mind to."*

She smiled with newfound resolve. She might not be able to get a clear shot at the convict but she could at least fire a warning shot, both to warn the convicts she meant business and to alert the picnic goers that they were in danger.

Using both her hands she lifted the pistol above her head and shot into the air.

Everything then happened so quickly. The sharp crack of the pistol thundered above all else. Birds screeched. A dog howled. The air became alive with echoing sounds, bouncing back and forth from the surrounding cliffs, continually magnifying until the reverberation became almost unbearable, almost as if one of the Kings Town cannons had been fired along the beach. The convicts cringed and looked around, startled. In one lightning fast motion, Edmund and Richard lunged forward. Annie tumbled to the ground. Sarah stared, trying in vain to still her trembling body.

Not thinking of her own safety she grabbed up the hem of her skirt and multiple petticoats with one hand while still holding onto the pistol in the other and ran, in a most unladylike manner, she was sure, towards the unfolding drama.

One of the convicts was holding a pickaxe menacingly over Edmund.

"Edmu-un-nd!" Sarah screamed. Forgetting that the pistol had but one shot, she tried to fire again but only heard a blank click. In a last desperate attempt, she threw the pistol as hard as she could and hit the convict square on the temple. It had been more luck than skill, nevertheless the convict fell to the ground with a heavy thud.

Edmund turned in time to see Sarah's dazed face as she tried to keep her balance. He smiled at her audacity and nodded his head in thanks. Sarah nodded back, proud of what she had achieved and of Edmund's acknowledgement. Just in time, she gathered her wits and grabbed Annie before she could get any closer to danger.

In the confusion, Richard Saunders took control of the other convict, struggling with him to the ground. Edmund pounced on the first fallen convict, securing him by pulling the man's shirt over his head and pinning his arms to his back with it. Richard did the same with the second convict.

The fight had been won.

Within minutes, new sounds echoed throughout the enclosed bay. The sound of thudding soldiers' boots, the sound of their heavy breathing, the sound of shouted orders and clanking weapons, frightening to some, but a welcome relief to Sarah.

The soldiers spread out across the bay's entrance, muskets cocked and ready, each one pointing directly at the convicts now in custody.

"What's all this then?" yelled Major Boyce. Seeing his officers struggling with convicts and the hull of an upturned boat, he quickly took stock of the situation. "You men, quick, search, there may be others." And then, turning his attention to Edmund and Richard, he said, "It seems, gentlemen, you have it all under control." The officers nodded and handed their captives to several of the waiting soldiers. The soldiers removed the captives' temporary restraints and replaced them with heavy manacles before marching them back to the settlement at the end of their bayonets.

Major Boyce scanned for his daughter, his fears allayed when he saw Lieutenant Saunders gently lifting Annie to her feet and leading her towards him. He gasped as though he had been kicked in the stomach as he looked at Annie's torn, sand encrusted dress and pale, tear-stained face. "Since your mother heard the pistol shot she has been frantic with worry. She will be very pleased to see you are safe." Removing his coat he covered her with it so as to preserve her modesty. Looking back to Edmund and Richard, he mouthed his thanks and then said loudly, "You did well, gentlemen, to fire a warning shot."

"Actually, sir, it was Miss Henshall who had the where-with-all to fire that shot." Edmund was full of awe and respect for her. Never had he imagined her to be so brave.

"So we have an unexpected heroine on our island this day. How can Mrs. Boyce and I ever thank you, Miss Henshall?" He kissed her hand.

"It was nothing sir. Just to see everybody safe is thanks enough," Sarah said.

"Miss Henshall, would it be too much of an imposition to ask you to escort Annie to her mother? These two soldiers can accompany you."

Edmund and Richard stared after Sarah as she accompanied Annie back to the picnic. "Well, that was a bit of unexpected sport, eh Thornton? Quite a girl you have there. Never have I seen a lady show so much gumption under stress. She's a good one, all right." Saunders slapped his fellow officer on the back.

"Yes, but what if…" Edmund could not bring himself to finish the thought. Sarah had been in real danger, mortal danger. He steeled himself. "We were lucky today, very lucky. We may not be so lucky tomorrow."

Things had now changed. His determination hardened. No more would he show leniency towards the convicts as he had. Nobody threatened one of his own, especially Sarah. From this moment on, he vowed, they would know the full wrath of his vengeance. By God, they would know it well.

Sarah's mind was muddled as she watched Mrs. Boyce and the other woman fuss over Annie. She thought back on the afternoon's events and could not help but feel a little sorry for the convicts. They must have laboured long and hard to build that boat. They must have been filled with such hope, such dreams, she was sure. For all she knew they were men with loving families back in England who missed them as much as she missed her Michael. Yet the reality of what these men were capable of doing to gain their freedom filled her with horror. Had Michael also turned into one of these animals? She shuddered at the thought.

"Michael. Not you. Please, not you."

She whispered a silent pleading prayer, forcing the thought to the back of her mind and tried to concentrate on comforting Annie.

"Quite a welcome to the island today's picnic proved to be," chuckled Judge Forsyth as he joined the gentlemen for brandy and pipes on the veranda of Government House that evening. "How is Annie faring after her ordeal, Major Boyce?"

"Actually sir, she's doing remarkably well for a young lady. A good night's sleep will do her well to forget about it and move on."

Major Boyce picked up a bottle of brandy and refilled the men's glasses. "But to more serious matters. Now that we are out of the ladies' gentle hearing," he said. "I have been receiving hourly reports regarding the investigation's progress. It seems your party was lucky only to stumble on two of the dastardly felons today. So far, at least fourteen have been implicated in the deed. In fact, it seems they were nearly ready to cast off. Many casks of maize, tea, sugar, and even water have been found stashed in the surrounding caves, as well as stolen tools and materials, even a compass I am told. I wouldn't have thought these scoundrels had it in them, but for convicts it's been a well thought-out plan."

"Sir, if I am able to be of any assistance, please do not hesitate to ask. I would relish the opportunity to show these convicts just who is in charge on this island," Edmund said with the eagerness of his newfound fortitude.

"Ah, but Thornton, you are usually the champion of convicts," Saunders, said slurring drunkenly.

"No longer, Saunders, I can assure you." Edmund said.

"Lieutenant, I have an offer for you." Judge Forsyth looked over toward Edmund. "Before we left Sydney I was given permission to appoint a personal assistant of my own choosing once I arrived on Norfolk Island."

"Sir?" said Edmund, standing erect.

"I understand that you have had minimal interaction with the convict population since being stationed in Australia."

"A little, sir."

"He's but a babe in the woods," slurred Saunders.

The judge glared at him.

Saunders burped, wiped his mouth with the back of his hand, then said, "I know when I am not wanted. I think I will go commune with nature." He stumbled down the stairs.

Judge Forsyth turned back to Edmund. "Your inexperience is the very reason you are perfectly suited for the position, Lieutenant. I will require you to help in the finding and presenting of evidence against those who are being tried. And as you have not been tainted by past experience, your findings will hopefully be impartial, no matter the station of the man brought before you, be he civilian, officer or convict. I took it upon myself to make some discreet enquiries about you and have so far only received very favourable reports." He paused, allowing Edmund time to think. "It would mean considerably more responsibility, Lieutenant, and only a little extra pay to compensate."

Edmund considered the judge's proposal. He lent on the veranda railings and stared out over the garden and thought of Sarah and the danger she had been in. Saunders was right about him. The week before, even the day before, he would have baulked at the opportunity now being offered. However, things had changed. His Sarah had been in real danger, and then there was Michael Hanlan, of course. Sarah must never discover his whereabouts. The judge's offer could be a blessing in disguise. It could afford him the opportunity to keep a much closer eye on Michael's movements. Now that would be definitely to his liking. He smiled. And then he remembered Saunders' taunt that other officers were starting to talk about his lenient dealings with the convict population. He had heard them. It would not be of any benefit to him if that sort of talk got out of hand. The gossips might begin to get a little close to the truth and that would never do. *No, by golly!* Edmund brought his hands down hard on the railing. The judge's offer really was too good to refuse.

He swung around. "Thank you, sir. You have my word I will, at all times, endeavour to be fair and just."

"Good man. Then it is settled."

Chapter Sixteen

Sitting in her front parlour, Margaret Forsyth was in quite a conundrum that morning. She thought back over the events that had led up to today. She had watched her husband leave each morning to work at his judicial duties these past six weeks since their arrival. She had listened tirelessly each evening as he unburdened the day's trials and tribulations. More and more she felt the need to help the convicts in some small way, but try as she might she could not think of anything suitable for a lady of her standing to undertake. *Yes*, she had told her sister in a long wordy letter. *I could, of course, give comfort to the sick or even read to them but I want to do more.*

And then the perfect idea had come to her. She could write letters for the convicts. Many were illiterate and would surely welcome the opportunity to communicate with loved ones back home in England, she told her husband. Judge Forsyth had agreed to approach the Commandant and communicate her idea. To their surprise, the Commandant agreed.

She had been well pleased with her new project but now that the time had come to begin 'The Experiment', as her husband had labelled her idea, she had to admit she was nervous. Even the logistics of such an undertaking brought despair. As she stood in her parlour that morning, many questions were beginning to worry her. Exactly where to meet the convict, seemed to her the most pressing. She could not go to the convict barracks herself, the smell would be unbearable, and under no circumstances could she invite men into her parlour.

The squeaking of the front gate took her attention. Walking down the garden path she greeted her visitor.

"Good afternoon, Mrs. Forsyth," said the reverend. "Your house and gardens are looking lovely. You have done yourself proud indeed and in such a short time. I am truly amazed at your efforts."

"Thank you kindly, Reverend Bayley. I must confess I do enjoy my gardening. There is still much to be done. But see here," and she bent down to touch a leaf of a nearby flower. "This geranium I bought with me seems to be dying. I have dusted it with flowers of sulphur but I will have to wait and see I suppose." Then she beamed with the sudden dawning of her answer. "Of course, the garden! Why did I not think of it before?"

Reverend Bayley cooled himself with his large fan. "I beg your pardon, ma'am?"

"Reverend, would it be too presumptuous of me to ask your help this afternoon?"

"My dear lady, I am at your disposal. What can I do?"

Margaret Forsyth outlined her scheme to him.

"Ah, yes," the reverend said after considered thought. "Your husband is definitely correct in choosing the Bard as your first endeavour. A good God-fearing man, I can assure you. May I suggest that I take advantage of the shade of your veranda while you meet with the man? That way I can act as chaperone."

Michael Hanlan walked with a lighter step that afternoon, looking again in delight at the slip of paper in his hand. He hastened his pace toward Military Road, eager to be out of the dark, cold shadows of the stone buildings that incarcerated him. Soon he began to feel the sun on in his face. It was warm and inviting. He felt as if he was walking from confinement into freedom. He listened as he walked. The sounds of the waves crashing on the shore grew softer and the sounds of birds grew louder. He thought he could even make out the distinctive kek-kek-kek-kek chirps of the Norfolk Parakeet, those mischievous green parakeets he had taken a particular liking too.

115

Thankfully, he could no longer hear the raucous shouts of soldiers and convicts from the prison.

He slowed for a moment and jealously watched a group of soldiers playing a game of cricket in the open field. It brought back memories of playing in the fields back home, memories of freedom. The batsman swung at the next delivery and sent the ball hurtling toward him in a high arc. It was all he could do to resist the temptation of catching it and throwing it back.

"Oi there! Where do you think you're going?"

Michael froze as one of the convict overseers strode over. Michael doffed his cap and fell back into the ditch off the road to let the man pass, bowing deeply.

The man stopped directly in front of him and peered so closely that Michael could smell his foul breath.

"Oh, it's you, Bard. Don't think I have to worry about you, do I, eh? Presume you have a pass to be wandering about on your own? We don't trust ye that much!" He punched one of Michael's shoulders in jest.

Michael ignored the urge to rub his sore shoulder. "Yes sir, I have, sir." Michael handed him his crumpled pass, but by the look on the overseer's face it was obvious that he was unable to read it.

"Lucky, wasn't I, that old Parsons saw fit to reward me with a pass for good behaviour this morning. I am on my way to Judge Forsyth's house just over yonder. The good lady has offered to write letters home for well-behaved convicts like me."

"Right then. But mind what you have written though, Bard, I am sure the Commandant will enjoy reading and erasing any juicy bits. Be on your way." He handed Michael back his pass.

Michael bowed low once again and waited for the man to pass before coming out of the ditch.

"Blast all overseers, nothing is going to ruin my day," he said aloud. Luckily there was no-one close by to hear him. He slowed down, relishing every moment of freedom. All seemed brighter, the sky bluer and the clouds fluffier. The trees, the grass and the bushes seemed greener and the birds definitely whistled more sweetly to his ears than he had ever heard them before. He was as a free man; at least he was for the time it took to walk to the judge's residence.

All too soon he reached the pillared stone entrance with its heavy iron gate. He stared through the gate to the interior of the garden that was bordered by stone walls. It seemed the occupants of the house were trying to create their own world, locking out the grime of Norfolk Island and protecting what civility they had within. A green parakeet flew very close to his head, making him flinch and duck out of the way. 'Kek-kek-kek-kek', it called. He watched as it flew towards the well in the judge's garden and settled upon it.

Michael removed his woollen cap, smoothed his hair and wiped his face on the sleeve of his jacket. Taking a deep, unsteady breath he pushed open the gate and inched his way up the flagstone path, not daring to look up, feeling out of place and out of his mind.

Reverend Bayley glanced up disinterestedly when the Forsyths' new convict servant acknowledged Michael at the bottom of the stairs. Michael glanced up and stood rigidly where he was, waiting for the next instruction, half expecting to be ordered away.

"You be the convict me mistress be expectin'? Let's be seein' your pass."

Michael held up the scrap of crumpled paper. The manservant stomped down the stairs, grabbed it and gave it a cursory look, pretending to read it.

"Hmmph. Wait 'ere then. I'll tell her you've fin'lly made an appearance."

Finally made his appearance? What did he mean? Was he late? Would the lady be angry? He had seen men punished brutally for much less than being late. He shuffled uncomfortably and waited.

Very soon a kind faced, matronly woman appeared at the top of the stairs, tying a bright blue bonnet with a wide brim under her chin. "I am so glad you have come, I have been so looking forward to meeting you. My husband has told me so much about you." Seeing Michael's confused reaction she stopped mid-sentence. "You are the one known as the Bard, are you not?"

"Yes, ma'am, that be what they call me." He twisted his cap nervously and stood back as the lady descended the stairs. She indicated the chairs that had been set up near the well and, like a scolded puppy, Michael followed at a respectful distance.

"I am Mrs. Forsyth, the judge's wife. He has often lightened our dinner conversation retelling some of your delightful stories. You have a gift, young man, one that you should cherish."

"Thank you, ma'am," was all Michael could stammer as he shuffled uncomfortably behind the woman. It had been such a long time since he had been spoken to in such a civil manner. Mrs. Forsyth showed him to a chair and bade him sit down. "I am much obliged, Mrs. Forsyth, for this opportunity to write a letter home."

"Not at all. It is nothing really. I see it as my charitable duty. I understand from my husband you are truly deserving of this reward for good behaviour."

Michael blushed.

"Fetch a fresh pot of tea, and a new pen, ink and paper. Bring two teacups and saucers," she instructed her manservant Matthews, who was awaiting her orders nearby. She tried not to sound too irritated, but the man always needed prompting. He didn't have any sense of anticipation of what was needed. He was certainly no Jefferies. By the Lord, the Boyce's had struck gold with him. Then again, what could she expect on this island of convicts and soldiers? She should count herself lucky at all she had found Matthews. He might only have been a luggage porter back in London, but at least he had some idea of what was expected of a manservant.

Then, remembering her company and his fallen status, she reminded Matthews, "But mind you, not the good ones. The older ones from the kitchen will do nicely. Here are the keys to the tea caddy. Use the Indian tea not the China tea. Make sure to offer Reverend Bayley China tea though." And then she added almost as an afterthought, "And some fresh bread, butter and jam are in order I think."

Michael stared at her with gratitude. He thought he knew his place. He was just a convict, one who did all he was ordered to with no questions asked, not to be acknowledged in any way. But here was a thoughtfulness he had not experienced in many years and suddenly he was unsure of his situation. Finding his voice, he stood up as a sign of respect for the lady, "Th-thank you Mrs. Forsyth, that be most kind of ye." He bowed his appreciation.

Margaret Forsyth gestured for him to sit. "I am not one to stand on ceremony. I see you admire my garden, at least what little there is of it." The gardens were sparse indeed, at least compared with the majestic gardens of Government House. Two lofty pine trees spread their shade from one side of the garden, and bushes that she was still having trouble identifying randomly dotted other parts of the grounds. "As you can see, I still have much to do but I am sure we will manage. I have started to plant the saplings and cuttings we so carefully packed back in England. I am still to see if they have survived and will flourish after that long sea voyage. That remains to be seen, I suppose."

Matthews cleared his throat to let his mistress know that the tea was ready. He served only his mistress and indicated to Michael to serve himself.

"Well, we had best begin, I suppose," his hostess said as she drained her teacup and wiped away the crumbs of her piece of bread and jam. She spread a clean sheet of paper in front of her and dipped her quill in the ink pot.

2nd June, 1848. Kings Town, Norfolk Island, she wrote with a flourish.

"Now, to whom will you be writing?" she enquired.

Michael paused. "Sarah," he whispered

So with another flourish, Margaret Forsyth wrote, *Dear Sarah.*

She presumed it was his sister to whom he had chosen to write and the first few sentences seemed to confirm her suspicion. But then the tone of the letter changed and it was obvious to her now that it was actually his sweetheart. She did not flinch, but continued to write as Michael dictated in pleasing well-educated English tones, only stopping to ask for clarification on some point or other or for him to repeat what he had said. Occasionally she looked up with surprise or concern, but the more she wrote the more she wanted to weep for these two separated young lovers.

Finally the letter was finished. "Would you care to sign your own name?"

Michael took the offered pen, charged it with ink but instead of signing it with his name he wrote:

Lavenders blue dilly, dilly,
Lavenders green.
When I am king, dilly, dilly,
You shall be queen.

Margaret Forsyth tried not to look up at the convict sitting across from her, with hot tears running down his gaunt cheeks. In an effort to keep her own emotions in check, she rang the little silver bell she kept on her person at all times to summon Matthews, who arrived promptly.

Glad of the convict servant's interruption, Margaret Forsyth turned her attention to matters where she felt more in control. "Please bring out the salver I use to put my letters on. You will find it on my writing desk."

Margaret Forsyth watched as Matthews scuttled away and then handed the finished letter to The Bard.

Michael tried to read the neat, closely written words, staring at the page through misty eyes. He noticed how it was already yellowing with age. He felt the crispness of the paper in his calloused hands and his grip on the page tightened. His Sarah would soon hold it in her own small delicate hands.

Out of the corner of his eye he caught Matthews returning. Blinking, Michael's attention was drawn to the silver salver in the servant's hand. He felt perspiration beading on his forehead, his hands felt clammy. He dropped the letter on the table. He could not help but stare.

Margaret Forsyth followed his stare. "My mother gave me this as a wedding gift when I married the judge. It was her mother's before, you know." She took the salver from the servant. "Thank you. That will be all."

Matthews bowed and backed away.

"It is a beautiful piece, is it not? It has my family crest engraved in its centre. See?" She removed the letters already piled on the salver to show Michael. She did not see him flinch. "I use it now as a place to keep my letters while I am waiting for the next ship to deliver them. Unfortunately, one of its feet is slightly shorter than the others." She turned it over and gently caressed each of the three clawed feet. "Every time I use it I remember my dear mama."

"It's no use… it's just no use." Michael grimaced. He pushed his chair away back from the table, shoved his cap back on his head and clumsily stood to take his leave. Regaining his composure, Michael said, "I am sorry for wasting your valuable time, Mrs. Forsyth."

"Wasting my time?"

"You cannot send it, the letter I mean. Please ma'am, do not send it. I beseech you." Once again he lost his self-control. "She will not want to hear from me. It is best she forgets all about me. Please, please forgive me." He raced down the path towards the gate. As he pushed through the gate to escape the Forsyth home, he collided with another man who was entering. Their eyes met for but a second. Michael's, blinded by tears, showed no sign of recognition. For the other man recognition was immediate. Michael touched his cap, more out of habit than respect, and then pushed past, not caring who it was he had run into.

Chapter Seventeen

Confused, Margaret Forsyth carefully folded the Bard's letter. It was such a beautiful letter, much too sincere to discard. Maybe once he had calmed down he might change his mind regarding the sending of it. *Just in case, I will keep it safe, in my bureau. No-one should find it there.* She took her time to move across the gardens toward the house. Out of the corner of her eye she spied Edmund. "Lieutenant, I did not see you arrive. Please excuse me. I will be with you presently."

"Ah, it's you, Lieutenant Thornton. I am glad to see you," said Reverend Bayley, jolted from his napping. "I suspect my presence here is no longer required so I will bid you good day. Please be good enough to pass on my compliments to Mrs. Forsyth."

Edmund bowed to the reverend but kept his eyes on Mrs. Forsyth as she disappeared behind the heavy wooden door. Confused he scanned the garden observing the table set up near the well. He noted the two chairs, one neatly pushed against it, the other lying on its back. He turned toward the gate, in the direction Michael had run. *What on earth was Michael doing here?* he asked himself.

On closer inspection he saw the discarded pen and the near empty ink pot. He saw two teacups and saucers and next to one of them a half-eaten piece of bread. *Surely she is aware that it's against the Commandant's implicit rules to give a convict rations that he is not entitled to, under any circumstances,* he thought with disgust. Then a more terrifying realisation washed over him. Where was Sarah? In panic he scanned the garden and towards the house. To his relief, the front gate then creaked open and Sarah entered the grounds.

"Miss Henshall, it is a pleasure to…" Edmund began but Sarah ignored him.

She glided past him toward Margaret Forsyth who had re-emerged from the house and was standing once again on the veranda.

"Was that the Bard, the one you were writing the letter for, Mrs. Forsyth?" Sarah pointed towards the convict now disappearing down the street. "By his countenance I presume the letter writing did not go well."

"No, indeed, my dear, it did not go well at all."

Sarah looked back in the direction from which she had come, hoping to catch another glimpse of the Bard. "I cannot help but think that I have seen that man before." She paused. "No matter, I have probably seen him on one of my strolls."

Relief surged through Edmund. At least, he reassured himself, Sarah had not recognised the Bard as Michael Hanlan. But he would now have to do all in his power to keep it that way. This had been a close call indeed. He had never expected Michael's and Sarah's paths to cross, even on such a small island. But he also had not reckoned on Margaret Forsyth's wish to be involved in some way with the convict population. It was obvious he would have to undertake a more devious plan if he was to win Sarah. He almost delighted in the idea of ruining his old foe in the process.

"I hadn't expected him to be so well-mannered," Margaret Forsyth murmured. "What on earth could he have done to find his way here?"

This was too much for Edmund. "Rest assured ma'am, every convict serving out his sentence here on this island is here deservedly."

Sarah turned around, surprised by such an outburst, and saw Edmund standing behind her for the first time. "I am sorry, Lieutenant. I wish you would not speak that way. That man was truly disturbed."

To change the topic before his emotions got the better of him, Edmund said, "The judge has asked me to meet with him here, ma'am. Is he available?"

"Unfortunately, Lieutenant, you seem to have come out on a wasted venture. The judge has not arrived home as yet. I will be sure to tell him you called as soon as he returns."

Edmund, however, was not so willing to waste an opportunity of spending time with Sarah. "It is such a beautiful day though, ma'am. It seems a pity to waste it worrying about the feelings of some incorrigible convict. May I offer to escort you on a walk?" Both women stared at him, almost in disbelief at his apparent lack of feeling towards another human being.

Margaret Forsyth was the first to regain her composure. "Miss Henshall may accompany you if she wishes, but I am much too exhausted to enjoy a walk, no matter how perfect the weather."

Surprise touched Sarah's pale face. "Without a chaperone, Mrs. Forsyth?"

"I just ask that you do not go far. The judge should be arriving home quite soon." Margaret Forsyth paused, and then as an after-thought said to Edmund, "I am putting my trust in you, Lieutenant. I believe it is well founded. You have known Miss Henshall for some years now, I understand. I am sure you will not allow any harm to befall her. I hope you understand me? I am sure you do."

"Rest assured, ma'am, I will allow no harm to befall her. Will you do me the honour of accompanying me, Miss Sarah?"

Receiving her guardian's nod of consent Sarah turned and wandered back down the flagstone path toward the front gate.

Edmund fell into step close behind Sarah, taking pleasure in her nearness. The faint scent of lavender wafted toward him and he inhaled deeply of its perfume. He knew then he would follow her anywhere, even if it meant giving up his commission. Nothing and no one would stand in his way again. Lost in his own thoughts he was taken by surprise when Sarah stopped abruptly at the gate. Eagerly he stepped forward to unlatch the heavy lock. She softly touched his hand to stop him but did not look at him. He followed her gaze and found her staring in the direction the Bard had earlier taken when he left the garden.

"Do not fret so, Miss Sarah. He was only a wretched convict. Not one deserved of your gentle consideration."

"Lieutenant, I do not believe I hear what you are saying. All men have a heart and deserve to be loved."

"Some, Miss Sarah, are more deserving than others."

She ignored him and continued, "I think on that point, Lieutenant, we shall continually disagree." She shut her mouth with a determined press of the lips and looked away.

"Do not distress yourself so. I am sorry. It was not my intention to upset you on such a beautiful day. Let us forget about him, forget about where we are. Perhaps you would prefer to sit in the garden rather than go for a walk?"

Sarah accepted Edmund's suggestion and allowed herself to be escorted over to the chairs by the stone well. The convict servant was clearing away the last remnants of the letter writing session. As they approached, Edmund waved him away and helped Sarah into the nearest chair. Sitting opposite, Edmund openly studied her.

"Edmund, why do you stare so?"

"Forgive me, but I still struggle to believe that you are actually here on this island. I feared I would never see you again after that last day in Plymouth."

A remorseful expression saddened her face.

"Pray tell me, Miss Sarah, I cannot but wonder what brought you to such an isolated place." In his heart Edmund was sure he knew the answer. Even so her response struck him like a heavy blow.

"A huge sailing boat," she said, trying to be flippant. "No, I am being silly. Actually my father's will made Judge and Mrs. Forsyth my guardians. The will stipulated that I cannot inherit my father's fortune until I marry. Both you and I know that I will never marry until I find…" She left the words unspoken, fingering the gold locket hanging around her neck.

Edmund understood her unfinished words all too well. He clenched his fists so tightly in his frustration that he felt his fingernails biting into his palms.

"You see Edmund, the judge and my father were very close friends, since well before my birth. When I heard that the judge was to be sent to the colonies, my heart leapt. Do you not see it was the answer to my prayers? It was my chance to find Michael, to make sure he was safe, to perhaps even bring him home."

"I see," said Edmund with no real empathy.

"I am sorry that I have led both Mrs. Forsyth and Mrs. Boyce to believe that we are more than just friends. When Mrs. Forsyth thought I was looking for you in the colonies she asked the judge to help. I hoped that if I found you I might find Michael." She spoke eagerly at first but as she continued she began to sound more resigned. "But when we arrived in Sydney, the judge was immediately appointed to this island. I had no time to make even the most discreet enquiry about Michael." Her voice faded. Almost as an afterthought she added, "Do you think, Edmund, a godforsaken place such as this could make my Michael become like one of those inhuman creatures we witnessed the day of the picnic? They were as men without hearts, without feelings for anyone or anything, no better than the beasts. Following that horrible affair, I had nearly given up on all convicts. Then, seeing that poor convict leaving this very garden only a short while ago, a man obviously with a heart, with feeling, damned to this wretched island, I truly despair for my Michael." She trailed off, then, finding her voice again, she continued, "I could not believe my good fortune when we met on the ship. My hopes were renewed, but we have had so little chance to speak. Do you remember that last day in Plymouth, when I asked you to find him for me...? Do you think he is safe?"

Bitter jealousy burned throughout Edmund's chest. Once again her appeal for his help in finding Michael was more than he could bear, just as it had been that day long ago in Plymouth. The scheme he had been simmering in the back of his mind took on more immediate purpose. Moving closer to Sarah he took her hands in his. "I have news, Sarah," he said.

Sarah searched Edmund's face and became alarmed by what she saw. Fearing the worst, she fidgeted in her chair, anxiously looking around seeking any distraction. "Oh, look, Edmund, see the pretty green parakeets over there. I have seen them many times in the garden lately. Why, I do believe they are building a nest. See, one has a twig in its beak. Will it not be wonderful to see the young birds when they hatch?" She continued to prattle on nervously. "I wonder how many there will be? I think I will make it my duty to keep them safe from harm. Michael would like that, new free life on this island of the damned."

Edmund listened, at the same time weighing up his options. Looking into her distraught face, he nearly gave up his resolve. It would be so much easier to tell her that Michael was alive and well, that he was the Bard, a convict on this very island, but his own needs soon far outweighed the fear of hurting her. After all, he would be there to comfort her in her distress, would he not?

"I don't know how to say this," he began.

Sarah's voice trembled as she whispered, "Oh no, Edmund, I do not think I wish to hear what you have to say." She stifled a sob that threatened to escape and tried to look bravely upon Edmund's face.

Edmund took a deep breath but he could not look directly into Sarah's pleading eyes as his deception began to take on a life of its own. "Dearest Sarah." He tightened his grip on her hands. "Did you not know that when he was sentenced to be transported his destination was here, yes, this very island, Norfolk Island?"

Sarah's eyes opened widely in surprise and she clutched her breast feeling for the precious locket. "Here? You mean he is on this island? He is so close. Where, where Edmund? I must see him. Take me to him at once!"

Closer than you think, Edmund thought, but he chose his next words carefully. "His transport, the ship we both watched him board, carried the fever, Sarah. It has been said that a soldier brought it on board when they berthed in Cape Town. After so long at sea, all on board were vulnerable and it spread unchecked both above and below deck. The surgeon was one of the first to be afflicted. Many lives were lost. Michael is dead, Sarah. He died on that fever ship."

"Dead, no, Edmund you are mistaken," Sarah replied with a calmness that surprised him. "He cannot be dead. He promised me faithfully that he would return to me. He has never broken a promise to me."

"He is dead, Sarah. I am so sorry to be the one to tell you. I have it on reliable witness that the convict Michael Hanlan was counted among those who died. He was buried at sea, Sarah."

"Buried at sea? No memorial. Oh, Edmund," she whispered. "Nothing to show that my Michael ever walked this earth, nothing?" A flash of unrestrained grief ripped through her. She grasped frantically for the locket, holding it tightly. Then her world went dark.

Chapter Eighteen

"Good grief! What on earth has happened, Lieutenant?" Judge Forsyth said as he strode over to where Sarah lay slumped in Edmund's arms. "Matthews!" he yelled for his servant. " Matthews, man, bring the smelling salts! Bring brandy! Hurry man, hurry! Give her to me, Lieutenant, you have obviously done enough here."

Edmund stood back clearly distressed. He knew she would be upset, but somehow his own vanity had not let him suspect such a calamitous turn of events.

"Give her air, man." The judge pushed Edmund even further away. "Stop crowding her. Ah, Matthews, good, let me have the smelling salts."

"Mr. Forsyth, Mr. Forsyth, what has happened? For the love of God, do tell me what has happened!" Margaret Forsyth arrived breathlessly and then stopped dead in her tracks when she saw Sarah.

Judge Forsyth waved the bottle of smelling salts under Sarah's nose. "It seems my dear that the lieutenant here has been too forward with our young ward. So forward it seems that it has made her swoon!" He glared at Edmund.

"I trusted you Lieutenant, to think I trusted you. Oh, it's all my fault. What have I done? What have I done?" She wrung her hands in despair.

Edmund tried to stutter his denial, totally taken aback by the judge's accusations. "Not at all, sir! I take offence at the suggestion."

"Edmund," Sarah cried weakly.

"Good! She's waking up. Everything will be all right, Sarah, you are safe now, we won't let anything or anyone hurt you." He looked accusingly at Edmund, and continued: "Matthews, help me carry her to the veranda. You had best come too, Lieutenant. She is asking for you, although why I do not know."

Edmund shuffled after the small procession making its way to the veranda. Margaret Forsyth fussed over her ward, ordering blankets, pillows, brandy, so much so that Sarah politely brushed her away.

"I am all right, Mrs. Forsyth, truly, I am. I did not mean to scare you."

"Are you able to tell us what happened, Sarah? Your aunt will never speak to me again. Did he hurt you? God forbid if he hurt you. How will I ever forgive myself?"

Sarah shook her head and held out her hand towards Edmund. "Tell them Edmund. Please tell them. They deserve to know. I do not think I have the strength."

Edmund felt the alarmed, yet judgmental gaze of both the judge and his wife boring right through him. It was one thing lying to Sarah for his own benefit but now he was trapped in his lie with nowhere to go but to perpetuate it. He thought carefully before he began. "Mrs. Forsyth, you may wish to sit, ma'am."

Margaret Forsyth stood protectively over Sarah, making no attempt to move.

"You may leave us, Matthews," Edmund said, but the convict did not move until his master impatiently waved him away.

"I would never hurt Miss Henshall, you must believe me. But today it was my unfortunate task to bring her very sad tidings."

Margaret Forsyth gasped and slumped into the nearest chair. "Go on, sir."

"When I left Plymouth, over two years ago now, Miss Henshall charged me to find a close friend of hers, indeed a close friend of mine as well." His voice grated.

Sarah managed a small smile through her tears and encouraged him to go on. Edmund looked at her in her anguish and his heart melted. How could he be doing this to the one he loved so dearly?

But he knew that if he was to win the prize there was no other alternative. He hardened his heart and went on.

"He was sent to Australia about a month before my regiment was ordered to the colonies. Until recently, I had not been able to find any information about his whereabouts. But now I have reliable information that he was on his way to this very island. On the fever ship, sir!"

"Oh dear God." The judge looked up. "But I was told all dispatches and records from that ship were burnt for fear of spreading the fever. How did you…"

Edmund congratulated himself on having the foresight to use the fever ship to further his ruse. "Sir, I have made it my duty to try to fulfil Miss Henshall's request so I continually sought the truth." The lie was becoming easier as he continued. In fact he was beginning to almost believe it himself. "The fever ship was a topic of conversation in the soldiers' mess the other day and I happened to chance on a man who had survived and had a close acquaintance with our friend."

"Umm, I am sorry to ask, but your friend he was a…"

Edmund nodded and sunk his chin to his chest, feigning shame.

"Look, Mrs. Forsyth," Sarah pointed toward the mischievous parakeets, still resting on the well. "See the pretty green parakeets. See how free they fly in a place such as this. Oh, Mrs. Forsyth how they chatter, they must be hungry. There is no one to feed them. We must find them food…" Tears flowed freely down her cheeks.

"Hush now, my dear." Mrs. Forsyth gently pushed her companion's hand back into her lap. "Yes, darling, I can see the birds. I am sure they will be all right. Almighty God looks after all his creatures, even the smallest…"

"Does He?" spat Sarah.

"The child's delirious, quite delirious. I think we had best take her inside and settle her. Perhaps a small dose of laudanum will help."

The judge sighed and chose his words with care. "I apologise, Lieutenant, for the earlier misunderstanding. I hope you bear me no ill feeling. However, I think my wife and I can manage now. We will speak more about the matter on the morrow."

Edmund took one last look at Sarah. "If you are sure, sir?"

Mrs. Forsyth answered. "You are most welcome to visit in a day or two, Lieutenant. We must give Miss Henshall time to get over the shock of your sad tidings."

"Thank you ma'am, I would like that."

Edmund tried to walk as sedately as he could towards the gate, as though everything was as it should be, yet he was struggling to take control of his emotions, to think clearly. The deed was done. There was no going back. It had been easier than he thought. Sarah would soon come to terms with the loss of Michael and he would be there to comfort her. Soon she would forget and learn to love him, he was sure. Judge Forsyth would not ask too many more questions because there were no records to check. There was just one small matter left in his way before victory was complete. He had to take control of Michael Hanlan's destiny. The judge unknowingly had given him the perfect opportunity to do just that.

Edmund laughed. As a duly appointed Assistant Magistrate, Edmund could now drive the final nail into MichaelHanlan's coffin.

That night, feelings of remorse tormented his sleep. All night long he fought a raging battle between guilt and victory. By morning he woke exhausted but convinced that the path he had chosen was the righteous one, the most honourable one for all concerned. He lay back on his bunk, hands laced comfortably behind his head, staring at the ceiling, letting his thoughts run free. After all, he told himself, if he had let Sarah know that Michael was alive, that she had in fact already seen him, word would quickly spread through the tiny settlement. She would soon find out that once a respectable person was known to be associated with a convict, she would rapidly become a social outcast. Judge and Mrs. Forsyth would have to struggle between their duty of care for their friend's daughter and their social standing in the settlement. If Sarah was associated with Michael they could not do both. He could picture in his mind's eye their pleasure when he, a respectable Lieutenant in Her Majesty's Eleventh Regiment of Foot, an Assistant Magistrate, asked permission to court Sarah. He sighed triumphantly. He could not see any drawback to what he had done the day before.

As for Michael, Edmund stopped mid-thought as guilt racked his body. Once more his mind raced back to the day that he and Sarah had followed the sad procession from Pentonville Prison to the London docks. He himself had gone under sufferance and had done all in his power to sway Sarah from her intent. But she had been so insistent. In the end, he had relented, as long as she remained hidden in the shadows and did not reveal herself to him. Edmund remembered the sense of victory he had felt as he watched Michael disappearing into the bowels of the convict ship. He had worked so hard to endear himself to Sarah, to make her forget, but he had been assigned to duty overseas too soon.

Sitting bolt upright he thumped his bunk in fury. He was not going to waste this second chance!

His devious scheme began to take shape. A scheme dredged from a place beyond all logic, beyond all reason, but to Edmund it was righteous and worthy. Jumping out of his bunk he pulled on his trousers, snapping the braces into place over his broad shoulders and then shoved his feet into his long black, leather boots.

Michael Hanlan, your fate now lies in my hands, my friend. Even you will see and understand that what I am doing is best for both of you. Sarah is out of your reach. If you really love her, man, you will understand that what I am about to do is in her best interest. The day you were charged, Michael, you lost all rights. You lost Sarah.

"Serves you right for not running fast enough, and for being so damned noble," he mumbled under his breath.

"Are you all right in there, sir?" Corporal Evans called from the other room. "I will have your breakfast ready directly, sir."

"Good. No, everything is all right. In fact, it could not be better." Edmund stood tall in the narrow doorway. "I am famished!"

Evans laid out a plate of freshly baked scones and jam. "Sorry there's no butter, sir, we have already used up our weekly ration."

"No problem," Edmund answered, spreading jam over a hot scone and contemplating whether or not he could trust Evans in his endeavour.

"Evans," he spoke with his mouth full, and then struggled to swallow it. "I was speaking to the judge yesterday and he has given me a special project to undertake, in my role of Assistant Magistrate."

"Well done, sir. How can I be of assistance to you?"

"Good man, I knew I could depend on you. There is something you can do." He took another huge bite and chewed thoughtfully. "When I first arrived, Mr. Vessey, the superintendent of convicts, spoke to me of a system of convict informers on the island, those who would report on the actions of others for reward. I understand the practice is common place, but as yet I have had no need of its services. Do you know of such a system?"

"Yes sir, many learn early that to truckle…"

"Truckle?"

"To inform on your fellows," Evans continued. "It is seen by many of our unwilling guests as a means to survive. It plays nicely into the constabularies' hands. It should be easy enough for me to find some willing participants to help you if the rewards are well placed."

"Ah, yes." Edmund scraped a thick layer of jam onto another scone, trying not to appear too eager. "That should do very nicely. There is a convict who has recently come to our attention, and both the judge and I believe that he warrants close watching at present. It is best you do not know who just yet. It might all come to nothing. Can you get a couple of these men here this afternoon?"

"I'll do my best, sir."

"By the way, where is Saunders?"

"Out the back, sir, cleaning his guns. I believe he's going hunting."

"Just what the doctor ordered." Edmund laughed. "I think I will join him. I will see those men on our return."

Edmund returned from the hunt feeling exhilarated. The hunting had been exceptionally good and the walk had helped to clear his head.

While he and Saunders cleaned their guns and bantered over whose catch of rabbits and pigeons was the greatest, Evans entered the room and politely coughed. "Please, Lieutenant Thornton,

I have done as you asked. The persons you wished to speak to are waiting just outside."

Bemused, Saunders asked, "Need any help?"

"No, this is something I must do on my own."

Edmund peered into the darkness and soon found himself facing two very desperate looking men. His lips twisted into a cynical smile. "And so it begins," he mumbled, and then barked, "Names?"

"I be Bush and he be Cook," the heaviest set of the two men said.

"I have been told that I can trust you?"

"If the price be right," Bush snarled. The other man standing beside him punched him in his ribs.

"If the price be right, sir," his mate corrected him.

"I can assure you the rewards will befit the service you give. I am the Assistant Magistrate now, so I have the power to hand out rewards and punishments as I see fit."

The men nodded; broad, toothless grins breaking across their faces.

"To business then, sir, it seems we can be of much benefit to each other. Just who be the man we need to rat on?" Cook queried.

Edmund scrutinised both men, sickened by their stench and revolted by their toothless sneers, but he needed them and he knew it. "First of all I must swear you to secrecy. If word ever gets back to me that this man knows I am watching him, it will be you who will pay a very dear price. Do you understand?"

The men nodded.

"I need him watched both day and night and any misdemeanour reported to me immediately, no matter how insignificant you might think it is. I will reward you handsomely, I assure you."

Edmund hesitated before he went on. Sarah's distraught face flashed in front of him but he stubbornly pushed it back into the recesses of his mind. "The man I want to know about is the Bard."

There was a stunned silence.

"The Bard, sir? Clearly, you be mistaken."

"If the lieuteni' say it's The Bard then it be The Bard. I, for one, will enjoy seeing one such as 'im get his just deserts." Cook rubbed his bony hands with glee.

"Then, it's settled." A smug expression of satisfaction curtained Edmund's face and his stance grew more determined. "I will organise for you two to be transferred to his gang and to be promoted to sub-overseers as soon as practicable."

"Thank ye, sir, thank ye. Ye won't be sorry." With that both men disappeared into the shadows.

Edmund stood very still for a moment and watched until he could no longer recognise their ghastly forms in the blackness. He congratulated himself. Now all that remained was to ensure that Sarah never crossed paths with the Bard again.

Chapter Nineteen

"I did not think I would need this dress again so soon, Mrs. Forsyth," Sarah said. "I thought I would find him...save him..." With tears blinding her eyes Sarah angrily threw her black taffeta gown onto her bed. "He had no right dying. We were supposed to be married. I came all this way to find him. He should have been waiting for me!"

"Black!" exclaimed Margaret Forsyth. "Oh, no, my dear, that would never do. How would we ever explain that you are in mourning for a... a convict? No, it would never do. Think of our reputations, my dear. I am sure this man meant much to you, but I think it would be best for all concerned it you mourned him privately."

"But Mrs. Forsyth..."

"Please understand, my dear. I do not expect you to dress lavishly, just appropriately. Now, let me see what would be suitable?" She rummaged through Sarah's clothing chest fingering each dress in turn and comparing colours. "Ah, here is one that might suit if you must see yourself in mourning, my dear." She held a pale lavender dress for Sarah to consider. "I wore a dress just this colour when I was in the half-mourning period after my mother's death." She glanced at Sarah, seeking her approval. "You must see, my dear, that this is the perfect solution. We will know that you are in mourning and you will feel that you are respecting your friend's demise but others may not form any connection."

Sarah fingered the soft folds of the lavender dress chosen and looked dolefully across to the chest. "But..."

Margaret Forsyth put her finger to Sarah's lips. "Hush now, dear. I will have no more discourse on this matter. I truly believe that I am asking you to do what is right under the circumstances. I am sure your young man would have agreed with me."

Even in her muddled state of mind, Sarah could see the truth in her guardian's words. So, with no further argument, she let herself be dressed in her many petticoats and the lavender overdress. She then sat staring blankly into the looking glass as Mrs. Forsyth brushed the knots from her hair, only wincing occasionally as the unskilled hands found a particularly difficult one.

As she brushed, Margaret Forsyth asked, "Are you able to speak now, my dear? Sometimes the world does not seem so bleak if you share your troubles with another." She stopped brushing and placed the hairbrush on the bureau. "Come, sit by me on the window seat. I would like to hear of your young man if you are willing to tell me."

Torn by conflicting emotions, wanting dearly to speak of Michael yet afraid of admonishment, she looked into her guardian's kindly face through a veil of tears. With immense effort, she stood, then stumbled across to the window and stared unseeingly out of it. Finally, she said, "He is... was a good man, a kind man, Mrs. Forsyth. I think you would have liked him. He always thought of others before thinking of himself; put their needs before his own. His mother is a widow. Oh my God, does she know? I must write to her."

"Calm yourself my dear. I am sure that the authorities would have taken care of that. Now go on with your story."

"Yes I suppose she already knows. You see Mrs. Henshall and Lieutenant Thornton's mother are great friends and now she lives on the Thornton estate. That is how Edmund and Michael met."

Margaret Forsyth nodded and bade her go on.

"It was a silly prank really, one that went terribly wrong, I can assure you." Sarah's eyes pleaded with the older lady to understand. "They never proved he actually committed the crime he was being accused of, ma'am, but he could not deny that he had been there and knew of it. That was enough to convict him. I have always believed he was covering up for someone, protecting them. But it was he who was caught running from the chapel."

Mrs. Forsyth looked up surprised. "Chapel?"

Catching her breath and wiping away the tears, Sarah struggled on. "It was a Chapel of the Catholic faith, ma'am, a Romanish Chapel. Of course, as you would know, such chapels are not looked upon kindly as they are not of the One True Faith. A large group of men had been celebrating Lieutenant Thornton's new commission into the early hours of that morning and had become quite drunk, or so I was led to believe. What actually took place, I am not sure. It was never made clear to me. The sacred vessels reported missing from the chapel that night..."

"What on earth got into him, stealing from a place of worship?"

"I fear I do not know, ma'am, the drink I suppose. Whoever took the vessels must have had a conscience as they were later found placed carefully behind a headstone in the cemetery. It was said that it looked as though they were there to be found. However, because Michael was the only one caught running away, he was the only one to be charged. The others apparently disappeared into the night." Her voice had become harsh and raspy.

"The crime of sacrilege, a serious crime indeed," murmured Mrs. Forsyth.

"But, ma'am, if you knew my Michael, you would know that he would never desecrate a House of God. Never have you seen such a devoted Church member as my Michael. When my mother was dying he would sit by her bedside for hours reading aloud from the Bible, putting her mind at ease. When mama finally went to her eternal reward he comforted me, reciting passages from the Bible that eased my pain. No, Mrs. Forsyth, he was not a man who would willingly destroy or take Church property."

"Could no-one help him? Would no-one stand up for him?" Margaret Forsyth said.

"The constable who arrested Michael that night did his best. He reported that, in his opinion, Michael would have had no time to place the sacred vessels where they were found before being arrested. It was obvious to all in the courtroom, except apparently the judge, that someone else must have been involved. But no other perpetrators ever came forward, so Michael was left to stand trial alone. No matter how much he was urged he would not give up the names of any others who were also there. So like my Michael, always protecting others, but this time at a very great cost."

"Very great cost, indeed."

"The judge on duty was angry that day. Michael's trial was the last of a long, arduous list. At first he sentenced Michael to death, but then Michael's counsel pleaded that he had obviously not been alone in the deed, so his sentence was commuted to transportation across the seas to a place of Her Majesty's choosing."

She fell silent then.

"And what of Lieutenant Thornton, he seems such a loyal friend. He could have helped, could he not?"

"The trial was over so quickly, ma'am. Edmund, I mean Lieutenant Thornton, tried to give evidence as to Michael's good character but to no avail. The good Lieutenant stayed at my side throughout the whole ordeal. He was my rock, ma'am. Michael saw him that way too." Sarah shivered. "Michael never took his eyes from Edmund. I am sure he was pleading for him to help but the lieutenant had no power in such a court. I do know, though, that he made every attempt to make my Michael's time in prison as comfortable as was possible."

Great sobs then racked Sarah's body and for some time Margaret Forsyth let her cry.

"That's right, my dear, cry. Cry as hard as you want, no-one can hear you. Much has been taken from you," she said. "In time, my dear, the wound will heal although you may not believe it at this moment." Sarah's guardian sat without a word, putting a comforting arm around the young girl's heaving shoulders.

"I fear, Mrs. Forsyth, that I accompanied you to this place under false pretences," Sarah said after a while. "I hope you do not think less of me now that you know the truth."

"Quite the contrary child, I applaud you for your bravery. I only wish the outcome could have been a happier one for you."

"At least I found Edmund. I am so sorry that I misled you about my association with Lieutenant Thornton."

"Misled me?"

"Letting you believe that I was searching for him."

"Think nothing of it, my dear. I am glad you found him. I think, perhaps, that having him here will be a comfort for you."

"I suppose so, but he is not Michael." Sarah wiped the tears from her eyes. "The judge, Mrs. Forsyth, he must think very poorly of me."

"On the contrary, child. It is not widely known but the reason the judge accepted this position in the colonies was because he hoped he might be able to do some good for these poor unfortunates. When you tell him what you have told me I can assure you he will not condemn nor criticise."

Sarah hugged her guardian. Slowly she pulled the locket from beneath her bodice and held it up for Mrs. Forsyth to see.

"A secret betrothal, Mrs. Forsyth. See, locks of our hair entwined forever. You are the only person I have told, ever shown. Not even Aunt Elizabeth… But now all is lost."

Sitting in the front parlour the next morning, Margaret Forsyth studied the cushion cover she had been working on. "Vermillion red, I think," she said and held up her needlework frame with the suggested thread displayed upon it. "Yes, vermillion red roses. It is a good contrast to the yellow roses on my last cushion cover. What do you think Sarah?"

Sarah gave a disinterested glance, nodded and then turned her attention once again to the window.

Margaret Forsyth looked with concern at her young companion. "Come now child, it does not do well to dwell in the past. I am sure your young gentleman would not want you to hide yourself away and wallow in your grief."

Sarah only moved to a more comfortable position in answer.

Margaret Forsyth shrugged and turned her attention to the task at hand. "I do wish some resourceful soul would come up with a way to easily thread a needle." She readjusted the light of the small oil lantern she had set up on the table beside her. "Dear, dear, the sight in these old eyes of mine is slowly fading, I fear." Finally accomplishing it, she picked up the cover and began to sew a row of small, delicate, vermillion red stitches.

The front gate creaked open and both women looked up.

"It is probably Mr. Forsyth." Margaret Forsyth started to gather up her sewing when there was a sharp knock at the door.

"Begging your pardon ma'am, miss," Matthews acknowledged both women. "A messenger from Gov'nment House is on the veranda. He has a letter from the Com'dant for you Missus."

"Me? Why on earth would the Commandant write to me? No, no, clearly he is mistaken. It is probably for Mr. Forsyth. He will be home directly Matthews. Just leave the letter on his desk."

"Very good, ma'am." He bowed and backed out of the room.

"When Matthews comes back I will get him to make us a strong pot of tea, it might make us both feel better."

Sarah smiled and turned once again to stare out the window.

"Scuse me, ma'am."Matthews was once again in the doorway.

"Yes, what it is now? Will you kindly bring a tea tray and a plate of those small cakes you made yesterday for Miss Henshall and me?"

"Yes, ma'am. But, ma'am, the messenger, the one from Gov'nment House, is very sure that the letter he be tryin' to deliver be definitely for the mistress of the house an' not for the judge."

"Then bring it here immediately, my man. Oh, how exciting Sarah, probably an invitation. Mrs. Boyce has been talking about organising a ball in the not too distant future. I had hoped, that she would ask my help. I do so love to arrange social events. I believe I have quite a talent for such things. Ah, Matthews." Margaret Forsyth took the stiff yellow parchment from the silver salver. "Go on." She waved him away. "Miss Henshall and I will die of thirst waiting for our cup of tea!"

She broke open the red wax that secured the paper.

"I do declare. What a day I have had. Six hundred lashes, two solitary confinements..." Judge Forsyth stomped into the room and slumped into his favourite chair. Matthews!" he yelled. "Where is that man? Bring me a brandy and my pipe!" Then more quietly, he said, "Here, young Sarah, help an old man off with his boots, will you?"

Sarah got up from her seat and pulled up a stool in front of the judge.

"Thank you, my dear," he said. "It has been a very tiring day, a tiring day indeed. We finally tried the convicts from the boat building fiasco, today. You know, Mrs. Forsyth, I do believe not one of them showed any remorse. In fact they yelled that they would try again given the chance. What to do, what to do?" His voice trailed off. For the first time he noticed his wife's distraught face and the letter she was holding. "My dear, what on earth is it? Not bad news I hope. You look like you have seen a ghost."

Margaret Forsyth did not look up, but two tears rolled down her wrinkled face. The judge looked to Sarah for an explanation.

"It is a letter from Government House, sir. It has only just this minute arrived."

Margaret Forsyth burst into tears and handed the letter to her husband.

Adjusting his monocle, he scanned the page, and then read it aloud:

"Mrs. John Forsyth,

Ma'am, I refer to my recent unfortunate approval of your request that you might be allowed to write letters for deserving convicts. I must now admit that I agreed to your suggestion at the time with quite some reservation but, in recognition of your husband's fine work on our island, allowed you to go ahead.

Now I find my reservation was well founded, after all. It has been brought to my attention that not only did you write a letter for the convict known as the Bard, but you also offered him privileges forbidden to the convict population.

143

Not only was it highly improper, but, is in fact a gross violation of the Regulations of a convict settlement.

Under normal circumstances, I would call for the immediate removal of yourself and your husband from the island forthwith. But in consideration of your husband's valuable services to the settlement, I am willing to overlook this transgression. But stand warned, only this once, ma'am.

I hereby demand that you cease your letter writing activities forthwith.

I have the honour to be, ma'am.
Your obedient servant,
Major John Boyce,
Commandant, Norfolk Island

PS: The convict in question has been punished and placed on a diet of bread and water for the period of two weeks."

"What have I done?" Margaret Forsyth wailed. "I never thought." She took several deep breaths. "That poor man, I never meant too..."

Edmund rolled his tongue over his teeth and smacked his lips with satisfaction. "Once again a magnificent repast, Mrs. Forsyth," he said.

Margaret Forsyth simply nodded, with just the hint of a smile, but continued to pick at her food, deep in thought. She had come to the table full of ideas of how to encourage a union between the young couple, but as the meal progressed, her enthusiasm for her plan paled as she watched Sarah pushing her food around her plate, taking no interest in their dinner guest or his conversation.

Edmund looked enquiringly from one to the other but received no response from either. Confused at the unusually quiet Forsyth dinner table, he looked towards the judge for an answer.

The judge could only shrug and raise his eyebrows in response. He placed his cutlery neatly on his now empty dinner plate and made to leave the table. "Would you care to join me on the veranda for a brandy and perhaps a pipe, Lieutenant? The last supply ship from Hobart Town brought me a wad of particularly fine tobacco. I would be pleased to get your opinion."

"It would be a pleasure, sir." Edmund stood up, relieved to leave the table. "If you will excuse me, ladies?"

"Yes, of course, Lieutenant, but you must promise that you and my husband will join us later in the parlour."

"You have my word, Mrs. Forsyth."

Sarah pushed back her chair and stood up. "I, too, must ask permission to leave the table ma'am. I must feed my parakeets." She disappeared in the direction of the kitchen.

"Her parakeets?" enquired Edmund as he followed the judge onto the front veranda.

"Oh, it's nothing really. Ever since she heard the news that you brought the other day she has been continually worried about that pair of parakeets nesting in the bush near the well. Still, I suppose it gives her something else to think about."

The men settled themselves into the wicker chairs on the veranda, exhaling smoke into the cool night air. Edmund saw this as his chance to speak about the dinner he had just experienced. "Could I be so bold sir, to say I hope nothing is amiss in your household? Your wife and Miss Henshall, they were both unusually quiet at dinner tonight."

The judge drained his glass of brandy before answering. "Yes, it is so unlike my wife to be so withdrawn, isn't it? And of course, Miss Henshall is still poorly I am afraid. Fretting for her...shall we say her friend?"

Tinges of guilt surged through Edmund. He squirmed in his chair, fully aware who was the cause of his beloved's grief.

"My poor wife received a disturbing communication today."

"Not bad news from home, I hope, sir."

"Oh no, nothing like that, thank goodness. She may like to talk to you about it though, when we re-join the ladies, presently."

Surprised that Mrs. Forsyth would even consider taking him into her confidence, Edmund lamely answered, "I would be glad to help in any way I can, sir."

145

"Good. I, too, would appreciate your guidance in the matter. But mind, let her broach the subject first."

His curiosity was aroused. "As you say, sir."

They both drew deeply on their pipes and lazily blew smoke rings into the air. The judge then stirred. "You must forgive me, Lieutenant. I have been pre-occupied by my own family's problems. You wanted to speak to me?"

Edmund sat forward on his chair. "Yes, sir, but if this is not a good time?"

The judge nodded.

"I have been meaning to ask you," Edmund began, grateful for the opportunity to raise the subject that was the reason behind his visit.

Judge Forsyth looked at him inquisitively. "Yes, Lieutenant, please go on."

"I understand, sir, that you are able to promote trusted convicts to positions of overseers."

Pipe in mouth, the judge nodded in recognition.

"Well, sir, I believe I may have found two likely candidates for such a promotion. Would you care to meet with them, sir?"

Judge Forsyth drew deeply on his pipe. "Thornton, you are now my assistant, so I trust your judgment. If you say they are good men for the job I shall take the necessary steps to instate them. Just give me their names and numbers."

Before Edmund could reply, a rustling sound in the side yard grabbed both the men's attention. Edmund rose to his feet to investigate. He squinted, trying to see through the dim light of the moon that was emerging from behind a dark cloud. He saw, what he could only describe as a ghostlike apparition, gliding slowly across the lawn towards the well.

The apparition was Sarah.

Two small parakeets chattered noisily above her head. Every now and then, one would find the courage to swoop down and pluck the scrap of bread from her limp hand. Edmund went to call her but the judge, who was now standing beside him, put a cautionary hand on his shoulder.

"I think it's best if we do not disturb her. Come, let us join Mrs. Forsyth inside."

Edmund took a last wistful look towards Sarah and then reluctantly followed the judge indoors.

Mrs. Forsyth looked up from the umpteenth reading of the letter from the Commandant and shook it angrily in the air towards the two men as they entered the room.

"Of all the nerve," she said. "Here, read this Lieutenant." She shoved the parchment into Edmund's hands. "Tell me what you think of it."

Edmund took hold of the letter and manoeuvred into a better position near the oil lamp. Every now and then he looked up at the judge and his wife, trying to gauge their reactions. He was grateful for the dull light. It hid his true emotions from his audience. So the Commandant had acted on his advice? Excellent! He regained his composure and considered his response, refolding the letter he handed it back to Mrs. Forsyth.

Clearing his throat, he said, "I believe the Commandant is only acting in your best interests, Mrs. Forsyth, and those of Miss Henshall. One can never be absolutely sure of how these scoundrels will act in the presence of a lady. "

"But," Margaret Forsyth interjected, "the man from the other day, I could never believe he would…"

"You were lucky that day, Mrs. Forsyth. One cannot depend on luck to keep you safe during all other such meetings. No, I believe the Commandant is only acting in your best interests." *And mine of course.* This was the chance he needed to remove one more possibility of Sarah unexpectedly meeting up with Michael.

Mrs. Forsyth looked at the letter. "I can see your point Lieutenant, but I am sure no harm was done by sharing my afternoon tea with him. I do not believe the Commandant has the right to threaten me or my husband on that count."

"I am afraid, Mrs. Forsyth, that in fact Commandant Boyce is quite within his rights to actually punish you."

Margaret Forsyth looked from her husband back to Edmund in shock.

"It is clearly written in the ordinances of this convict settlement, that no convict shall be given any sustenance other than that determined by the ruling authority, particularly not by any person in the civilian population. So, you can see, ma'am, that in actual fact you breached the law. Unknowingly, I admit. Still, if it became common knowledge among the convict population that you held a soft spot for them, who knows what mischief they might get up to... I am sorry to be the one to tell you this Mrs. Forsyth, but I truly believe that for your and Miss Henshall's safety, you must desist from such activities."

Before Margaret Forsyth even had time to consider Edmund's words, the first drops of rain sounded upon the shingled roof, soon followed by a great deluge. Edmund hoped Sarah had made it to the veranda in time and escaped the downpour.

Suddenly, Sarah ran into the room, drenched and weeping. Edmund wrenched off his jacket and ran to put it around her trembling shoulders.

"What on earth has happened, my dear? Here, sit and catch your breath." Margaret Forsyth removed her newly embroidered cushion from the closest chair and Edmund gently guided the distraught Sarah to sit down.

"My birds," she wept into her hands.

"Your birds?"

"The rain, do you not understand? The rain! How will my birds stay safe? They have laid three eggs, did you know? Their nest is so very flimsy. This rain will surely destroy it."

Judge Forsyth tried to placate her. "There, there, my child. If you would like I could build a cage on the veranda and keep your birds in there."

"No!" she yelled. Then she repeated more quietly, "No. None of God's creatures should ever be caged. All should be free, all should be safe. I will care for them, then, if the Almighty above sees fit to take him from me ..." she gulped hard. "Oh, if only I had been there, maybe I could have saved him. Now I will never know."

Only Edmund seemed unmoved by her tears.

Chapter Twenty

Edmund put the basket of fruit he had bought with him on the stone gatepost of the Forsyth home. "Good morning, Mrs. Forsyth."

"Ah Lieutenant we have not had the pleasure of your company for about week now, have we?"

"Yes, I am sorry ma'am. Unfortunately duty took me to the other side of the island."

Margaret Forsyth laid down the trowel she had been using to dig out a particularly stubborn weed from her garden bed. Removing her gardening gloves she held up her hand toward Edmund. "Here, would you be so kind, Lieutenant? I am afraid these old legs of mine are not what they used to be.

Edmund helped the awkward lady to her feet.

"We heard the alarm bell earlier, Lieutenant, another escape?"

"No, no, all's well, Mrs. Forsyth, just an over eager sentry. He apparently saw something crawling through the long grass and when it did not stop at his warning shot, he fired directly at it."

"A convict?"

"No, it was only a poor innocent dog. I am assured that it was only nicked and should make a full recovery, although it will walk with a limp now."

"Good grief. Still it makes one feel safe in ones' bed, knowing that the sentries are keeping good watch and taking no chances."

Edmund looked over toward Sarah. She was propped up with cushions on a chair on the veranda. "How is our young patient today?"

"Not much better, as you can see. I have been able to encourage her to take a little toast that I softened in boiled water."

"She has eaten nothing else?"

"Nothing of any substance, Lieutenant, not since your news, and she drinks only a little. What to do, what to do?" She wrung her hands. "I tell you, Lieutenant, though she is frail what I am most concerned about is her state of mind. I have urged Mr. Forsyth to secure passage for us both on the very next ship that is going to Sydney. Perhaps a period of convalescence away from this place may be the answer."

Edmund was alarmed at the prospect of Sarah leaving, but looking at her he had to admit that she did indeed look very pale and withdrawn. Even the blanket she was wrapped in seemed to engulf her wasting figure. He had not reckoned on his little scheme having such a devastating effect on his beloved Sarah.

"Do not, I humbly urge you, Mrs. Forsyth, make any hasty decisions about Sarah's future. Let me see what I can do." He picked up the fruit basket and tiptoed up to the veranda, so as not to wake the sleeping patient. Quietly, he pulled over a chair and set it close to Sarah's makeshift bed.

Bleary eyes looked up at him and a hint of a smile passed over Sarah's thin pale lips in recognition. "Ah Edmund, how good of you to visit."

She held out her hand and he took it in his, unnerved by her fragility. Her hand seemed dwarfed in his grasp. He then poured her a small glass of brandy and lifted her head, trying to encourage her to drink, but she only spluttered and refused to swallow.

"Come now, Sarah. What's this I hear; you are not eating or drinking? That will never do. We all need you to keep up your strength."

She made no reply. There was a long silence between them, Sarah staring unseeingly into the garden and Edmund intently watching her.

"Edmund, I abandoned him," Sarah said after a while. "I abandoned him when he needed me most." Tears flowed down her ashen cheeks and she slumped further down into the cushions. Then, more hysterically, she cried, "I *abandoned* him."

Edmund cupped her trembling chin gently in his hand and turned her face toward him. He smiled and wiped her tears away. "There now, my dear, tears will not bring him back."

"No, nothing will," she sighed.

He continued to caress her cheek as he thought out his next words carefully, trying to hide the immense sense of victory he felt. "He must have been aware of the consequences of his actions. He should have thought it out more clearly before joining in such a silly prank. He must have known that if he was caught he would be giving up his freedom."

Sarah pushed his hand away. "I do not believe it. Someone else put him up to it. I am sure of it."

Edmund felt the wind forced out of him. He could no longer look into her eyes but stared directly ahead, worried that his own expression would betray him.

Sarah continued. "He was a man who valued his freedom so very much. He was a true friend, Edmund, a true friend. He would never turn on another, even if it meant losing his own freedom. He must have had his reasons. You knew him well, too, Edmund, surely you can understand? Oh, I miss him so very much. If only…" Her words trailed off into silence.

Edmund understood all right. He was seething. Sarah's feelings for Michael ran much deeper than he had anticipated. Her love would not be so easy to win as he had initially thought. His original intentions needed adjusting.

"I know," he said, covering her hands with his own. So petit and frail, they disappeared from view, as though they had been swallowed whole. "That is how we should remember him. That is exactly the reason you must get well, Sarah." His words left a sour taste in his mouth and he swallowed hard, trying to be rid of it.

She smiled. "Of course, you are right, Edmund. You were always such a good and loyal friend to both of us. I will always love you for it. I am so very glad you are here on this Godforsaken island."

Platonic love? Edmund wanted to spit. *Will she always see me as a brother and never a lover?*

Sarah stared at the garden. "Do you remember the time when you and Michael scared me so…?"

They spent the rest of the afternoon reminiscing about Michael and their exploits together. Sometimes laughing, sometimes crying, Sarah continually leaning on Edmund for support, just as he had hoped.

Margaret Forsyth waddled up the stairs toward the couple. "I heard laughing."

"Oh, Mrs. Forsyth, Edmund, I mean the lieutenant, has been wonderful this afternoon. It has been so good to speak of Mr. Hanlan with someone who knew him almost as well as I did. Have you tasted the lovely fruit he brought with him?"

"No, I have not. But I can clearly see, by the look on your face, my dear, that Lieutenant Thornton has been the best tonic I could have possibly hoped for."

Edmund smiled and returned his attention toward Sarah. "Perhaps we might soon be able to resume our walks, Miss Henshall?"

"Perhaps, lieutenant. We shall see."

"A man can ask for no more." Once again he gave an exaggerated bow and made to take his leave. Then stopping on the first step he turned, and said "Mrs. Forsyth, ma'am. May I beg your indulgence for a moment? I need to speak with you regarding a delicate matter. Perhaps you might consider accompanying me to the gate?"

Margaret Forsyth excused herself willingly from Sarah's company.

Sarah watched with admiration as the tall, strong lieutenant led the waddling, short matron down the flagstone path.

The couple stopped at the gate and Sarah watched as they discussed their topic with great zeal, often looking towards her. It seemed from their stance it was something of great importance. She could see Mrs. Forsyth shaking her head with some conviction but Edmund, it seemed, was very persistent and continued to implore the lady until she reluctantly nodded in agreement.

Mrs. Forsyth waddled back up the pathway, finally, reaching the top of the veranda stairs. Sarah looked up at her expectantly, sure that she would be told what was happening. She was soon disappointed.

"We must rise and dress before sunrise tomorrow, Sarah. The lieutenant will be here with a horse and carriage as soon as the sun breaks the horizon." With that she waddled into the house and firmly shut the door behind her.

The sun had not yet risen above the horizon the next morning when the rhythmic sound of horses' hooves and carriage wheels along Military Road alerted Sarah to the arrival of Edmund. With reservation, she tied her bonnet ribbon and threw her cape around her shoulders, unsure of what to expect.

In the dim light of false dawn, she followed her guardians down the garden path towards the waiting carriage, curious as to why Mrs. Forsyth was carrying a large bunch of freshly cut flowers, but she asked no questions. She became even more perplexed when Reverend Bayley greeted her as Edmund helped her to board the carriage. She looked with uncertainty toward Edmund but he only smiled and put his finger to his lips.

Edmund climbed back onto the driver's box as the judge joined him. "Move on," Edmund encouraged the horses.

Sarah sat very still, keeping her eyes firmly fixed on the passing vista. A heavy, queasy feeling settled in her stomach as she realised they were heading in the direction of Kings Town cemetery. She closed her eyes and only opened them when the carriage came to a halt. As she alighted, she was thankful that the cemetery was no longer in sight. Edmund guided her and Mrs. Forsyth out onto a cliff top, the judge and minister respectfully followed. Only when Sarah looked down did she see the cemetery spreading to the left of her, the sea lapping at its fence line.

Reverend Bayley's deep voice droned on. "We have committed the body of, umm," He looked questioningly at Edmund, who mouthed the name to help the minister's memory. "Oh, yes, of course." He raised his prayer book once more. "We have committed the body of Michael Hanlan to the deep, looking for the Resurrection on the last day, and the life of the world to come, through Our Lord Jesus Christ; at whose second coming in glorious majesty to judge the world, the sea shall give up her dead, and the corruptible bodies of those who sleep in him shall be changed, and made like unto his glorious body, according to the mighty working whereby he is able to subdue all things unto himself."

Sarah stood motionless on the edge of the cliff, staring at the raging sea below her, the dreaded sea that took her Michael from her. She could just hear the monotonous voice of the minister above the wind as it whipped through the pines behind her. She tried to comprehend the words but their meaning was too painful to contemplate. She could taste the salt spray on her lips as the waves crashed on the jagged rocks below her.

Her arms felt numb and her legs suddenly gave way under her. In a lightning-fast movement, Edmund caught her in his strong, muscular arms. She clung to his powerful body for support, feeling the strength in his embrace, the warmth of his breath on her cheek, as he whispered in her ear.

"Hush now, Sarah my darling. I am still here. I will not desert you. I will protect you always."

For a long moment she stared back at him. A sense of much needed security engulfed her. Confused by the emotions that his closeness and his voice stirred within her, Sarah broke away from his hold, not yet ready to forget her Michael.

"Here, Sarah." Margaret Forsyth handed Sarah the large bunch of flowers that she had cut from her garden that morning. "I know my dear; that Mr. Hanlan will never have a permanent monument to mark his death, a place for you to mourn, but that does not mean we cannot mark his burial ground with flowers."

Swallowing a sob that rose in her throat, Sarah took the flowers, lifted them unsteadily to her lips, paused a moment, and then tossed them over the cliff into the violent sea below.

"Please accept my sincere apologies for the loss of your cousin, Miss Henshall. Lieutenant Thornton tells me that he was a fine sailor and will be sorely missed."

Sarah looked from Edmund to the minister, her thoughts clouded in confused, emotional turmoil. "Cousin? Sailor?" She tried to comprehend what the minister had said. She wanted to shout. "He was not my cousin! He was my lover!" But then she caught Mrs. Forsyth's warning look and demurely thanked the minister for the service.

"I must admit, Miss Henshall," Reverend Bayley said, making an annoying smacking sound with his lips. "This morning's service was, to say the least, a little unconventional. A burial service so long after the event... not usually done. No, not usually done. But, the lieutenant was very insistent."

Sarah managed a small, tentative smile of appreciation, her eyes filling with hot, stinging tears. Once again she turned with contempt to the ocean that had taken her lover away. The waves were playing with the flowers she had thrown. One moment they were being lifted to the crest of the wave as though peacefully floating. They then disappeared into the belly of the same wave, only to reappear on the next. She felt as if they were taunting her, playing with her emotions. At first giving her hope, as the flowers floated freely on the crest of the wave, then all too quickly the wave took control and dragged the flowers and her heart to the very depths of the dark ocean, only to rise once more in defiance on the next wave. Sarah watched mesmerised. Soon, the sea tired of its game. With one almighty, violent wave her flowers smashed onto the jagged rocks below her. Grief and an extreme sense of loss tore through her heart.

Sarah sat alone that evening, the light of a candle her only comfort. No more tears would come. She watched the shadows thrown by the flickering flame across her bedroom wall with morbid curiosity. It aroused thoughts of ghosts and of death, of Michael. She wished she had died with him. She tried to think of happier times, but none would come.

Sarah became aware of her bedroom brightening as the full moon emerged from behind scudding clouds, banishing the eerie shadows. Through her window she could see the dark silhouettes of the tall pines. Somewhere close, she could hear the night birds calling.

Then she caught sight of her journal lying abandoned on her writing desk. Reaching for it, she fingered its well-worn edges, trying to remember all the happy memories it held within its pages. Small glimpses of Michael in happier times began to break through her guard. Michael, who could always see the good in all people, Michael, always generous and loving, Michael, who could always make her laugh. She surrendered to the memories and let them wash over her like a cleansing bath. She began to feel his strength and love surge through her and it gave her the confidence to finally face a future without her beloved.

With newfound resolve she searched for a pencil stub, opened a fresh page in her journal and began to write in large, even letters:

I WILL ALWAYS LOVE YOU MICHAEL.

Turning the page she continued.

But today will be the beginning of my new life, a life without you. My life will not be as I had envisioned, being your wife and being the mother of your children. I feel your spirit within me, urging me on, pushing me forward. I know you will continue to protect me. You are gone and I will always mourn for you and keep you locked in my heart, but I now know that our good friend, Edmund, is right. You would not want me to give up. So with the help of Judge and Mrs. Forsyth, and Lieutenant Thornton also, I will go on living, just as you would have wanted.

Chapter Twenty-One

Michael sat hunched up in the corner of the cell, using the damp stone walls for balance, his knees crushed up against his chest for want of room. Anger still knotted up inside him. No matter how he looked at it he could not understand what he had done to warrant being locked up in this hell hole. He had heard stories of the horrors of being incarcerated in the 'nunnery'. He had thought them exaggerated – until now. Twelve men cramped together in a cell of no more than six by twelve feet, he had estimated, no room to sit let alone lie down. It was a space with no ventilation and was now rank with human excrement and other vile odours. Even breathing had become an arduous task. How he longed – how he *needed* – to stretch his stiff legs, breathe fresh air again, feel the cooling force of the wind on his skin once more.

He tried to calm himself by listening to the now familiar sounds that he could hear on the other side of the thick stone wall. The cries of the seabirds filled his mind and he could imagine them darting and diving into the depths of the water in search of prey. He could hear the roar of the waves crashing against the rocks. All sounds of freedom.

But then the grunts and groans of the men around him bought him back to the reality of his incarceration. He traced the thirteen rough scratches he had painstakingly etched into the stone wall next to him – one for each day of his confinement as best he could judge in the dark confinements of the cell. Only the turnkey's arrival with each day's ration marked the passage of time. Picking up the rock he had been using as a writing tool he began to scratch a fourteenth mark when the sound he had been anxiously listening for finally reached his ears. He heard the key turn in the rusty lock and the unwieldy latch being lifted. Edging back against the wall, he allowed the surgeon easy access as the turnkey pushed open the heavy door.

"So which one is it today?" the surgeon said to the turnkey.

"O'r there, sir, the Bard, sir." He pointed a pudgy, dirty finger at Michael, who struggled to his feet, encumbered by the heavy leg irons riveted around his ankles. He touched his forelock in recognition of the surgeon.

Trying to hide the pain that was now coursing through his stretching muscles, Michael allowed the surgeon to check him over.

"My God, Bard, you must have a fine constitution." The surgeon laughed as he cast a cursory glance over Michael's lean, yet still remarkably muscular body. "A diet of bread and water for two weeks would have laid many a man low." He nodded toward the turnkey. "Right then, this one's fit for work detail. See to it, man."

Michael shuffled out into the sunlight, rubbing his eyes to help them accustom to the unfamiliar glare. Every muscle in his body ached and every limb protested as he tried to stretch as he walked.

"It's to the saw pit for ye, Bard. Your new overs'rs are waiting for ye," chuckled the turnkey, shoving him towards the smithy's forge to have his leg irons removed.

Sweat poured freely down Michael's back. His arms burned with the exertion needed to pull the long saw downwards through the thick pine logs, his eyes continually blinded by the falling sawdust, his nose and ears constantly blocked. But even here, standing ankle deep in sawdust and dirt, he could still smile. It had only been a week since his fourteen day confinement but the prison mess food, although meagre, had helped him to regain his strength as quickly as could be expected.

Once again he was grateful for his good fortune at being paired with his old sawing partner, O'Malley. They enjoyed working together. It seemed that they could read one another's movements, so the sawing went more often than not without hitch. They were easily the most productive pair in the pit, but had he or O'Malley ever heard a word of praise? Hardly, just threats of feeling the cat if they slackened even for a moment.

The quitting bell finally rang and Michael and O'Malley joined the crowd of unwashed, unkempt convicts trudging toward the mess. They shuffled to a sheltered spot near the high boundary stone wall.

"I'll go get our mess kits for what they're worth," O'Malley mumbled. "No knives and forks, they expect us to eat like pigs. We're human beings not animals!" he yelled to no-one in particular.

"Right'o to, believe it's my turn to get the rations," Michael called after him as he joined the long queue of impatient men waiting to claim their gang's canvas bag of boiled meat. As he got closer to the large boiler at the other end of the yard the smell became more rancid and the men more agitated.

"Wait your turn!" The convict in charge of the boiler yelled.

"His bag has more in it than mine!"

"Yeah, not fair!"

More convicts joined in the rabble, shoving and jostling one another. One convict was pushed back against the boiler, almost toppling it over. Two heavy constables, truncheons in hand, pushed their way through the mob and dragged away the main offenders, restoring calm.

At long last, reaching the head of the line Michael claimed his steaming, hot bag of meat. Still not trusting the men around him he carefully held it high above his head so that it did not drip on him, but at the same time protecting it from potential scavengers. Cautiously he made his way back to his gang.

"Took your time, Bard. Here, quick give me my share!" A pair of gnarled hands grabbed the bag from Michael. Hungrily opening it, the convict shoved his hand into the bag not wanting to miss his share.

"Hold on, mate. Let the Bard share it out. He's always been fair," a quieter voice implored.

The first convict held onto the bag for a moment, but then reluctantly withdrew.

At the rest of the gang's insistence Michael took the bag and shared the salt beef as equally as he could onto each man's tin plate.

"Bless us O Lord, for what we are about to receive and make us truly thankful." O'Malley crossed himself, then looked at Michael and laughed heartily. "Don't reckon praying over this food will make it any bett'r but at least it delays havin' to eat it immed'tely!"

Michael looked across to the next table where the two men he had nicknamed his 'shadows' were sitting deep in conversation. Never had he felt as closely scrutinized as he did now by these two new overseers. Since his release from the 'nunnery' they seemed to be always hovering close about him. Michael stuffed another chunk of the tasteless salted beef into his mouth, wondering what they might be discussing so earnestly.

"These two new overseers, O'Malley, know much about em'?"

"Not much," replied O'Malley, his mouth full. "They were made our gang's overseers just before your release. Ever'one was real surprised. They have quite a reputation here and it's not all good, let me tell you." And then more thoughtfully, he added, "Wouldn't be surprised if they were flashmen in the employ of some officer or other."

"Well perhaps that explains their promotion but it does not explain their apparent interest in me." Michael considered the pair. The two overseers were hunched over their food, their heads close together as though they were afraid someone might overhear them.

Grinning a grotesque, toothless grimace, one looked straight at the Bard and mumbled something to his pal. Michael could only make out one word: chains.

Edmund skulked in the shadows of the high stone wall of the lumberyard as the men finished their meal and reformed their gangs ready for the afternoon work details. He scanned the unkempt mass of humanity, as it was herded before him, for any sign of Michael. He located him, surprised at how well he was looking after his stint in the 'nunnery'.

"Still smiling," Edmund said and scowled. "Well he won't be smiling for long." He watched with satisfaction as his two chosen overseers pushed and shoved their gang on towards the rest of their day's labour.

Michael and O'Malley made easy work of the long timbers from their pile, the saw moving in regular rhythm through the thick timbers.

"Hey, hold it there O'Malley. I'm coming up," Michael shouted.

"What's up Bard?"

"Can't you feel it?" Michael puffed as he climbed out of the pit. "The saw's blunt, no use trying to cut through any more till we get it sharpened."

The overseer, Cook, saw his chance and pounced. "You there! Bard! What do ye think you are doin'? It ain't quitten time yet! Bush," he yelled to his partner, "get the chains, we got ourselves a malingerer."

Bush grinned from ear to ear.

"Come on, Cook, be reasonable. The saw is blunt…" Michael didn't get a chance to finish his sentence; instead he felt the blow of the overseer's truncheon across his shoulders.

"You dare speak back to me, ME?" Cook growled. "It will be the bridle for you, no doubt about it."

O'Malley looked on helplessly as his friend was manacled and marched away.

"I was sent here for bloody reformation, not to be a bloody slave," yelled Edward Lawton, as he was escorted from the police court.

"Slave, eh? Well maybe we will just keep you a little longer then. Add another month to this man's sentence." Judge Forsyth ordered his clerk to record the sentence as one more month of hard labour in the crank mill.

Michael gaped open mouthed at the man who was being dragged past him, amazed at his close likeness to his old friend, Edmund Thornton.

The next man was then bought before the bench on the charge of not pushing his cart hard enough.

"You are sentenced to twenty five lashes, convict 89276."

"Much obliged, sir." The convict gave the magistrate a mock salute. "Cues me, sir, could I be as bold to ask if you could order those lashes to be delivered on me legs. Me poor back is still not healed from me last meeting with the flogger."

A chuckle passed throughout the court.

"And if you would be so kind, sir," the man continued, "I would be much obliged if you would order half to one leg and half to the other." He shook his wooden leg to the whole company. Laughter broke out and the sound of clanking chains reverberated throughout the court as the convicts in the dock stomped with solidarity for the man.

Banging on his desk with his gavel the stipendiary magistrate tried in vain to regain control of the room. It was only when Judge Forsyth stood up and motioned for silence, that order was restored. He ordered the guards standing by the door. "Get that man out of here, at once!"

"And increase the braggart's dose of the flogger's switch to fifty," yelled the stipendiary magistrate.

The man waved defiantly as he was led from the court.

Finally Michael's case was called. Rough hands unshackled his chains from the rails and he staggered over to the bench behind which the judge and magistrate sat.

The stipendiary magistrate did not look up at the convict in front of him, only snarled and shuffled through the pile of papers on his desk, but Michael felt reassured by Judge Forsyth's encouraging smile and touched his forelock in recognition.

Before the judge could speak, the stipendiary magistrate took control of the proceedings, and, as it was not a capital offence, Judge Forsyth could only shrug, sit back and watch. Michael was forced to listen as the charges against him were read out. The overseers' version of the event was meticulously recorded in the ledger by the court clerks. When he tried to interrupt and correct the account, he felt the butt of his guard's rifle in his ribs.

"Still speaking to your superiors without permission, eh, Bard?" The stipendiary magistrate tapped his pencil stub on his desk.

"That silken tongue of yours is going to get you in trouble, Bard. I think being gagged by the bridle may teach you a lesson. Yes, six hours I think. Bailiff, see to the sentence being carried out."

Michael looked disbelievingly from the stipendiary magistrate to the judge, his eyes imploring the judge for mercy as he was being dragged toward the courtroom doors. Judge Forsyth only looked apologetically at him, but made no comment in Michael's defence. Instead he rose, gathered his belongings, and hastened outside into the fresh air.

"Are you all right Judge Forsyth, sir? You look uncommonly pale."

"Ah, is that you, Thornton?" the judge enquired, shading his eyes from the sun. "Yes, yes, I am all right I suppose, just a heavy list this morning. By the way, we missed you at this morning's sessions. I had expected you to attend."

"Beg pardon sir. I had some pressing business that required my immediate attention. I did not think I would be needed."

"You are probably right. The stipendiary magistrate had it all in hand, I suppose."

Two constables strode past them, dragging a struggling convict between them.

The judge watched the group pass with sadness in his heart.

Edmund tried to look surprised. "If I am not mistaken, that was the Bard, was it not, sir?"

"No, you are not mistaken, Thornton." The judge paused for a moment. "He was charged with stopping work to talk." He watched as Michael was being chained to a lamp post some distance off. "Good grief, the poor man was only asking to sharpen his saw."

Edmund stepped back into the shade of the building as though to get out of the sun, but in fact trying to blend into the shadows so that he could watch the punishment being administered without being seen. A feeling of triumph flooded through him.

Judge Forsyth stepped back with him, not taking his eyes from the Bard. "The stipendiary magistrate, in his wisdom, determined that six hours in the bridle would teach the poor unfortunate a lesson. In my opinion, Thornton, this is a blatant case of the overseers reporting a convict for their own gain. I cannot help but wonder what they got in compensation for their treachery."

As if in resignation, the judge averted his eyes and said, "Well, I suppose we cannot be of any help here." He gave Edmund a friendly nudge. "I am sure there are two ladies who would welcome our early return today. What say you Thornton? Would you care to join me?"

Edmund's face split into a wide grin at the unexpected invitation. "It would indeed be my pleasure, sir."

Michael struggled at the chains that bound him to the lamp post, his hands behind his back. He had seen men after the bridle had been administered, teeth missing, unable to eat for days afterwards. He clenched his lips, shaking his head every which way, trying to thwart the constable's efforts to push the cylindrical, wooden gag into his mouth.

"Look 'ere, Bard. Don't struggle so. It will be all the better for you, if you don't struggle. I don't wanna break y'r teeth but I w'll if you force me to." Once again he tried to push the gag through Michael's clenched lips. "Come on Bard, you know me. I will be as gentle as I can, no one else need know, just you and me, eh?"

Caught unaware by the man's sympathy Michael released his lips ever so slightly but the man quickly took advantage and shoved in the wooden pole and tightened the leather strap around Michael's head. Horror passed through Michael. For a moment he could not breathe. He struggled for breath, looking imploringly at the man in front of him.

"Just relax, Bard," the man coaxed. "The breath will come, I promise you."

Michael could feel a trickle of blood running down his chin and this panicked him more, tears streamed down his face. He sucked hard for breath. Slowly it came. He found that if he sucked deeply he could breathe through the small hole in the gag, although with much difficulty and pain. Every time he took a breath, he heard a low, long whistle as the air passed through the small hole, like the sound of a lute. As long as he could hear it, he figured, he knew he was still alive.

At first Michael was grateful for the shade afforded by the nearby stone wall of the barracks, but as the sun moved across the sky the heat became oppressive. He could feel his uncovered skin burning. His jaw ached unrelentingly, and his throat was so parched he feared he would either choke or die of thirst. Other convicts trudged past, muttering sympathy, but no-one spoke to him, for fear of facing punishment themselves.

Michael lost track of time. He began to hallucinate in the heat. Frightful apparitions filled his thoughts. The most vivid of these was that of a large black bird in full flight coming straight at him. He tensed waiting for it to attack. Then it began to talk.

"Bard, I have only just heard of your ordeal. I am so very sorry. I have been in Longridge all day." Reverend Bayley rushed over to the lamp post, his cassock flying out behind him in his haste. Taking a square of linen from his pocket he tried to wipe away some of the dried blood from around Michael's mouth. The convict flinched in pain. The minister turned and said, "Get over here and release this man at once." He dragged a reluctant constable towards him. "How long has he been here?"

"Nigh on six hours, as was ordered, sir."

"Well then, release him. Get on with it man. Release him this very minute!"

As the constable clumsily tried to unlock the chains that bound Michael to the lamp post Reverend Bayley unbuckled the gag's strap.

Michael felt the strap loosen around his head and the gag dropped from his swollen lips. As his binds were loosened, he found he could not stand on his own and he slumped into the minister's arms. Through his dry, chapped lips he managed a hoarse whisper of thanks to his rescuer and answered a heartfelt "Amen" in response to the minister's prayer of deliverance.

"Get some water immediately, before this poor man expires, and find some salve for his burns."

A mug of water being offered, Reverend Bayley moistened the linen square in his hand and wiped it gently over Michael's lips and then offered him a drink. Michael choked and gagged, then finally swallowed.

Chapter Twenty-Two

Sarah crumbled some stale bread onto the veranda ledge and watched as her green parakeets flew eagerly over to it. She smiled, holding out her hand so that the birds might feed from them.

Mrs. Forsyth was glad for the distraction. "It has been a few weeks now Sarah, since you heard of your... your friend's passing, God rest his soul, perhaps you should now be considering the terms stipulated in your father's will. He wanted you to marry, and I believe that Lieutenant Thornton would be a kind and considerate husband. You really should think about it, my dear."

Sarah blushed, but did not answer.

The birds were startled from their feast by the creaking of the front gate and they flew swiftly to the safety of their nest in the nearby pine tree.

"My goodness, Reverend Bayley." Margaret Forsyth straightened her dress. "How kind of you to visit. Sarah and I are becoming quite bored with only one another for company. Would you care for some refreshments?"

"Most kind of you." The minister climbed up the stairs onto the veranda and made himself comfortable in the chair indicated by Mrs. Forsyth. "If the wonderful smells emanating from your kitchen are anything to go by, Mrs. Forsyth, we are indeed in for a treat."

Margaret Forsyth glowed in the praise. "It is an old family recipe of my grandmother's. Sarah, would you help Matthews bring out some tea and cake, then come join us. Where is he, anyway? He should be here greeting our guest. Oh, and when you find him, would you please remind Matthews to use the best china? Here is the key to the tea caddy." She handed Sarah the large bunch of keys that she always kept on her person. "I am sure you know which key it is."

"Yes, Mrs. Forsyth. Please excuse me, Reverend Bayley." Sarah disappeared inside, fumbling with the keys.

Returning to the veranda, Sarah quietly fussed over pouring tea and cutting slices of seed cake for them.

Reverend Bayley reached for a discarded book left on the table and opened it to the title page. "Ah, Shakespeare's sonnets. I am very partial to them myself."

"Yes indeed, Miss Henshall reads aloud to me. It is a pleasant way to pass these long afternoons."

"I agree whole heartedly, Mrs. Forsyth. I have a fine library of my own in my house. If ever you should want new reading material, please, do not hesitate to come and browse my bookshelves."

Taking a large sip of tea, Margaret Forsyth set her teacup down upon its saucer and said, "Now, my dear Reverend, what do we owe the honour of your visit today?"

"Yes, of course, I do beg your pardon," he said. "You may have heard that the Lady Franklin landed at Cascades earlier this week carrying another load of convicts to our shores. But, this group is different."

Both women leaned forward in their seats.

"Different, how?" asked Sarah.

"Different, in that many of their number are juveniles, some as young as nine years of age."

Sarah gasped. "Those poor children, what they must have been through."

"Yes indeed, Miss Henshall. We must remember though that they are still convicted felons even though they are so young. The Commandant though, in this case, has been very generous. He has bid me take the younger children under my wing, keep them from learning the ways of the more hardened criminals and give them a chance to reform. He has given me permission to teach them in my own home for two hours each day."

"Very admirable of the Commandant." Margaret Forsyth sat back in her chair. "A pity he was not so considerate of my letters for the poor unfortunate men."

"Be that as it may, Mrs. Forsyth. I believe my teaching can only go so far. What these young souls really need is a mother's influence. I was hoping that I might impose on you ladies to take on such a position. You will be helping save these young boys from a life of misery."

"Upon my word, what a strange request," declared Mrs. Forsyth.

"What a wonderful request!" Sarah jumped up from her chair. *Michael, oh Michael, this is your doing. I can feel it. I might not have you to fuss over now but I will have children. I love you, Michael Hanlan.*

"What exactly would be required of us, Reverend?"

Without waiting for an answer Sarah cried, "Why, I can read to them, even teach them to read if they are so inclined. I can teach them to write, I can even teach them to draw!"

"Slow down young lady. Let us hear from Reverend Bayley what is actually expected of us."

"Your young ward has understood my request well, Mrs. Forsyth. Perhaps you could include the teaching of a few social graces too."

"It seems simple enough." Margaret Forsyth pushed the crumbs of her cake around her plate.

Sarah looked at her guardian. "Please, Mrs. Forsyth. We will be doing so much good. Please," she begged.

Margaret Forsyth patted her ward on the hand. "It seems Reverend that you have found a tonic stronger than any physic prescribed by the surgeon. I have not seen Sarah so spirited in such a long time. It is so good to see. So the answer has to be yes. Yes, we would both love to help you in your venture."

Sarah rained kisses of gratitude on Mrs. Forsyth's cheeks. "Thank you, thank you!"

The ladies became so engrossed in the discussion of the new project with the minister that the judge and Edmund's arrival went unnoticed.

Sarah was the first to notice them. "Judge Forsyth," she threw her arms around the startled man. "Something wonderful has happened. Reverend Bayley…"

The men nodded acknowledgement of each other as Sarah raced on. "He has asked Mrs. Forsyth and me to help him teach the juvenile boys!"

There was stunned silence from the two men.

Edmund found his tongue first. "But, sir, you cannot expect these fine women to visit the convicts' barracks. They would meet all manner of men there. " He stumbled over his words. "All manner of ruffian. One could not possibly guarantee their safety."

"Do not be silly, Lieutenant, as if the Reverend would put our lives at risk."

"You insult me, sir," the minister interjected. "Let me assure you Judge Forsyth, and you, too, Lieutenant, that I would never put the welfare of these kind ladies at risk by even suggesting they visit the convicts' barracks. They will be working with about a dozen of the youngest boys in my own home, under my strict supervision."

"I meant no harm, sir," Edmund said with a stammer. "You must understand that it is quite a surprise to hear of your plan. Surely the Commandant has not approved it, has he?"

"Indeed he has. In fact he is quiet enthusiastic about the prospect. It was at his suggestion that I approached these good ladies. On reflection I realise now that I should have probably spoken to you first, Judge."

"I am sure that Miss Henshall and I can speak for ourselves, sir. So you may expect us on the morrow," Margaret Forsyth said, hands on hips.

"Well it all seems to be settled then." Judge Forsyth smiled at his wife. "Now, Lieutenant Thornton and I have news that should please you greatly."

He handed his wife a sealed parchment.

Margaret Forsyth looked from her husband to the lieutenant. Not finding any hint in their expressions about its content, she handed it over to Sarah. "Here, my dear, you open it. The last letter I read did not please me at all."

Sarah broke the seal and read:

July 23rd, 1848

The Officers of Her Majesty's Eleventh Regiment of Foot request the pleasure of Judge and Mrs. Forsyth's company, and the company of Miss Sarah Henshall at an Evening Party, on this coming Saturday, in the mess room of the Military Barracks.

An answer will oblige.
Dancing.

Chapter Twenty-Three

Mrs. Forsyth gave a breathless sigh of delight as she stood in the doorway of the officers' mess, now transformed for the evening into a ballroom. "I do declare, would you look at that, Sarah. You could almost believe you were in a forest glen."

Sarah nodded in agreement as she gazed around the room. The officers had meticulously fashioned cuttings of the Norfolk Pine, Cabbage Tree Palm and other palms, ferns and grasses to form a graceful bower across the room. It did indeed look lovely, a perfect setting for the Officers' Ball. "Beautiful," she sighed, lifting her nosegay to smell its scent. "Absolutely beautiful."

"I cannot see the Major and Mrs. Boyce. Can you Sarah?" Margaret Forsyth strained her neck trying to see over the milling crowd of Norfolk society. "All and sundry seem to be here tonight. Oh dear it seems such a small space for nigh on a hundred people. I do hope there will be room to dance don't you, Sarah? Still there are so many more gentlemen than ladies it won't take long to fill your dance card. I do declare, so many eligible gentlemen in one place."

Sarah only smiled, well aware by now that an answer was not expected.

"Sarah! You have come at last!" Annie Boyce appeared next to her friend.

"Your gown is very becoming, Annie. Pink is most definitely your colour."

"Do you think so, Sarah?" Annie looked unhappily down at her dress. "I was unsure. It is last year's gown, you see. Father would not agree to another coming from Sydney so mother fancied it up with some old lace to make it look new."

"Truthfully Annie, you would not know to look at it."

"But look at you! Your gown is probably the latest fashion in London." Annie sighed, staring at Sarah's lavender gown with its low cut neckline and full sleeves.

"Do not be so sure, Annie. Fashion is notorious for changing so very quickly. You must remember that it is nearly twelve months since I left England. Who knows what they are wearing now?"

Both girls laughed good-naturedly.

At that moment Judge Forsyth and his wife approached.

"Ahem." The judge cleared his throat to gain the girls' attention.

"Oh, I do beg your pardon. Good evening Judge Forsyth." Annie dropped a curtsy to Judge and Mrs. Forsyth. "Good evening Mrs. Forsyth. Please forgive my enthusiasm."

"Quite understandable, my dear, and may I say you look very well in your ball gown."

"Thank you, ma'am." Annie bowed politely.

Margaret Forsyth looked past the girl. "Tell me, Miss Boyce, did your mother and father accompany you this evening?"

"Yes, indeed ma'am. Mother is waiting for you, just over there. She asked me to bring you to her directly you arrived."

The party weaved their way through the crème of Norfolk Island society. The women dressed in white and pale coloured silks and satins, skirts rustling as they brushed past each other and the men magnificent in the reds of their military uniforms or regal in the formal black trousers and jackets of the civilian staff.

Glancing around the room, Sarah enquired, "Have you seen Lieutenants Thornton and Saunders, Annie?"

"They have sent their apologies."

Sarah's face fell.

"Oh dear no, Sarah, you misunderstand me. They are not gone for the whole evening. They are only occupied at present, helping set up tables so that those who wish to play cards can do so at their leisure. But look!" She held up her dance card, her hand trembling as she did so. "Lieutenant Saunders has already near filled my card! I believe, if I had let him, he would have asked every dance of me! Can you believe it?" Leaning in closer to her friend she whispered, "Do you think it proper, Sarah, to allow him to be so demanding?"

"Of course it is proper." Sarah hugged Annie. "I am so very pleased for you."

Captain Travers appeared without warning in front of the ladies, greeting them with an exaggerated bow.

"Good evening, Captain Travers," Margaret Forsyth answered for them all. "I must say, Captain, your regiment has certainly done you proud this evening. The decorations are truly delightful."

"Thank you ma'am, I will pass on your compliments," Captain Travers said. "I hope you do not consider me forward, ma'am, but Mr. Vessey, over there, has expressed a desire to be introduced to you and the young ladies. I have taken it upon myself, as master of ceremonies for this evening, to ask your permission."

The girls looked at each other, but it was Margaret Forsyth who answered, looking over at the man. "We would be delighted, sir."

Captain Travers motioned to Mr. Vessey to join them and then introduced him to the women.

"Yes indeed, it is a pleasure to make your acquaintance again, Miss Boyce." George Vessey bowed, but immediately looked toward Sarah.

"Lastly, may I present Miss Henshall, the ward of Judge and Mrs. Forsyth?"

"The pleasure is mine, I am sure." George Vessey bowed deeply.

Sarah dropped a bobbing curtsey. As she rose she found herself staring into the mischievous, blue eyes of the Superintendent. *So like my Michael's.* Her breath caught in her throat. *The same tight curls also,* she noticed, *but thankfully blond not ginger.*

"It is a pleasure to meet two such pretty ladies on such a desolate island as this," George Vessey said.

Annie looked away.

Sarah was confused by her friend's off-handed reaction to such a handsome, well-spoken man.

Captain Travers bowed toward the women. "Well then, I believe my task is done here. I will take my leave now. Other duties pressingly call." He strode off in the direction of the small stage set up at the front of the room.

"Mr. Vessey," Sarah ventured. "Your accent is strange to me. From what part of England do you hail?"

"Actually, Miss Henshall, I am colonial born. Sydney Town was the place of my birth. I am what is known colloquially as a currency lad!"

"How exciting, Mr. Vessey. Then you are the first actual colonial we have met. Is he not, Sarah?" Margaret Forsyth said.

Sarah nodded but had no time to answer before George Vessey spoke. "May I be so bold as to ask, Mrs. Forsyth, if your ward, Miss Henshall, might still have the first two dances free?"

Margaret Forsyth looked toward Sarah. "Of course, she will accept, sir."

Annie grabbed Sarah's hand tightly. Surprised, Sarah pulled away.

"Please take your partners for the first quadrille of the evening," Captain Travers bellowed to the attending crowd.

Sarah threw Annie a look of astonishment as she found herself being whisked onto the dance floor by the handsome Mr. Vessey.

Music began to echo through the hall. Sarah could hear the violin and clarion, but could not see the musicians. The resonance of sound seemed to be coming from behind a floral decorated screen. "Do you think the musicians might be convicts?" she asked her partner as they twirled around each other. Mr. Vessey looked toward the screen and shrugged.

Sarah turned her attention back to the dance. The chalked wooden floor echoed with the step of every dancer, a strange rhythmic beat. Muffled voices tried to compete with the music. George Vessey's face started to fade the more involved in the dance she became. She let herself be led in the dance steps by the man she was with, dreaming of the man she wanted.

Richard Saunders surveyed the crowd in front of him. "I am glad that task is well finished, Thornton. I have asked Miss Boyce to save me the first dance and now it seems I have let her down."

"I am sure she will forgive you, Saunders. It is obvious, that the girl is smitten with you."

"I confess the feelings are well returned." He watched the line of dancers as they stepped through a quadrille. "Will you look at that, Thornton? It seems your Miss Henshall has not missed the first dance."

"I beg your pardon?"

"Look, over there. Is that not your Miss Henshall under the spell of our Mr. Vessey, no less?"

Edmund glared across the room, seething with rage. It was all he could do to stop himself from walking over and dragging them apart. Trying to sound calm and unconcerned, his voice could not disguise the anger he was feeling, Edmund inquired, "Just what do you know of Vessey?"

"I do know that all the ladies, whether they be young or old, seem to swoon at his feet." He screwed up his brow. "He is not that good looking do you think, Thornton?"

Edmund did not answer but stayed focused on the dancing couple.

Saunders went on. "Rumour has it that he is actually born of convict parents, a convict uncle as well… if the rumours are to be believed."

"I see, well that explains it I suppose," Edmund replied, failing to conceal his animosity. *Why is she always attracted to the underdog?* Then, changing the subject, Edmund asked, "Is that not Miss Boyce over there, speaking with Mrs. Forsyth? I am sure she would welcome your company."

"I can see your thoughts are elsewhere, Thornton, so if you will excuse me, I believe I will go and ask the lady's forgiveness for being unavailable for the first dance."

For two dances Sarah twirled and stepped, oblivious to all that was happening around her, deep in another world, a world where she was with Michael, a world where she was in love and was loved passionately.

She heard George Vessey ask, "Miss Henshall, would you care to get some air? It is very close in this hall."

Sarah looked vaguely at the man, the trance broken, and nodded.

Sarah shivered as they stepped out onto the parade ground. The air hummed with the sound of night insects and the soft whispering and giggling of other couples strolling around the grounds.

"Are you cold, Miss Henshall?" George started to remove his jacket.

"No, I find the weather here quite balmy, so very different from England."

They stopped under a spreading tree. A full moon shed dappled lights and shadows across the ground, filtering through the branches above.

Sarah stared at her partner, his facial features partially obscured. No words passed between them. Her heart still ached for Michael. She could think of nothing else. It was easy to allow herself to live in the illusion that Michael was with her on that moonlit night.

She then felt his hands entwine with hers, sending a tingling sensation through her whole body. She could feel the warmth of Michael's body as he moved closer towards her. Her body began to ache for her lover's touch. She closed her eyes, feeling her knees go weak. She did not pull away when he caught her around her waist. There was a warning tingle in the base of her stomach but she took no notice. His searching lips found hers and she responded willingly. Michael was in her arms once more and she did not want to leave his embrace.

Without warning Sarah found herself being roughly pushed up against the trunk of the tree, pinned with nowhere to go. Reality instantaneously returned. Panic surged through her.

She could hear George Vessey's ragged breathing. She watched with great apprehension as his gaze dropped from her face, to her bare shoulders, to the line of her breast. With all her might she tried to struggle free, to pull away, but the man was too strong.

"Mr. Vessey! Sir!" Edmund's response was swift and violent. He dragged the man off Sarah, his first punch winding him, his second sending the man to the ground clutching his face in agony.

Sarah pulled away, fighting back tears. "Edmund, Edmund, what have I done?"

"It is not what you have done, Sarah, but what this cad has done to you. If he has hurt you in any way, I swear, he will feel the cold steel of my blade."

"No, no, Edmund. I am all right, he has not hurt me. Please, for my sake, leave him be." She looked at the ground, hoping that the guilt she felt could not be heard in the sound of her voice.

"For your sake then, Sarah, but he had best not approach you again."

He pulled the now bleeding George Vessey up from the ground by his collar. "You are very lucky, sir," he spat, "that it is only a broken nose. I warn you, if you come anywhere near Miss Henshall again the consequences will be far worse."

Holding his nose, the man struggled away without saying a word.

The mournful cry of the ghost bird filled the air, giving the night an eerie, cold feeling. Sarah shivered violently. "Take me inside, please."

Edmund escorted Sarah into a vacant room at the front of the barracks. He found her a chair into which she gratefully sank, arranging her heavy skirt and petticoats around her, scolding herself for the dirt that soiled the hems. The cheerful sounds of the ball filtered through the room. But it was too much for Sarah. She put her hands to her ears trying to block it out, but Edmund removed them and laid them in her lap. She looked up at him, her cheeks stained with tears, her eyes reddened, puffy.

"I am so sorry, Sarah, that I was not there to protect you."

"Don't look at me so, Edmund. I do not deserve your kindness, not tonight."

"You are not yourself, Sarah." Edmund chose his words carefully so as not to show how he really felt. It was not the right time or place, he calculated, to make his final bid to win the prize. "You have not given yourself time to mourn. First losing your father and then so soon after, losing…"

"Michael," she finished his sentence with a whisper.

Edmund hesitated, torn by conflicting emotions. He wanted to grab her and kiss her fiercely to try to expunge Michael from her mind. But, at the same time, he had to fight hard not to take her head in his hands and squeeze out the memories of the man.

"Will you please fetch Judge and Mrs. Forsyth? Tell them I am unwell and need to return home."

The sound of Sarah's strained voice brought him back to his senses. Glad to be given a task, Edmund left to do her bidding.

Chapter Twenty-Four

A month after the Officers' Ball Judge Forsyth paced his office staring at the pile of files sitting on his desk. Then looking up he saw Edmund through his window. He stopped pacing, stepped outside his door and called, "Lieutenant Thornton. Will you come with me to my office? There is a file I would like to discuss with you."

Edmund turned round at the sound of his name being called. Hurriedly, he had handed a parcel to each of the two men he had been speaking to, and then waved them away.

"Of course, sir.".

The judge watched as the two uncouth men disappeared around the corner of the barracks. "What on earth have you got to do with the likes of them, Thornton?"

"Just a couple of overseers, sir," said Edmund, trying to sound nonchalant. "They are keeping me well informed on the activities of a few of the more notorious guests on this island. In exchange I give them a little tea, sugar and if the information warrants it, sometimes even tobacco."

"Flashmen, I see. I cannot say that I trust a man who is willing to send another to punishment for his own gain."

The disapproving tone of his voice was not lost on Edmund.

Stepping into the office, Judge Forsyth indicated a chair for Edmund. Sitting down himself he started to thumb through some papers in front of him. "Ah, here it is." He pulled out the relevant pages and scanned down them. "This man known as the Bard, he perplexes me, Edmund."

"You should not concern yourself, sir." Edmund's voice was hoarse with frustration. "He is only a convict, sir, and seems to be a poorly behaved one at that."

"That is exactly what perplexes me. Firstly, I can find no record of the man's true identity."

Edmund turned away and pretended to look out of the window, trying to hide the smile that threatened to break across his face. Obviously his spies in the record office had done their job well, eradicating all personal documents regarding Michael Hanlan.

"Are you listening to me, Lieutenant?"

"Yes, of course, sir, sorry sir."

"Not only can I find no record of his identity, according to this," and he waved the Bard's file in Edmund's face, "he has always been a model convict, a model convict from the time he landed here on Norfolk right up until it seems the letter writing incident." The judge handed the file over to Edmund. "Since that day his behaviour has changed dramatically. I tell you Edmund, it baffles me."

Edmund took the paper, trying not to smirk as he perused it.

"I agree sir, he has an extensive record." He read the list of misdemeanours and punishments aloud. "Speaking without being spoken to – the bridle. Whistling while working – two days bread and water. For tying his bootlaces when muster was called – two days bread and water. For walking across the prison yard to make an enquiry – five days solitary…" And so the list went on. The only punishment the Bard seemed to have avoided was the whip o' the cat.

Despite his initial smugness, Edmund became increasingly uneasy as he read through the list of punishments. Punishments that in all probability, if it had not been for him and the diligent work of his spies, the Bard would never have had to endure. But he consoled himself, firmly believing that he was actually protecting Sarah and her reputation. After all, it would probably ruin her in this small settlement if her close association with a convict became common knowledge. And by all reports the Bard was standing up to his punishments well.

Judge Forsyth sighed with disappointment. "I heard a convict talking the other day. He said something like – 'Let a man's heart be what it will when he comes here, his man's heart is taken from him, and he is given the heart of a beast.' Truly, I believe I have not heard a truer word spoken on this desolate island. And, mark my words, Edmund. I do not think that it only pertains to the convicts here. It seems that this blessed island changes us all, all but the strongest. Here, give me that list, I have another to add."

Taking a pen he charged it with ink and wrote: *For in subordination – one week in chains grinding maize in the crank mill.*

Putting his pen down, he looked hard at Edmund. "Let us hope that such hard labour may finally break him and make him become a better man." He blotted the sentence and pushed the file away.

Firmly squaring his feet on the rough floor, Michael gripped the crank handle with both hands and began to push forward with as much force as he could muster, making the giant grinding wheel move. He willed his hands, hands now so gnarled and calloused from manual labour, to keep on turning the crank, though every other muscle in his body burned in protest. He turned the wheel with such force that his half naked body glistened with perspiration and every fibre and muscle in his body strained to its full capability.

"Rest time!" the overseer bellowed.

Michael opened and shut his fists trying to relieve the cramps now assaulting them. With the cramps relieved, he stared at the blisters that were still healing and the rough calluses that were forming on his palms.

Not the hands of a gentleman anymore, he reckoned, dreading to think what Sarah would make of them. *Sarah, darling Sarah, what will you see when you look at my poor hands again? Will you be revolted by them? Or will you see them as the hands of a man who has done his work honestly, served his term and come home to you?*

The rest period was over too soon. The words "Back to work," sounded through the mill.

Every muscle in Michael's arms and legs now burned fiercely, but he kept moving in a steady rhythm. Then, unbelievably, he saw something that appeared as much a vision of Sarah as any he held dear to his own heart: a vision of an almost forgotten friend, a friend now garbed in the refinery of the British army. "Edmund?" he said, and shook his head, unable to believe what he saw. "Edmund? Is that truly you?"

The man turned, not noticing him, and then moved out of sight.

Michael crawled into his hammock that night, every frustrated movement making it swing alarmingly. He tossed, punching at his thin pillow, visions of Edmund in his red uniform following every turn, toss and twist he made.

Guards armed with batons patrolled between the hammocks, checking that all was in order. "Right then, lights out!" called the dormitory supervisor.

The sound of the heavy doors of the dormitory being slammed and bolted was the signal for the area to come alive. Hidden candles were lit and blankets were hung between hammocks to give the occupants privacy. Men scrambled from one hammock to another, some for intimate meetings and others to carry out their clandestine crafts.

Trying to break free from Edmund's face, Michael did not feel the inclination to be sociable that night so he hung blankets on either side of his hammock. Plaiting flax was by now second nature to him. His fingers worked deftly crossing each strand to make a neat squared plait.

No matter how hard he tried to concentrate on his craft he could not get the man he had seen earlier that day out of his thoughts. *Of course it could not have been Edmund. Surely if it were him he would know that I, too, am here on this wretched island. If indeed it was him, undoubtedly he would speak up for me, save me from this hell.* Missing the plaiting pattern he cussed himself and pulled apart the last couple of crosses. He started to plait with more force, with each crossover getting angrier. Of course, it *had* to be him. *Why didn't he acknowledge me? Why didn't*

183

he recognise me? Confused, he put away his plaiting materials and blew out his candle, a rancid smell engulfing his small space. Michael lay back in his hammock, calming himself, and tried to think more clearly.

Of course, he couldn't say anything to me. He would not want to be seen fraternising with the convicts. He felt more comfortable with this thought. *Maybe I should just let Edmund know I'm here. Then he can help me.*

Elongated, haunting shadows made by the silhouettes of the convicts working on either side of him played on the blankets hanging between them. He rolled over and tried to sleep, but blinked awake with a start.

Oh my God! If Edmund is here, who is looking after my Sarah? He set his resolve to approach Edmund as soon as he could for news of her. But then his sister's frightened face flashed before him and he remembered his debt, the debt of honour he owed to Edmund. He could not compromise Edmund's position of authority. It would only make it difficult for Edmund to admit he had a close relationship with a convict.

No, he consoled himself. *I will have to respect Edmund's privacy and wait for him to help me. I only hope it's soon.*

Michael shuffled into the crank mill the next morning with less enthusiasm than was usual. The fetters chained to his feet made walking difficult. The only relief he found working in the mill was that the two overseers who seemed to shadow him everywhere were no longer there. Still, he could not help but wonder what would befall him next. He could feel himself becoming weaker, less determined to survive. He had had enough. He did not even want to tell stories any more.

"If me reckonin's right, it be your last day here, eh Bard?" The overseer cackled as he marked Michael off his list and bent down to check that his fetters showed no signs of tampering.

Michael half-heartedly knuckled his forelock in respect. He then took his place with the other forty nine convicts sentenced to hard labour in the crank mill.

Without warning the crank mill erupted into loud cajoling and profanities. Michael looked over towards the window where he could just see the flowing black cassock of Reverend Bayley as the man hurried by. Overseers started stomping through the mill trying to restore order.

All fell silent when the minister appeared at the door. The only sound to be heard was that of the loud, rhythmic clanking of the crank wheels as they turned. All eyes were on the minister as he handed the head overseer a letter. Michael panicked when he saw them look in his direction. Instinctively he lowered his eyes so as not to draw attention to himself. When he looked up again, Reverend Bayley was tapping at the paper as though to emphasise a passage of some importance. He was looking sternly at the overseer, who was vigorously shaking his head. By their stance, Michael could see that they were arguing.

At length, it seemed the overseer conceded and pointed in Michael's direction. Michael felt his stomach lurch and held more tightly to the crank handle for balance. As the minister passed each convict, they stopped working. The sound of the working mill became quieter and quieter until it finally stopped all together. Everyone was staring at Michael. Michael tried in vain to turn his wheel on his own. The minister put his hands on Michael's and motioned for him to stop.

"Yes, this is the man I want. Unfetter him immediately."

The overseer begrudgingly did as he was ordered and Michael, dragging his feet, followed the minister into the bright sunlight.

Reverend Bayley guided Michael by his elbow down towards the shore.

Michael stared at the minister, wondering what new punishment was about to befall him. Was it so serious that the minister had to tell him?

"Bard," Reverend Bayley began in earnest. "I have been speaking to Judge Forsyth."

Michael felt himself begin to shake uncontrollably. "Sir?" he questioned. "I swear, sir, I have done nothing wrong. I have been in the crank mill for the last seven days, sir. On my oath, I have done nothing wrong." He fell to his knees in desperation, too weak to stand.

The minister coaxed him back on to his feet. "Calm yourself, Bard. This be good news for ye."

"Good news, sir?" Michael's heart began to pound.

"The judge, Bard, still thinks very well of you. He agrees with me, that there must be other forces at work for your record of good behaviour to have become so blighted."

"Thank you, sir," was all Michael could think to reply.

"It has come to our attention, Bard, that you possess a skill, other than your wonderful ability to tell stories."

"I do not understand, sir."

"I speak of your ability as a hatter, Bard."

Michael's heart sank. It seemed his nightly work had been discovered. All he could do now was confess and take his next punishment, whatever it might be, hoping that the other men in his mess had not been discovered as well. "Sir, I am sorry. I know that my nightly craft is against regulations. But I beg you to understand, I must say in my defence, that the proceeds have helped the men in my mess to supplement our meagre rations. It has bought us tea and sugar, some fruit and vegetables and, yes, sometimes even tobacco." Michael hesitated, realising he was confessing all to one in authority. He bowed his head and awaited judgement.

"It might surprise you Bard that the authorities are well aware of the nightly tasks undertaken by so many of your fellow convicts. They have been turning a blind eye to much of the black market. Many of you are offering products not readily available in such a closed settlement. In fact, many ladies on the island proudly parade, wearing your bonnets. Even the commandant's wife. It has even been said that they have not seen finer work, even in England."

Michael reddened. "Th-that is v-very high p-praise indeed, sir," he said in both confusion and amazement.

"You should indeed be well pleased with yourself, Bard. Now, that brings me as to why I liberated you from the crank mill today.

Judge Forsyth and I have another task for you. One I believe that is of great importance."

Michael listened as the minister continued.

"You may have noticed some very young convicts in the barracks of late."

Michael nodded.

"These young boys, forty or so of them, arrived about two weeks ago now, although why the powers that be see fit to send such impressionable young minds into this den of iniquity I will never understand." He stared out to sea for a moment. "I thank God though, that our Commandant has seen fit to separate them from the masses as much as possible. As such, he has commissioned me to look after them. I have been trying to teach them myself. I have also been able to obtain the help of Mrs. Forsyth, you may remember her."

Michael thought back to that day in Mrs. Forsyth's garden. Long ago he had reconciled himself to the fact that she was in no way to blame for his misfortune.

"And her ward," the minister continued, "to help me teach some of the younger boys in my house."

"I am sure she will teach them very well, sir. I have very fond memories of the lady."

"It was, in fact, her husband, Judge Forsyth, who suggested that I should speak to you. You see Bard, we would like you to become the boys' overseer, live with them, eat with them, tell your fine stories and teach them to make bonnets. It will give them a trade. I can assure you, that all they make will be sold and the monies spent on books and writing implements, to help them in their studies. What say you then, Bard?"

Shock and disbelief momentarily kept Michael's mouth firmly shut. With a great effort he forced out the words he had been trying to say. "I am overcome, sir. I hope that I can do justice to the confidence both you and the judge are showing in me."

"Good then, so you will take up the position?"

"My mess mates, sir, what of them?"

The minister patted him on the back. "Never fear, your mates will not be forgotten. I have been reliably informed that at least one of them is competent in boot making, another in tailoring and yet another one is very competent in, shall we say, negotiating skills."

Michael bowed low in gratitude. "How then could I refuse such a generous offer, sir? Thank you, you have given me much more than a position, sir, you have given me hope."

Chapter Twenty-Five

Sarah swirled her brush, trying to blend the paints on her pallet to her liking. "Dash it all Annie, I just cannot make these colours true. The green of their feathers is proving to be the most difficult."

"You are much too hard on yourself, my dear Sarah. Why, your work is absolutely delightful." Annie sorted through Sarah's previous attempts. "These two little birds must be the most painted birds on the island."

"They remind me of someone very dear to me," Sarah replied.

"And who, pray tell, might that be?"

"He is gone now, nothing can bring him back," Sarah whispered, her hand clutching for the locket at her breast. "No matter." She brightened up. "It is such a fine day, one must not live in the past. Come with me." Sarah put down her brush and pallet. "Come, I'll show you. Quietly now." She led Annie over to the parakeets' nest. Three baby parakeets, with their wide mouths opened, chirped at them.

Annie beamed. "New life, how wonderful."

But Sarah went suddenly mournful. Confused by Sarah's reaction, Annie comforted her friend back to the veranda. "Do not be so sad, Sarah. My old gran used to say that new life was the promise of new beginnings, the promise of a more fulfilling future."

"I hope so," Sarah sighed.

Mrs. Forsyth stood up trying to get a better view of the street in front of the house, startling the green parakeet that was sitting on the veranda post. "Look girls, I do believe it is the two lieutenants and they are coming this way." She watched the progress of the men with interest and clapped like a school ma'am. "Make yourselves respectable. Sarah, for goodness sake, please take off that dreadful painting smock."

Sarah's face coloured, but she untied her smock and folded it over her chair, as Mrs. Forsyth waved to the soldiers and pleaded with them to join her and the girls on the veranda.

Both officers removed their hats and gave exaggerated bows to the older lady.

"Mrs. Forsyth, we were hoping that you might allow Miss Henshall and Miss Boyce to accompany us on a walk, perhaps toward Emily Bay?"

"What a lovely idea, Lieutenant." Margaret Forsyth began to stand up. "I will just get our bonnets. We will be with you directly."

Sarah noticed a suggestion of annoyance in Edmund's demeanour as he watched the older lady walk inside.

"We had hoped it would only be the four of us, Sarah," Edmund whispered.

Sarah looked towards Annie who was already deep in conversation with Saunders. "Leave it with me," she said.

Mrs. Forsyth scurried back onto the veranda wearing her bonnet and carrying another in each hand.

"Mrs. Forsyth, I think you may have forgotten that Mrs. Boyce is to visit later this afternoon. She is hoping you will help alter her gown. It would be truly unfortunate if you were to miss her."

"Oh dear, I had quite forgotten." She looked crestfallen at the idea but turned to the young people and, removing her bonnet, gave her consent for them to walk without her.

Each of the lieutenants offered his arm to one of the young ladies and escorted them down the path and out into the street. Only Sarah looked back. She waved and blew a kiss to the old woman standing despondently at the top of the veranda stair.

To his annoyance, Edmund spied a young, slim man in black religious attire hurrying toward them. "Miss Henshall! How fortuitous to meet you on this road," the man held up what Edmund supposed must be a Bible considering his occupation. "I was making my way to Emily Bay to read."

Sarah called back cheerfully, "Very fortuitous indeed, Mr. Fletcher, as we ourselves are walking in that same direction. We would be delighted if you would join us."

She turned to the others.

"I am not sure if you have all been introduced. Miss Boyce, Lieutenants Thornton and Saunders, may I present Mr. Fletcher, the new curate assisting Reverend Bayley."

Silently fuming, Edmund made to move ahead of the group by himself.

Sarah grabbed him by the arm. "Why are you being so pretentious Edmund? The curate is only newly arrived. Would it really be such a bother to walk with him? He is a very learned man."

Edmund paused in his stride and turned towards Sarah. "For you, Miss Henshall, I will do anything to make you happy."

Turning to the curate, Sarah said, "Mr. Fletcher do come and join us."

She linked arms with both men and moved them forward, chatting incessantly while the gentlemen took stock of one another over her head.

"Oh, look, up there in this pine tree. Can you see it, Lieutenant? It looks like a child's green ball."

"I think you will find that it is actually a pine cone, Miss Henshall," said the curate.

"How curious," responded Sarah. "You are such a learned man, Mr. Fletcher. I have never seen one on the ground. I do so love the smell of burning pine cones. Don't you?"

"Indeed, but when the cone of this tree falls," said Mr. Fletcher, "they break up and rattle through the branches. I have heard it said that the sound is akin to the watchman's rattle, a sound that surely haunts many a man on this island."

"He's right you know," Saunders laughed. "I have heard tell of a group of convicts who all started running wildly when they heard the rattle of the cones. For all intent, they thought it was the night watchman alerting the authorities of their whereabouts with that dreaded rattle. It is said they were so frightened that their overseer had quite a task to stop them before they ran off a cliff!"

Sarah noticed the colour drain from Edmund's face.

Regaining his composure Edmund managed a small smile and retorted, "Guilty consciences, all of them, I'd say."

Sarah's immediate thoughts went to Michael. Had he heard the watchman's rattle? Is that why he ran? She looked across to Edmund's distressed face and misread the meaning. *He knows more about Michael's arrest than I do.* A lump rose in her throat and she moved closer to Edmund, trying to let him know that all was well.

"I believe I must take my leave of you, Miss Henshall, Miss Boyce." Mr. Fletcher bowed low to the two ladies. "It has been a very pleasant afternoon but I fear I have imposed on you and your friends long enough."

Sarah glared at Edmund and then turned her attention toward the curate. "Please Mr. Fletcher, do stay. You are not imposing at all."

"You are very kind, Miss Henshall." The curate looked directly at Edmund. "But I fear I am becoming very tired. I bid you all good day."

Sarah watched the curate walk back towards the settlement and then turned on Edmund. "You were very rude, sir," she said. "I believe that, if you tried, the two of you could become good friends, but you will not even make an effort."

"Can you not see what that man is really after, Sarah? He pretends to be your friend but... Sarah, I need you to listen to me."

Saunders and Annie discretely strolled on ahead.

"You sound so serious, Edmund."

"I am serious, Sarah. Judge Forsyth has taken me into his confidence and has explained to me the conditions of your father's will." He stopped and stared into Sarah's eyes to sense her reaction. "You must realise Sarah, the judge only spoke to me because he respects you so. He knows that we have been friends for some time now so I suppose he thought he could trust me to keep you safe," and his voice hardened, "from cads like Mr. Fletcher!"

"I am not sure I understand, Edmund."

"Cads like a penniless curate, as I am sure your Mr. Fletcher must be, my dear, are only after your money, your inheritance."

Sarah looked shocked.

"Although we only met today, I have already heard of the curate's arrival. I've also heard that Fletcher is only here because he has extensive debts in Sydney."

"I see, so I presume you are referring to my having to marry in order to inherit my father's money, Edmund."

Edmund nodded and then fell to his knees at her feet, putting his hands over hers. "I can look after you, Sarah. Keep you safe. You can depend on me. Please..." His voice trailed off.

"I know I can depend on you, Edmund." She clasped his hands tightly, urging him to his feet. "You are, and always will be, my closest friend. And, you can be sure, Edmund, my father's fortune is quite safe. I will never marry, I cannot. You of all people know best that my heart will always belong to Michael."

"Michael is dead, Sarah. You cannot go on loving a ghost."

"The watchman's rattle, Edmund, the one Mr. Fletcher spoke of, do you think Michael heard it? Is that why he ran?"

"Devil's breath, Sarah! You can sometimes be so exasperating. How should I know if he heard the rattle? I was not there!"

Sarah tried to look into his eyes, surprised at the outburst, but he turned away.

"You there, Saunders!" Edmund called. "Are you and Miss Boyce ready to return?"

"Right you are, Thornton. You and Miss Henshall go on, we'll be right behind you."

Damn Michael Hanlan and damn everything about him! It was not my fault, Edmund assured himself again. *Anyway, how was I to know the runt couldn't run to save himself?*

Edmund reported for duty that night. Without doubt, he preferred the night watch above all others. He liked the anonymity, and tonight he was engulfed in blackness, with just the occasional star breaking through the mosaic pattern of the clouds. The tranquillity that surrounded him was only interrupted by the rhythmic crashing of unseen waves on the reef and the mournful cry of ghost birds as they returned to their nest.

Edmund raised his collar higher and blew on his cupped hands, trying to warm them. This was the hour when he could think, clear his head and concentrate on what was most important to him. He climbed the stairs to the guardhouse that towered above the convicts' barracks.

The sentry on duty saluted him. "Evenin' sir. Bit brisk out tonight, ain't it?"

"Suppose it is," Edmund answered. "All well, private?"

"Not even a rat stirrin', sir. See for y'self."

Edmund took the soldier's spyglass and panned the barrack grounds. The glass lingered longer on the boys' dormitory. He heaved a deep angry sigh.

Hanlan is sleeping soundly, I suppose, he thought. *All the little boys tucked comfortably in their hammocks, I am sure.*

He handed the spyglass back to the sentry and stormed back down the stairs. He could still taste the fury he had felt when his flashmen had come to him with the news that Hanlan had been posted to another gang and was no longer under their supervision.

Edmund sobered as the shape of the gallows reared in front of him, silhouetted against the dark sky. He quickened his step to pass it, his throat constricting. He loosened the top button of his jacket, trying to calm his breathing.

Just when he had accepted the fact that Sarah was going to be working with the convict boys, he now had to deal with the fact that his control over Michael's destiny had been wrenched away from him. The Reverend had really made a mess of things. Making Michael the boys' overseer, what on earth was the man thinking? Edmund could only trust that the minister would keep his word and never allow Sarah go to the prisoners' barracks. He kicked the ground, sending clumps of red dirt into the air.

As long as Sarah and Michael never know of each other, all should be well. I have been given no choice. At least, I will be able to make sure they never meet. Reverend Bayley will find that I am a very frequent visitor when the boys are with Sarah, and, for more than one reason! The man should be damned!

He stared across the darkened sea. He knew deep down that his behaviour was irrational, but he was adamant no-one was going to prevent his plans from having Sarah, not now. Then the inkling of an idea crept inside his thoughts. He slapped his thigh in jubilation.

Yes indeed, he did like the darkness of the night for thinking.

Chapter Twenty-Six

With growing pride, Margaret Forsyth and Sarah watched their twelve young charges march in two straight lines back to the convicts' barracks under the care of Mr. Fletcher. As they watched, the youngest boy turned and waved.

"Little scamp!" Sarah waved back, while smelling deeply of the hibiscus the boy had given her earlier. She was fond of all the boys in her charge, but of all of them she felt closest to this boy, his curly ginger locks, his freckled grin and his mischievous blue eyes. "I truly wish they did not need to go back every day. What must happen to them there?"

"We do not have to worry in that regard, my dear. The judge tells me that the commandant, himself, appointed the Bard as their overseer. Do you remember him?"

"The convict from the garden? Yes, I remember. The boys tell me he tells better stories than we do. He makes them up, so they tell me that they do not need to learn to read." She laughed. "At least he teaches them that they must work very hard to get back home. I am told he relates stories to them of a particular friend he has home in England. He tells the boys that everything he does is for her, to get back safely to her. I truly hope he does."

Sarah started to walk back into the minister's house. Suddenly she stopped and turned toward Mrs. Forsyth. "Did you know her name is Sarah, too?"

"Whose name is Sarah?"

"The Bard's particular friend. A popular name I suppose." She sighed and again inhaled deeply of the hibiscus. "I am actually jealous of this Sarah, Mrs. Forsyth. She is so lucky that her man is still alive and working so hard to get back to her. If only my Michael..."

"Yes I remember now, his letter was addressed to a Sarah. He would not allow me send it, you know. He said there was no hope. I still have it in my bureau. Maybe one day soon he will feel confident enough to ask me to post it."

"I hope so, for his Sarah's sake. She must be aching for news of him," said Sarah, and then to change the subject back to the boys, she continued, "I do enjoy working with the boys, Mrs. Forsyth. It is a very worthwhile task, is it not?"

"Yes indeed, I find it very rewarding."

"That young Billy, he is certainly my favourite. Have you seen how inquisitive he is?"

"Yes, he is a very conscientious student, I agree. Yet, apparently old habits die hard with that young one."

"What do you mean?"

"I mean... take for example the hibiscus he gave you. The one you now hold in your hand. One of the boys told me that young Billy picked it from Reverend Bayley's own garden, under his very nose!"

"That little imp! If the truth be told, though, he was probably sentenced to this island for little more than that as his crime."

Sarah smiled thoughtfully. *He will be my special project. I failed Michael. But I can help Billy. I can make sure that Billy stays safe.*

"Here are your charges all safe and sound, Bard," said the curate.

The Bard bobbed his head. "Right then, you boys, spread out amongst the older boys. Come on, be quick with you. Some of you over there stripping the flax, others plaiting, and the rest of you practice with your needles so you can stitch the finished plaits together."

Without further urging the boys dispersed and set to work.

Michael turned to the curate. "Mr. Fletcher, sir, the older boys have just finished an order of hats. Will you deliver them to Reverend Bayley for me, please?"

"Certainly." Mr. Fletcher examined one of the finished hats, a particularly pretty bonnet. "The work is of a very high quality, Bard. You are proving to be an excellent teacher."

"Thank you, sir. Your praise will be well received by my boys."

"Your boys? How curious you speak of them so."

"They have become my family, sir." He looked fondly around the room. "I do have another request, Mr. Fletcher."

"Go on."

"We are running low on flax, sir. Could you request that Reverend Bayley organise a guard for my boys and me on the morrow, so that we can cut more?"

"What? All the boys? All forty of them?"

"If that would not be too difficult, Mr. Fletcher? Most of the boys have not been out of the barracks for many a day now, sir. Not all are so lucky as to visit the good ladies at the minister's home."

"Yes, yes, of course, you are right Bard. I will request a guard of five or six be assigned. That should suffice. I am sure Reverend Bayley will approve of it."

Michael watched with some jealously as the curate left the dormitory, carrying the bag of finished hats and bonnets. He heard the guard acknowledging the curate, then the latch was clicked across and the key was turned in its lock, all reminders of where he really was – *who* he really was – exiled to an island prison, unable to do what he pleased or see whom he pleased.

Michael felt a tugging at his jacket. Looking down, he found the youngest of his boys staring up at him.

"Bard, can I make a bonnet for Miss Sarah? Please Bard, please!" Billy implored.

Michael nodded and patted the young boy on the head. "Ask Albert, over there, I am sure he will help."

Albert, hearing his name, looked up.

"Young Billy here would like to make a bonnet for Miss Sarah." The Bard winked at Albert. "Would you assist him?"

"Sure, Bard. Come over here Billy."

Michael watched them set to work for a moment and then turned back to his own creation. *Why the devil does her name have to be Sarah? It is too cruel to always hear the name spoken. It is a torture in itself.* He stabbed his curved needle with force into the flax plait, then tugged the plait of flax so that it curved in just the right way to form the brim of the hat. *Still,* he consoled himself, *hearing her name, reminds me of her, reminds me of who is waiting for me, and that I must do all I can to return to her, so she does not wait in vain.*

He looked at his boys chatting amongst themselves and helping one another. He thought back to the squabbles of the first few days when he became the boys' overseer and smiled at the remarkable change the past weeks had brought about.

There had been a heavy deluge of rain during the night and the grass glistened in the early morning sunlight. As the group of young convicts made their way under guard towards the waterhole where a good crop of flax grew, they eagerly jumped into every puddle that they could find.

One of the guards winked at Michael and smiled. "Don't look so perturbed, Bard, they mean no harm. It's good to see the boys enjoying themselves."

The flax cutting went well considering the boys' inexperience. The older boys used scythes to cut the flax, while the younger ones collected and piled it up. A haphazard heap was soon piling up by the waterhole.

"Come now boys, this will not do," Michael said, deliberately chiding them. "You younger boys start sorting the flax into piles and tie it with this Sampson's sinew vine."

Young Billy tried to grab one of the long vines, his little fingers only just able to grip it. Michael looked toward the ginger-haired boy struggling with the length of vine and smiled at his efforts. "Sometimes I wonder at you, dear boy. Get one of the older boys to cut it into more useable lengths."

"Aye, Bard," the boy replied very seriously.

Even the five guards lounging on their muskets chuckled at the boy's comical attempts to drag the vine over to Albert who was working close to the water hole's edge.

"Careful there, Billy. Not so close to the edge."

Billy tugged hard on the vine trying to loosen it from a snag. Then all Michael's fears began to unfold. The vine loosened causing Billy to lose his footing and overbalance. His feet slipped on the moss-covered rocks and he fell backwards with a splash into the waterhole.

It seemed to Michael that all now happened in slow motion. It was not Billy he watched fall into the water but his own young sister. His legs felt heavy with indecision. He felt rooted to the spot. Then the screams came.

Michael ran over. "The vine! Grab the blasted vine!" he yelled. "Give it to me! Here, Billy grab hold! You can do it!"

"He's going down, Bard! For God's sake do something!" screamed Albert.

"Quick! Give me that other vine, you there, you guards hold onto the other end!" Pulling off his shirt and boots, Michael tied the other end around his waist and scrambled over the rocks.

Taking a deep breath, cheeks bulging, teeth clenched, his eyes tightly shut, he jumped. His fear of water overwhelmed him. He panicked when he experienced the initial shock of the cold water going over his head. The weight of his clothes pulled him down, his limbs felt like lead weights, limiting movement. He sank deep beneath the surface.

Visions of his sister raced before him, forcing him to open his eyes and search for Billy. Looking up, he could see sunlight playing on the water's surface, and the flaying arms and legs of his young charge. He kicked furiously, forcing himself upward. His head burst through the surface of the water, stale air exploding from his lungs, his mouth sucking in deep breaths of sweet air. He grabbed the boy.

"Quick there now, pull us in!"

With great difficulty the five guards and the curate hauled them to dry land.

Albert reached down to take the near lifeless body of Billy from Michael. "Come on Billy, breathe, breathe," he pleaded, slapping the young boy on his back.

Muscles burning and completely exhausted, Michael climbed out of the water, just as the young boy started to cough violently, dispelling the water from his lungs. Great cheering broke from all in the vicinity, both convict and guard.

Michael crawled over to the boy, hugging him close. Never before had he felt such elation. He had saved a life.

Reverend Bayley raced into the boys' ward, his black cassock flowing behind him. "Oh my God, Bard, I only just heard of your bravery." He strode over to the hammock where Billy lay and felt the sleeping boy's forehead. "How is the boy after such a horrendous ordeal, Bard?"

"He is recovering well, Reverend. It is good of you to come."

"Actually, I have been sent on an errand by Mrs. Forsyth and her ward. I have candy, handmade by the ladies for the boy." He handed over a large bag. "Enough to share with all the boys I am sure."

"That is very kind of the ladies."

With great excitement the boys clamoured around the minister, reaching for their share.

"Easy boys, there is enough for all. No-one will miss out." Michael tried to hand out the candy fairly. "We must leave a good chunk for Billy, mustn't we? After all, he is the reason we have such a treat to share." He handed the largest piece to Billy, who was stirring from his slumber.

Reverend Bayley pulled Michael aside. "I have a letter from Miss Sarah for you. It seems the young boy you saved is very dear to her heart. I believe she wishes to thank you. She would dearly loved to have come herself, but the Commandant and I have assured Judge Forsyth that his wife and ward would never visit the convict barracks. So it falls to me to be the messenger." He smiled and handed Michael a letter drenched in lavender.

Michael smelled deeply of its fragrance. Every fibre in his body tensed, tears swelled in the corners of his eyes. He reddened under the scrutiny of the minister, then, regaining control of his emotions he broke the seal and skimmed its contents. After a moment, he refolded it and tucked it into the rope that tied his trousers around his waist. "Please thank Miss Forsyth for me, Reverend. It is very good of her to recognise the deeds of a lowly convict."

"But, Bard, you are mistaken. She is not Miss Forsyth."

"Bard, Bard! Billy, he be chokin'! Come quick!" Albert screamed.

Michael raced to the boy's hammock and fell to his knees beside him. Sitting Billy up, Michael hit him sharply on his back. The boy coughed up the candy that had stuck in his throat and took a deep breath. Laying the boy down, Michael stroked Billy's forehead. "You are safe now Billy, me lad, you are safe."

Chapter Twenty-Seven

Margaret Forsyth picked up her embroidery and sat down near the window in her parlour. "Please make my excuses to the lieutenant, Sarah. I am not feeling myself today."

"Perhaps a glass of lemonade might help," Sarah suggested.

"No, no. Do not fuss so, Sarah. I am sorry, though, that I do not feel strong enough to join you at the regiment's cricket match. You will have to go without me. Now, go and fetch your bonnet. If I am not mistaken, the two officers and Miss Boyce are at the gate."

Sarah glanced out of the window to see Edmund striding up the path. Annie remained at the gate with Lieutenant Saunders. Sarah gave Mrs. Forsyth a quick kiss on the cheek, who shooed her away. Tying her bonnet, she met Edmund at the door before he could knock.

After greeting Annie and Lieutenant Saunders, Sarah linked arms with Annie, not noticing her friend's reluctance to release the arm of Lieutenant Saunders.

"You had best lead the way Lieutenants," said Sarah. "We would not want the two best players in your regiment to be late for the game now, would we?"

Both men reluctantly stepped forward. When the men were a good distance in front, Annie whispered to Sarah, "Do you not think Lieutenant Saunders a most dashing young man, Sarah? His manner is most agreeable, is it not?"

Sarah looked at her friend in disbelief. "I do declare, Annie, I had not noticed."

"He does look so becoming in his regimentals," Annie continued undeterred.

Sarah stared at the two men walking in front of them. She had to admit that both the officers did indeed cut fine figures in their uniforms, one tall and dark and the other a little shorter and fair in colour. She glanced at her friend and saw a new light in her eyes.

"Why Annie, I do believe..." She left the sentence unfinished, watching Annie blush a brilliant crimson.

After a short walk they reached the military playing fields. It was bustling with activity. Groups of soldiers with jackets off and sleeves rolled up, were stretching, throwing balls and swinging bats. Ladies were sitting on the perimeters, shaded by trees and parasols, deep in conversations, while children played at their feet.

"The enlisted men did a fine job preparing the pitch, eh, Thornton?" Saunders remarked.

Edmund surveyed the newly cut grass, the neatly cleared and prepared pitch and nodded.

"Ah, Thornton, Saunders, you are finally here." Captain Travers raced toward them, hurriedly accepting the men's salutes. "Do you play Thornton? You have not played with us before, have you?"

"I must admit, cricket is a passion of mine, sir."

"Capital, Thornton. You do not by any chance bowl do you? The Regiment is in dire need of a good bowler."

"I believe I am a very capable bowler, sir," he said, then quickly added, not wanting to sound too proud. "At least that is what others have informed me."

"Capital, capital! I have at least half dozen figs of tobacco riding on the outcome of this match, so I expect you men to do me proud."

"We will do our best," the two officers answered, almost in unison.

The captain then acknowledged Sarah and Annie, who were standing coyly behind the officers, and offered to escort them to the shade and join his wife and Mrs. Boyce.

Annie turned to Saunders and shyly wished him luck. Sarah was astonished to see such an unmistakable look of passion pass between the couple. A slight pang of jealousy swept through her.

"Ah, Miss Henshall, I am delighted you have come." Mrs. Boyce held out her hand in welcome. "Will you not join Mrs. Travers and me?"

"Thank you Mrs. Boyce, you are most kind." Sarah bobbed in curtsey and sat down between the ladies, apologising for Mrs. Forsyth's absence.

Mrs. Boyce looked around inquiringly. "I thought our Annie was with you. Oh yes, there she is, finally dragging herself away from that dashing young officer. It is a good match do you not think, Miss Henshall, our Annie and Lieutenant Saunders? I must declare he is a very considerate suitor."

Sarah nodded. "She had not told me," murmured Sarah, almost to herself, disappointed that Annie had not thought her worthy of her confidence.

"I am not surprised, my dear. I believe it only became a serious attachment these past few days. I am sure she will speak to you soon."

"I hope so."

"You know, my dear, I have noticed the same look of pleasure in Lieutenant Thornton's eyes every time he sees you. It would not surprise me, if he will soon follow his friend's lead and seek a serious attachment himself."

Sarah blushed. She looked toward Edmund. He had taken off his jacket and was now rolling up his sleeves to reveal the sinewy curves of his muscled arms, clenching and releasing his fists in readiness for the game. She had to admit that she was indeed drawn to him. *But only as a friend*, she assured herself, never as a beau, never as a lover. The thought was simply absurd. Yet, as she watched him bowl his first delivery she felt a stir of arousal, and later, when it was his turn to bat, watching his athleticism between the wickets was truly tantalising.

As the day passed, Annie became more open about her attachment to Saunders. She spoke lovingly of him, she spoke of the future she hoped they would have together. She spoke of the wedding she hoped would soon be hers.

Sarah tried to sound happy for her friend but an intense feeling of loneliness, a feeling that was completely foreign to her, marred her happiness. She had always felt safe and secure in her father's house. She had felt secure in her love for Michael and his love for her. Now, listening to her friend, she realised that on this island she was now completely alone. Judge and Mrs. Forsyth were very kind of course, but now that Michael was gone what on earth was keeping her on this strange island with all its beauty and all its terror?

She still loved Michael with every fibre in her being. She could not imagine loving anyone else. But then she heard the rich timbre of Edmund's voice, mingled with others, appealing to the umpire for a decision. It was a voice that sounded comforting, that sounded commanding. It was a voice from her past, one she knew well, one she knew she could depend on and perhaps, she toyed with the idea, one she could perhaps even grow to love.

Polite clapping rippled through the audience when the game finished. Edmund dashed over to the women, struggling to put on his jacket.

"Great game wasn't it?" he said, puffing. "It was so good to play again. Pity we lost, though. Do you realize that not one man on our team has had a bat or ball in his hands since we left the mainland? The other regiment have been practicing for weeks. We'll beat them next time, eh, Saunders?" He playfully nudged his friend, who now stood next to him, on his shoulder.

"Yes, we will definitely defeat them next time." Saunders then excused himself and took Annie's arm in his, and strolled towards the sea.

Edmund offered his arm to Sarah. "Mrs. Forsyth will be thinking I have kidnapped you, Miss Henshall. We, too, had better be on our way. Would you allow me to escort you home?"

"I would be delighted, sir," Sarah replied.

Edmund proudly placed Sarah's arm through his.

Sarah was both surprised and confused by the warming sensations his touch caused throughout her body.

Edmund walked on in silence, not wanting to break the trance that enveloped him, a trance in which Sarah was his, loving him as much as he loved her.

Sarah, though, was the first to break the silence. "You played a fine game today, Edmund, although I must admit I understand little of the game itself." Edmund only nodded, but Sarah went on undeterred. "Tell me Edmund, did you know that Lieutenant Saunders and Miss Boyce were officially courting?"

Edmund sighed and nodded. "Yes, he told me this very morning." How jealous he was of Saunders. *Lucky devil*, he told himself. "Can you keep a secret?"

"Of course I can, Edmund. Pray do not hold me in suspense. Tell me what you know."

"Saunders told me that he plans to ask for her hand in marriage later today. Do you think she will accept him?"

"She would be a fool not to. How wonderful for her. I am sure that they will both be very happy together."

They reached the iron-gate on the border of the Forsyth's property. Edmund took a deep breath and held it for what seemed like an infinitely long time, trying to weigh up his options. It was now or never, he told himself.

"Sarah," he began.

Startled, she looked up at him. Edmund's expression told Sarah everything he felt. She became frightened about what he might say. She put two fingers to his lips to silence him. It was a futile attempt to halt what she was sure was coming.

Edmund tenderly removed them and held her hand in his, as he continued. "Please hear what I have to say, Sarah. It must be said. We have known each other for many years now. We have shared both good times and bad."

207

Biting her lip, she turned away from Edmund's intense gaze, but he gently turned her head back to face him. "Miss Henshall, Sarah, I ask that you, too, might consider me as more than just a friend." He paused and took both of Sarah's hands in his. Once more he was surprised at how her petite hands were swallowed in his grasp. "Please listen to me, Sarah. Although I am only the second son of a lawyer, I have been assured by my father that I will want for nothing after his death. I need you to know this, Sarah. I need you to understand that I have no desire to gain control over your father's fortune."

"I would never think that, Edmund."

Looking directly into her eyes, his voice becoming husky with emotion, he said, "Surely, it must be obvious to you that I love you, Sarah, love you most ardently. I humbly ask that you might do me the honour of being my wife. I hope with all my heart that you might allow me to ask Judge Forsyth for his permission to wed you."

Sarah's heart jolted and her pulse raced. Here was the security she yearned for, but he was not Michael. Could she be untrue to Michael's memory? Could she be happy again? Trying to mask her inner turmoil with a deceptive sense of calmness, Sarah answered, "Tomorrow, Edmund, you may speak to Judge Forsyth, tomorrow." She squeezed his hands, opened the gate, and hurried up the garden path without looking back.

In one quick moment all Edmund's fears were allayed and his greatest dream fulfilled. He had heard the words he had yearned to hear for many months now. A great burden had been lifted from him as he stared after her, reluctant to let her leave his sight.

Mrs. Forsyth greeted Sarah with a barrage of questions about the cricket match. Unable to handle them at that moment, Sarah feigned a headache and pleaded to be excused to her room. Margaret Forsyth began to protest, but her husband hushed her.

"Let her go my dear, she is obviously troubled. I am sure she will talk to us when she is ready."

Sarah kissed them both goodnight and gratefully retired to her room, closing the door behind her. She sat at her dressing table, staring with unseeing eyes at her reflection in the mirror. Her thoughts spun in turmoil, a war of emotions raged within her. All at once she felt an enormous sadness and then elation, followed by sense of peace, a peace she had not felt since she had accepted Michael's passing. She buried her head in hands and wept until all her tears were spent.

That night she struggled to untie the bow in the velvet ribbon tied around her neck. Removing the locket, her love token from Michael, for the last time she kissed it. Holding it close to her lips she whispered, "I am sorry Michael, I will always love you, please believe me, but I know you will understand. Edmund is a good man, even you must agree."

With great apprehension, she crept over to her bureau. Opening the top drawer, she removed a delicate, lace handkerchief. She unfolded it and placed it next to her writing box, still unwilling to let go of the locket. She fingered the brass trimmings of her writing box. She fiddled with the key checking that it still turned smoothly in its lock. Finally, opening the lid, she traced the gold trimming of the smooth black velvet that covered the writing surface with her finger. With great care she lifted the inkwell from its secure placement in the box and gently pushed the base of the space it had left. A secret panel gave way revealing three small mahogany drawers, each with its own small ornate brass handle.

With trepidation, Sarah opened the middle drawer. Not giving herself time to think, she hastily wrapped the locket in the lace handkerchief, placed the small package in the drawer and closed it.

Chapter Twenty-Eight

There was only the slightest clicking sound of the key as it turned in the lock of the boys' dormitory, but still, nearly as one, the boys stopped what they were doing. All eyes stared at the door with growing anticipation.

The heavy door was pushed open. Returning from a lesson with Sarah and Mrs. Forsyth, the lively younger boys rushed in, followed by Mr. Fletcher.

Young Billy was unable to control himself and, in the excitement of the moment shouted, "Tell the Bard! Tell him the news." He pulled the curate's jacket but, before Mr. Fletcher could even open his mouth to speak, Billy yelled, "Miss Sarah is getting married!"

Michael looked from the boy to the curate, who nodded in agreement.

"So the kind young lady is to be married. That is very good. And pray tell me, Mr. Fletcher, could the lucky fellow be your good self?"

"No indeed, it is not," Mr. Fletcher stammered. "I am told she is to marry a Lieutenant of her Majesty's Eleventh Regiment of Foot, a Lieutenant Thornton I believe, yes, that's his name."

"Lieutenant Thornton?" Michael's voice rose in surprise.

"You know the officer, Bard?" inquired the curate.

"Me?" Michael took a quick breath. "No, sir, I have just heard mention of his name."

"I fear, Bard, your boys are going to be kept very busy over the next couple of weeks.

Mrs. Forsyth has requested that your boys make the wedding bonnets. Here." He handed Michael four neatly written pages. "The lady has sent a description of exactly how she would like the bride's bonnet to be made. Oh, and she has included notes for her own bonnet and one for the bridesmaid."

Michael perused the pages. "Very detailed indeed."

"Do you think you and your boys will be up to the task?"

"Of course," Michael replied. He looked across at the dwindling pile of flax in the corner. "We had best then cut new supplies of flax, I suppose."

"Of course, Bard. Probably best, though, if you only take the older boys on this occasion, eh?" Mr. Fletcher playfully ruffled young Billy's curls. "Sorry, Billy, not this time."

Michael lay in his hammock that night, listening to the sounds of his boys' peaceful sleep, the regular breathing, the sporadic snores, the occasional wheeze and cough. But no crying, unlike the first week, when the nights had been filled with screams, nightmares and gushing tears, now all seemed to be calm. He, too, was able to sleep more soundly. The vivid nightmares that once tortured him were now gone. He could sleep in the certainty that he would, without doubt, be worthy of being reunited with his Sarah, when this ordeal was over and his sentence was at an end.

His thoughts wandered back to the curate's visit that afternoon. *So, my good friend Edmund is to be married. Good luck! I say to him. What a surprise! So his dearly beloved is a Sarah, also. What a wonderful coincidence. I am sure that our two Sarahs will become the greatest of friends when we all return home to England.*

He had to admit though, that he felt strong pangs of envy towards his friend. Still he could not harbour ill feelings for long. It had been some weeks now since he had understood that, of course, it had been Edmund who had been the architect of his good fortune. After all, he had been appointed the boys' overseer immediately following his chance sighting of Edmund outside the crank mill. He was now certain that Edmund knew of his interment here on Norfolk Island. He was just as certain that Edmund had been the one to approach the judge and convinced him to change his circumstances for the better. But what he couldn't understand was why did he still keep his distance?

He turned over in his hammock, trying to make himself more comfortable. The reason, then, seemed to become clear to him. Edmund was getting married. It would only complicate matters if his bride's family discovered his association with a convict.

Yet in truth, it still hurts. I hope, one day, that I will be able to thank my good friend for his part in my deliverance.

The next morning, Michael sorted through the pile of flax, only selecting unspoiled strands, comparing lengths, widths and colour.

This bonnet will be flawless, he said to himself, as he began plaiting. *I might not be able to attend my friend's wedding, but at the very least, I can gift his bride a perfect wedding bonnet.*

As he plaited, Michael pictured himself making his own Sarah's wedding bonnet. The thought filled him with hope.

Chapter Twenty-Nine

Sarah felt trapped. Trapped and over-awed by the ladies of Norfolk society who had come with their offerings of lace and beads to make the wedding clothes.

Trapped and stifled by this blessed island.

Trapped by life itself.

She paced her prison, too frightened to sit in case the whole event overwhelmed her.

She refreshed cups of tea and she cut slices of seed cake for these ladies, the ladies who had decided to make her life the centre of their attention. Margaret Forsyth sat in her high-backed wicker chair like an overseer. All questions went via her. All answers were given by her. Sarah had learned early in her wedding preparations that her own wants and wishes were of little consequence, so she, like everyone else, bowed to the wishes of Mrs. Forsyth.

"Can I pour you another cup of tea, Mrs. Boyce?" Sarah asked.

The lady held up her china cup and saucer. She watched the bride-to-be pour her tea, holding up her hand when the cup was full enough. "How quaint of you, Miss Henshall, to choose to have your wedding banns read at service these past three weeks."

"Quaint indeed, Mrs. Boyce," interrupted Mrs. Travers. "I understand that back home in England, only the lower classes bother to do so now. Persons of your social standing, Miss Henshall, are now choosing to be married by license."

"To be truthful, ladies, I wanted to give myself time to get used to the idea of being a married woman." Sarah tried to sound cheerful. "Can I refill your cup too, Mrs. Travers?" The lady nodded. As she poured the tea, Sarah admitted to herself: *If the truth be known, I was giving myself time to accept that I will be Mrs. Thornton and not Mrs. Hanlan.*

"If the lieutenant had his way, ladies, they would be married already," Margaret Forsyth declared. "But a Christmas wedding, so romantic," she sighed. "Pity though that your Aunt Elizabeth cannot be here, Sarah. But the Lieutenant was very insistent that they not wait." She looked smugly at the other ladies.

"Yes indeed, Mrs. Forsyth, never have I seen a man as smitten as our Lieutenant." Mrs. Travers sighed. "I understand, Miss Henshall, that you have known Lieutenant Thornton for some time."

"Yes, Mrs. Travers, we were friends back in England. We shared a close friend who is unfortunately no longer with us."

"How romantic," said Mrs. Travers, "to think that your destinies led you to a reunion here on this island. Good fortune has definitely smiled on your union, Miss Henshall."

All the ladies in the sewing party nodded in agreement.

"I understand, Miss Henshall, that upon your marriage, you will become a very wealthy woman in your own right," Mrs. Boyce said with some conviction.

At the mention of wealth, all the ladies on the veranda stopped their needlework and looked toward Mrs. Forsyth.

Margaret Forsyth admonished her friend. "Hush, Mrs. Boyce. I told you that in strictest confidence. We do not speak of such things in company."

Taken aback, Mrs. Boyce returned to her needlework and replied, "I only wanted to say how fortunate the lieutenant is to be marrying a lady who has such a generous dowry."

Annie Boyce spoke up in defence of her dear friend.

"I am sure, mother, that Lieutenant Thornton is marrying Miss Henshall for love and certainly not for her money."

Feeling upstaged by her friend, Margaret Forsyth said with an air of self-importance, "Well, now that it is out in the open, Sarah's father, Mr. Thomas Henshall, was my husband's closest friend. It was his wish that upon his death that my dear husband become Sarah's guardian. He also stipulated that his fortune be put in trust for Sarah until the day of her marriage. We have taken our roles as her guardians very seriously, very seriously." She took a breath wanting to give her words more importance. "We have now known the lieutenant since we arrived here. We could not be happier in Sarah's choice of husband."

Sarah was anxious to be free of the gossiping women. Discretely, she put down the plate of cakes she had in her hand, walked over to Annie and whispered in her ear for her to join her in the garden. As she descended the veranda stairs, Sarah heard Mrs. Boyce whisper that she must be suffering from nerves.

"My wedding preparations must be difficult for you, Annie. Have you and Lieutenant Saunders set a date for your nuptials?"

"Richard has asked that we wait until his parents have been informed. He hopes they might even consider undertaking the voyage from England to join us."

"That could be a year or more, Annie!"

"I know," she replied. "Oh my goodness! Look Sarah, look over there, on the well!"

There, sitting proudly, were the two green parakeets with the three young chicks Sarah had so carefully reared. Startled, the young birds flew into the air, followed by their parents.

"They are flying," cried Sarah. "They have finally left the nest. How wonderful!" Annie smiled. "Surely it is a good omen for your wedding day, Sarah."

"Yes, perhaps it is," Sarah replied thoughtfully, staring over the garden well.

"You seem troubled, Sarah. Is there anything I can do to help? You spoke to me once of the young man of whom they reminded you."

Taking a deep breath, Sarah spoke slowly. "His name was Michael, Michael Hanlan. He had such mischievous blue eyes, Annie. Oh, to see those eyes one more time. He was liked by all, young and old. He was a good man, Annie, and I loved him with my whole being."

Annie gasped.

"You are surprised? I loved him and I believe he loved me. I know he did. But he is gone now; he died of the fever. Edmund tried to find him. He knew I loved him, but the ship..." She saw her friend's confused face so did not continue.

The girls sat quietly for a long while, Annie holding her friend's hand.

Sarah looked up. "You think I am being disloyal to Edmund, don't you?"

"It is not for me to say, Sarah. I know the lieutenant loves you dearly and I am sure you will both be very happy."

"It is just that..." Sarah paused. "It is just that, in all my dreams I was sure I would marry Michael. Do not misunderstand me, Annie. I will make Edmund a very loyal and loving wife. I know that Michael would be pleased with the union. In fact, I truly believe that Edmund is the only other person on this earth I would even consider as my husband. You need not fear Annie. All will be well."

"It is not good to dwell on the past, dearest Sarah. Tomorrow will be the beginning of your new life, your life with Lieutenant Thornton. Past disappointments can now be put behind you and forgotten."

The next morning Sarah paused on the top stair of the carriage steps and stared at the chapel in front of her. She had worshipped in this same chapel every Sunday for the last seven months. In her mind she could see the congregation waiting for her to arrive. Still she hesitated. This morning was very different. This morning would change her life for ever. There would be no going back, not after this morning.

Leaning on the judge's proffered arm, Sarah stepped out of the carriage. Annie started fussing over her friend's wedding dress. "Your gown, Sarah, it is exquisite!" In excitement, Annie hugged her friend.

Sarah smiled sadly, and then adjusted the spray of flowers and seed pearls sewn around the waist and down one side of her blue silk gown. A gust of wind caught the muslin veil attached to her delicate straw bonnet. Annie laughed, reaching out to catch it and put it in place again.

Judge Forsyth chided, "Come along child, we cannot leave the lieutenant thinking he has been jilted at the altar."

Sarah allowed herself to be led toward the door of the chapel. She knew in her heart that what she was doing was for the best, but still she had to calm her nerves before entering.

It will be a marriage of convenience, she tried to convince herself. *That's all, a marriage of convenience. Edmund will understand.*

Judge Forsyth stepped into the sanctuary a little ahead of Sarah to allow her wide skirt, with its many under petticoats, to fit through the door.

When she entered, the congregation broke into delighted murmurings, discussing her dress, her hair, her bonnet.

Sarah kept her gaze steadfastly forward. Bright sunlight filtering through a chapel window momentarily blurred the altar and the two men standing there. Sarah blinked, trying to clear her vision.

"Michael," she whispered, her heart leaping into her throat.

But hope was short lived as a cloud passed over the sun. Edmund stood there, elegant in his uniform, Lieutenant Saunders at his side. He was smiling broadly at her as she walked up the aisle.

Sarah looked with apprehension toward Edmund. She felt lightheaded and held the judge's arm tighter for support. As she moved closer she could see his eyes were filled with tenderness and passion. *He does love me, Annie was right. I hope I can return his love in the way he would wish.*

Sarah took her place by his side. As the judge and Lieutenant Saunders eased into position just behind the wedding couple, Reverend Bayley held up his hand to begin the ceremony.

"Dearly beloved, we are gathered together here in the sight of God, and in the face of this Congregation, to join together this man and this woman in holy Matrimony. Which is an honourable estate, instituted of God in the time of man's innocence, and therefore is not to be entered by any, unadvisedly, lightly, or wantonly, to satisfy men's carnal lusts and appetites, like brute beasts that have no understanding; but reverently, discreetly, advisedly, soberly, and in the fear of God."

Sarah looked up at Edmund, surprised to find him reddening and perspiring profusely, even though the chapel was cool.

The minister continued. "I require and charge you both, as ye will answer at the dreadful day of judgement, when the secrets of all hearts shall be disclosed, that if either of you know any impediment, why ye may not be lawfully joined together in matrimony, ye do now confess it."

With her focus on the minister, Sarah was alarmed when she felt Edmund tremble violently next to her. Looking at him, concerned, she could see his eyes darting nervously back and forth. He looked behind him as though daring anyone to speak.

Looking satisfied, Edmund turned back to Sarah, easing into a carefree smile.

"Who giveth this woman to be married to this man?" Reverend Bayley asked.

"I do," said Judge Forsyth. He kissed Sarah on her cheek.

As Father used too, she thought with sorrow.

Sarah cast her eyes downwards, unnerved by Edmund's steady gaze as he recited his vows to her.

"I, Edmund Thornton, take thee, Sarah Henshall, to be my wedded wife, to have and to hold from this day forward, for better for worse, for richer, for poorer, in sickness and in health, to love and to cherish, till death us do part, according to God's holy ordinance; and thereto I plight thee my troth."

Reverend Bayley turned to Sarah and she repeated after him.

"I, Sarah Henshall, take thee, Mi…" She stumbled over the words, her voice sounding fragile to her own ears. She paused, took a deep breath, and then began again in a loud clear voice, looking directly into Edmund's eyes. "I, Sarah Henshall, take thee, Edmund Thornton to be my wedded husband, to have and to hold from this day forward, for better for worse, for richer, for poorer, in sickness and in health, to love, cherish, and to obey, till death us do part, according to God's holy ordinance; and thereto I plight thee my troth."

"You have the ring, Lieutenant?" Reverend Bayley asked.

Richard Saunders placed the small gold band that Mrs. Forsyth had kindly lent them until one could be purchased on the mainland onto the minister's prayer book.

Taking the ring from Reverend Bayley, Edmund placed it on Sarah's finger. His voice breaking with emotion he recited after the minister. "With this ring I thee wed, with my body I thee worship, and with all my worldly goods I thee endow. In the Name of the Father, and of the Son, and of the Holy Ghost. Amen."

His gaze caressed Sarah with a softness she had not expected.

Reverend Bayley then sealed Sarah's future. "I pronounce that they be man and wife together. You may kiss your bride, Lieutenant Thornton.

He kissed her gently, with no sense of urgency.

Trapped, Sarah's inner voice cried in anguish. *Trapped as another man's wife.*

Edmund proudly displayed his new wife on his arm, accepting good wishes freely from all who offered them, grinning broadly at one and all.

Sarah tried to go through the motions of being the happy bride but her heart felt empty. *Just a marriage of convenience*, she kept telling herself. *Just a marriage of convenience.*

The chapel doors were thrown open. The officers of the Eleventh Regiment of Foot had formed a guard of honour, drawn swords crossed in an archway above their heads.

"Three cheers for the Lieutenant and Mrs. Thornton," yelled Richard Saunders. "Hip, hip…"

"Hooray!" all the men responded.

Taking Sarah by the hand Edmund led his bride through the archway as his men cheered.

219

When the couple reached the end, another man yelled, "And one for luck, hip, hip…"

"Hooray!"

Chapter Thirty

The wedding breakfast was held in the officers' mess. It was decorated in much the same way as it had been for the Officers' Ball, Norfolk greenery gracing every table and wall. Sarah tried without success to repress memories of that fateful night, four months ago now. How easily she had allowed herself be deceived that night, but then she looked at Edmund and remembered how safe she had felt in his arms. Still, he was not Michael. She pushed her food around her plate, not joining in any of the conversations around her.

"Come now, my dear," Margaret Forsyth tried to console her. "Your wedding night is nothing to be so nervous about, Sarah. I am certain that the lieutenant will be a very considerate husband."

Sarah looked up startled. She had not considered the wedding night, not considered what it meant. Her stomach turned as nausea washed over her. Before she could gain control of her emotions and answer her guardian, the sharp chinking of a glass being struck with a cutlery knife filled the mess, gaining the attention of all the guests.

Richard Saunders stood and raised his glass. "May I ask you to join me and raise your glasses and drink to the health of the happy couple?" He waited until the loud scraping of everyone standing died down. "Long life and much happiness to two of the most deserving people it has been my privilege to call my friends." He toasted Sarah and Edmund and then drained his glass.

"Long life and happiness!" The words echoed throughout the mess.

Edmund stood to respond.

"I thank my close friend..." He was interrupted by a noise at the back of the room.

An uneasy silence rippled across the room as more and more anxious guests watched the progress of a pale-faced soldier pushing his way through the crowd, continually asking for the whereabouts of Captain Travers.

"Here I am." The officer met the young corporal half way. "On whose orders do you dare interrupt this wedding party?"

The corporal stood to attention, trying to catch his breath.

Every guest stared in astonishment, all straining to hear the low whispers passing between the two men.

Without warning the words, 'revolt' and 'convict revolt' began to spread from mouth to mouth. Ladies swooned, everyone began talking at once. Sarah gripped her husband's arm so tightly he flinched, but calmly he placed his hand over hers to give her reassurance.

Captain Travers strode toward the wedding table, trying to display a countenance of calm. The crowd of wedding guests bustled behind him.

"I am so sorry, Mrs. Thornton," the captain began.

Sarah felt an involuntary shiver at the sound of her married name.

"I am afraid that we require the services of your husband." He looked directly at Edmund, who instinctively stood to attention. "And you will be required too, Lieutenant Saunders." The other officer pushed back his chair so hard that it clattered on the floor. "It seems that someone has chosen this exact time to incite the convict population to riot."

"My wedding has been common talk among the convicts, sir. They would have counted on all the officers being here."

Sarah clutched her husband's arm. "Edmund," she cried. "I cannot let you go, not now, not today."

"Hush now my darling, I am sure all will be well. I must go." He uncurled her fingers from his arm and kissed each one. "I am not going to do anything reckless, my dear. Not now that I finally have everything my heart has ever desired."

"Edmund, I lost my true love to this horrid place. I do not want to lose another," she whispered.

Edmund's face went dark as Captain Travers dragged up the corporal who had delivered the news. It was Corporal Evans. Blood was running down his cheek, staining the neck of his uniform in dark claret. "Tell the lieutenants what you told me. It seems, gentleman, that this young corporal here was guarding the ammunition store. I understand that he fared better than the two guards on the outer door. They are both dead, their heads cleaved in. I will let him tell you what he saw."

Evans looked straight at Edmund. "Somebody was pounding on the door, demanding I open it. I only opened the peep hole, sir. Truthfully sir, I thought it was you. I saw his face, your face sir, through the peep hole, sir."

"Edward Lawton!" both Edmund and Saunders said together.

Captain Travers raised his eyebrows. "At least we know one of the ringleaders." He leapt onto the bridal table so that all present could see him. "Ladies and gentleman," he shouted. "Please do not be alarmed. I realise that you do not hear the settlement warning bell ringing. It was felt that it would be safer not to alert the convicts to our activities, but I must advise you that we are facing a very grave situation. All officers and enlisted men are to present at once to the barrack parade grounds. The troops are already under arms and preparing to march."

The hall erupted as soldiers gathered together in readiness, yelling orders to each other. Women clung to their husbands, crying, not wanting them to go.

"Attention!" Captain Travers yelled again. "I suggest that it would be safest for the ladies and other civilian staff to remain barricaded in here for the time being, until we regain control of the rioters." He jumped down from the table and went to Judge Forsyth.

Judge Forsyth leapt up from his chair as his wife tried to drag him back into his seat. "Can I be of any assistance, captain?"

"Yes, Judge, I believe you can. I will leave you in charge of the situation here. Please try to keep everyone as calm as possible.

Perhaps the musicians could commence playing. Above all though, after we leave, make sure the door is locked and barricaded."

"Of course, sir." The judge almost saluted in his enthusiasm.

Sarah stared after Edmund as he left the hall with the other officers and watched as the judge organised the remaining men to barricade the main door with tables and chairs.

"The boys! I have to get the boys," she heard Reverend Bayley yell.

"Sit down, Reverend, please sit down," pleaded Mrs. Forsyth. "The Bard will be with them, will he not? Surely he will not be party to this riot."

"I know that ma'am, but I believe he will try to bring them to my house to keep them safe, particularly the younger boys."

"Billy," Sarah cried with anguish, coming to her senses. "Oh my God, Billy!" Without thinking she grabbed the minister's arm. "This way Reverend, I know a side door."

"Sarah, you stay where you are. You do not have any idea of what is happening out there," said Mrs. Forsyth, terrified.

"I have to go Mrs. Forsyth. The boys will be so very frightened. Please understand."

Not waiting for an answer, the minister and Sarah exited the door.

Sarah and Reverend Bayley stepped into the yard. To Sarah, it was mayhem. Armed soldiers were running out of the barrack gates. Officers were bellowing orders. The settlement alarm bell was now ringing, a piercingly loud, incessant clanging. Shots sounded nearby, followed by yelling and screams.

"Stay close to me, Mrs. Thornton," Reverend Bayley said, taking Sarah's hand. "Pray, excuse the familiarity."

They crept along the sides of the buildings, not wanting to draw attention to themselves. As they moved closer to the gate, the minister produced a serving fork that he had secreted up his sleeve before leaving the wedding table. "Not much of a weapon, I know," he whispered to Sarah, glancing out of the gate with trepidation.

"But if I aim for the eyes of any attacker, you might at least, have a chance."

Sarah, trying to stay in control, smiled when she saw how serious the minister was being. "My life is in your hands then, sir," she whispered back. "And if by chance you fail, at least you will be near at hand to give me comfort in my last moments."

Reverend Bayley looked from the fork that he was brandishing to Sarah's eyes. They both stifled nervous laughs at the absurdity of the situation.

As they passed through the gate Sarah could see desperate convicts using picks and hoes to fight off the well-armed military. As she watched, many fell in agony, and it made her mission all the more urgent. Her own safety now became a secondary concern to the rescue of her boys. She urged the minister forward at a speedier pace, taking the lead, paying little heed to what was happening at the other end of the road.

Thankfully, they made it safely across the two-hundred or so yards between the barracks and the minister's home, the only casualty of their mission so far, being the hem of Sarah's wedding gown. It was torn and caked with dirt.

The minister had been correct in his expectations of the boys' overseer. No sooner had Sarah put a large kettle of water on to boil she heard the muffled sound of many running feet and urgent exchanges between Reverend Bayley and the Bard.

"You did well to bring them here," Reverend Bayley said, and smiled at the boys, trying to keep them calm.

"Begging your pardon sir, but not so loud. We do not want to bring attention to ourselves." The Bard doffed his cap awaiting the consequences for his being so forward. To his surprise, none were forth coming.

"Quite so, quite so." The minister lowered his voice. "Make haste then, come up onto the veranda. It will at least afford us a little protection. Where are the older lads? I only see the younger boys."

"They decided to stay and protect what is theirs. I do not think they will be in any real danger, sir."

"Have you any idea of what is happening, Bard?"

"The boys and I were kept in the dark, sir. It was only moments before we heard the first shout that a friend burst through our doors warning us that the men were in a very excited state, but he could tell me no more."

"Pity, it would help if we knew just what we are up against."

"True, but we thought it best to prepare for the worst. The boys and I… we hid all our working tools, only keeping close those pieces that we thought might second as a weapon if the need should arise. Hence, the hoes and shovels that the boys are carrying. But truly I cannot see of what use a hoe might be when faced with the muzzle of a gun."

It was then that Reverend Bayley noticed Billy hiding behind the Bard. "Hello there, young Billy, scared are we?" he ruffled the boy's hair. "No need to be, you know. We will look after you." Then to the Bard, "Well then, we had better get these boys inside."

The young boy clutched tighter to the Bard, shuffling closer to him, trying to hide behind him.

As soon as Sarah opened the front door many of the boys pushed past her, politely doffing their caps, then hurriedly hid behind furniture. She checked each boy as they came in looking for Billy. But he was not there. Her heart leapt into her throat, "Not Billy, not my Billy." She raced out on to the veranda, grateful that she had not removed her bonnet as the sun was glaring down. To her relief she saw the child hiding behind the convict overseer and clinging to his legs.

Sarah reached down to seize his hand, her gaze fixed on the boy alone. "Come along Billy," she said, as she tried to direct him into the house. "It's safer inside. I have a hot cup of tea waiting for you." She tried to cajole the child into obedience. But Billy refused to let go of the Bard's legs. "Come along my boy," she said. "Be a good boy." She grabbed for his hands to try and drag the boy away.

Michael was too shocked to move. He was staring into a face of his beloved, thinking this had to be a trick of the mind. But it was no trick. Her every smile, every tear had burnt deeply into his heart, a face he loved, more than life itself. His heart leapt, his pulse raced, his stomach knotted. He wanted to shout her name, but the shock of her sudden appearance had closed his throat, constricting it. All he could do was mouth her name: "Sarah."

Her nearness was overwhelming. For just a moment, just a short glorious moment, they were linked through Billy. Michael could feel his body tingling. He could feel her very being ebbing and pulsating through the boy and into him. His heart thumped erratically, every sense in his body burned with desire.

"Come along Billy, we need to get inside now." The urgent voice of Reverend Bayley broke through his trance making him remember, remember where he was, remember what he was, a convict... and she a lady.

The slender delicate thread that had joined them, if only for a moment, was broken, as Billy relented and took her hand. Michael's hands hung limp by his side as he watched his love hurry into the house. Not once had she looked into his face.

"You should be getting back, Bard. There is no telling what might be happening in the barracks. Go with care, mind. Mrs. Thornton and I will pray for the safe deliverance of you and the older boys."

It was only then that Michael recognised the bonnet Sarah was wearing, the bonnet he had made with his own hands, the bonnet for which he had meticulously chosen only the best materials. The bonnet he had made with pride for the wife of his best friend.

Mrs. Thornton?

Michael's thoughts screamed in in his mind. He doubled over as though he had been kicked in the stomach, the wind knocked out of him.

"Are you all right, man? What on earth-?"

"It is nothing, sir, I assure you nothing." He doffed his cap and backed away from the minister, keeping his gaze on the door through which Sarah had passed for as long as he could, hoping with every fibre of his being that she would come running out, that she would recognise him, that they would finally be together again.

But she never came to the door, never came running after him. *Mrs. Thornton, Miss Sarah.* Grief choked him.

He crumpled to the street, sobbing uncontrollably. "You promised me, Edmund, you promised me." He was vaguely aware that he was blubbering through his tears. "Have I not kept my word, Edmund? I have told no-one, not one person, of your own dirty secret. I am living in hell. Yet still I have kept my word. All I asked in return was that you look after her, keep her safe. Not damned marry her!" He screamed, all control leaving him. There was nothing left, no reason to live anymore. Picking up a nearby stone, he threw it in blind anger straight into an oncoming troop of soldiers.

Two soldiers rushed over and grabbed him under his arms. Dragging him to his feet, they shoved him in front of their sergeant.

Michael was too weak with sorrow to put up any fight. He let himself be taken without a struggle.

Chapter Thirty-One

The police court was crowded that afternoon with angry military personnel of every rank baying for blood.

Judge Forsyth subtly tried to stretch his aching back and legs. Sarah and Edmund's marriage, celebrated only that morning, seemed like a distant memory now. He read down his charge sheet. Never before had he ordered so many terms in solitary confinement, so many floggings. His head itched uncomfortably under his powdered wig as the afternoon wore on, his voice increasingly hoarse and painful as he yelled and bashed his gavel on his desk, trying to gain control of the court.

The riot had been short lived. From all reports the whole convict population had simultaneously exploded into violent physical action, with the intention to hurt and destroy all they could. The consensus was that it had been well planned, that the convict Edward Lawton had wielded incredible power over every convict and had been able to convince almost every one of them that he could take the island no matter the consequences.

Now, many of those underlings were paying the price for their leader's tenacity. He, however, remained at large.

As each accused convict was dragged before the court, the voices of the military personnel grew louder, more excited, more violent. Not for the first time that afternoon did Judge Forsyth wish that he had the steadier, more reliable Lieutenant Thornton sitting beside him in judgment, but the lieutenant had been called to other duties, searching for the ringleader. Instead, he had Mr. Vessey and the magistrate sitting with him. Both seemed to delight in inciting the already angry mob to even headier heights of agitation. He could understand their frustration. They had lost many good men that morning, including Captain Travers. Still, he knew he needed to remain impartial, needed to remain above the rabble.

He banged his gavel to gain attention. "Next," he called.

The Bard was shoved before him, his head bowed and despondent.

Edmund slipped into the back of the courtroom just as the two convicts he had employed to spy on the Bard were making their way to the front of the court. He was only taking a cursory interest in the proceedings until he heard the judge say to them, "If you two have something to say about the Bard, say it now or sit down and get out of my sight."

The two men mumbled to one another, one urging the other to speak.

"Well?" the judge asked impatiently.

"It was the Bard's stories, sir," one of them said, finally.

Edmund could not believe his luck. They were lying, pure and simple, yet no-one else in the courtroom could tell. They convinced the judge that one of the Bard's stories was the signal for the convicts to take up arms that morning.

The room erupted, yelling for retribution.

Judge Forsyth sat very still, looking directly at Michael. "Do you have anything to say, Bard?"

Edmund could not see Michael's face, but he heard no reply to the judge's request.

The judge looked exasperated. "I do not understand the curses of the Devil that seem to plague this man. I have witnessed, myself, the good works he has achieved with the boys. I see him as an honourable man and not as a man who could maliciously incite such a deadly riot. Will no-one speak for him?"

The court remained silent.

"As there is not one who will speak for the Bard, I have no choice but to sentence him to one hundred and fifty lashes, to be issued in part on two consecutive days."

Raucous cheers sounded through the room. Edmund thought back to another courtroom where he had remained silent as the same innocent man was sentenced. He made a mental note to pay those lying scoundrels well for their unexpected services.

Judge Forsyth stood up, exasperated. "I will have no more of this today." He stormed out of the room.

All convicts and military, without exception, were ordered to witness the afternoon's punishments.

Edmund had for the most part been able to avoid attending punishments. But today was different. He wanted to be there. He had a sense of great satisfaction, a sense of triumph even, and was eager to stand with his regiment at the stone gate of the convicts' barracks. He just hoped this would prove a permanent solution to his problems, realising that the need for a complete solution to the Bard had become more urgent. Now that Sarah was his, Michael could not be given any chance to ruin his perfect life.

The ground beneath the triangle was already saturated with blood by the time Michael was lashed to its frame. A constable ripped Michael's shirt off his back, revealing his white, unmarked skin.

Reverend Bayley stood with the older boys who had stayed to protect their dormitory. He began to recite prayers for the Bard's deliverance. The boys stood in staunch solidarity, repeating the prayers loudly and clearly.

The flogger, cat-o'-nine-tails in hand, took his position and waited for the assistant surgeon to decide just how many of the convict's seventy five allotted lashes he felt the man could stand straight off.

Without even examining Michael the man proclaimed loudly, "Thirty!"

Edmund watched with perverse curiosity as the flogger removed the cat-o'-nine-tails from its protective pouch. He watched him unravel the nine leather strips individually and run them through his fingers, gingerly fingering the knot tied in the end of each one. He watched as the man raised the cat-o'-nine-tails above his head and prepared for the first cut. With great satisfaction he witnessed the look of terror that momentarily passed over Michael's pasty white face but still Edmund did not protest at the harsh sentence. Still he didn't speak up for his friend.

The boys' strong melodic voices echoing around the stone walls of the barrack yard disconcerted Edmund. Imposing an iron control on both his actions and his emotions, Edmund stood rigid, looking straight over the boys' heads to the high stone wall behind them. He concentrated hard on the wall. At no stage did he allow his stare to waver.

But even the boys' recited prayers could not block out the whistling lash of the first savage cut, the sickening dull crack of the cat-o'-nine-tails upon naked flesh. "On-n-e... Tw-oo... Thr-ee..."

Edmund did not flinch as each lash found its mark. "Ni-ne... T-en... El-even..." Strong and clear, the constable's voice echoed through the barrack grounds.

Michael bit his lip, clenching his fists tightly, trying to subdue his sense of pain, gaining strength from the boys' prayers. He forced himself to concentrate all his thoughts on Sarah, the Sarah he remembered in England. Perspiration fell from his brow, but no sound left his lips.

The punishment continued until it became more than Michael could stand and his head fell forward.

Reluctantly, the flogger stopped his brutal work and looked towards the assistant surgeon for instruction. Edmund, too, looked toward the assistant surgeon. The man poked Michael with his walking stick. Michael flinched.

The assistant surgeon yelled, "Two more!"

The two were given and after another poke from the assistant surgeon and another twitch from Michael, two more were ordered. Thus the flogging went on until the full sentence was carried out.

At no time did Edmund let his gaze drop to the bloodied back of Michael as he hung, barely conscious, on the triangle. He stood straight and tall, gripping the burnished brass handle of his sword in its scabbard, tighter and tighter.

The sound of splashing water, as a bucket of seawater was being tossed over Michael's lacerated back, aroused Edmund from the trance-like state he had fallen into. He became acutely aware of severe pain in the palm of his hand. Hastily he removed it from the hilt of his sword. Only then was his attention drawn to the bloody sight in front of him. He looked directly at Michael. For the first time he saw his boyhood friend, the boy he grew up with, the boy he had shared childhood secrets and hopes with, lashed to the triangle in front of him. He felt the bile rise in his throat.

Michael's limp body was taken down in a state of collapse. Edmund stared as Michael was half-dragged and half-carried past him by two hefty constables toward a crude wooden cart, normally used to carry bodies to the cemetery, but today it was being utilised for transport to the hospital.

So engrossed was he that he jumped when he felt a tap on his shoulder.

"Hey, Thornton!" It was only Richard Saunders, his friend. "Bet you can't wait to get back to your bride, lucky devil!" He hurried away without waiting for an answer.

Michael also heard Edmund's name. The two men locked eyes.

"I loathe and despise you, Edmund Thornton. I curse you with every breath in my body." Michael spat in Edmund's face.

One of the constables lifted his truncheon to hit Michael. Edmund grabbed it before the constable had a chance to crack it down on Michael's head. He wiped the spittle from his face.

Michael went on undeterred. "You'll have to kill me Thornton, if you want to keep her. I swear you'll have to kill me!"

The soldiers picked him up and threw him into the cart.

Reverend Bayley matched his step with Edmund's as they left the barracks, shaking his head. "Bad business, hey, Lieutenant? And to think this is your wedding day. I suppose you are looking for your bride. I can tell you that she is safe in my home with some of the juvenile convicts and Mr. Fletcher. She followed me to my house just after you left. I tried to dissuade her but she would not hear of it. The Bard brought the boys there to be safe."

Edmund's brain exploded in rage. *Michael and Sarah have met?* Trying to control his voice, he addressed the minister and excused himself.

"Of course, I understand. You will want to see her safe. Go, go!"

As he hurried to the minister's home, Michael's words kept screaming through his mind. *I loathe and despise you, Edmund Thornton. I curse you with every breath in my body. You'll have to kill me Thornton, if you want to keep her.*

Well, Michael, he thought as he arrived at the minister's house, *it might just come to that.*

A plan began to form in his mind, a devious plan, a plan that called for deception and disguise, a plan that would rid him of the honourable Michael Hanlan for good.

Chapter Thirty-Two

Panic like she had never felt before pulsed through Sarah as she put down the book of fairy tales she was reading to the boys. All eyes were transfixed on the barricaded door as heavy footsteps could be heard thumping up the path toward it. With her heart pounding her chest, she put a shaking finger to her lips. She motioned to the boys to remain very quiet and very still. Not moving her attention from the door, she felt behind her for any form of weapon. Her fingers closed around the handle of the fire poker. Grabbing it tightly, she steeled herself in readiness as the barricaded door shook and rattled. Mr. Fletcher appeared in the doorway of the adjoining room brandishing a frying pan, visibly shaking. Sarah could hear a man cursing on the other side of the door as it began to edge open. All in the room seemed to hold their collective breaths.

Suddenly, the barricade gave way and the door burst open. Piled pieces of furniture tumbled and crashed to the floor. Sarah gave a startled gasp as her husband of only a few hours, hurled himself through the door. "What on earth?"

"Edmund! It's only you," Sarah cried in relief. "We were not expecting you."

"Obviously," Edmund replied, looking towards Sarah and the curate still brandishing their weapons.

"Oh, g-good h-heavens, Lieutenant Thornton, you gave us q-quite a start!" Mr. Fletcher said, and put down the frying pan.

Edmund ignored the curate and walked toward his wife. "We can put that down for a start, Mrs. Thornton." He released her whitened

235

fingers from the poker and then encircled her with his arms, pulling her close.

"Mr. Thornton, we are not alone, sir," Sarah said. She twisted and turned, trying to break from his grasp as his lips searched urgently for hers.

Sarah felt her heart sink. His kiss was nothing as she had imagined it to be. Where was the euphoria she should be feeling as a newly wedded bride? Where was the heady flutter she had always felt when in Michael's arms? She felt none of these emotions.

She tried in vain to push her memories of Michael back into the deep recesses of her mind. She tried to concentrate on Edmund. But her memories were too strong to remain buried inside. *No, it is all wrong, it is all wrong!*

She tore herself from his arms, shaking.

Edmund held his wife at arm's length. Sarah felt uncomfortable as her husband's eyes raked over her body.

"I must insist you let me go, sir." Sarah tried to sound surer than she felt. "If you will not consider Mr. Fletcher's feelings, please consider the feelings of these young boys."

Edmund dropped his hands and looked for the first time at the group of pasty, white faces that stared up at him. "Damned them all to hell!"

"Edmund!" Sarah gathered the boys closest to her into her arms. "You cannot mean that. What have they done to hurt you or others?"

"Eight good men lost their lives today, my dear, including Captain Travers and my batman, Corporal Evans, at the hands of their..." His eyes were blazing. "...of your boys' comrades! By God!"

Sarah tried to keep her voice steady. "These boys have been with the curate and me all day. They have had nothing to do with what has happened today. You can ask Reverend Bayley, if you do not believe me. He left us only this past hour."

"In fact, dear wife, I met the minister on the way from the convicts' barracks and was very surprised to learn that you were here. I particularly told you to remain in the military barracks until it was all over. What on earth were you thinking? You could have been killed!"

Sarah cringed under her husband's outburst. "I am sorry," she answered. "But the boys..."

"Damn the boys, Mrs. Thornton. I am your husband now and when I give you an order I expect you to obey it!"

"Yes, Mr. Thornton."

"Also Mrs. Thornton, if reports are to be believed it was not only the younger boys you entertained here this afternoon."

"I am sorry, Edmund, I do not understand. What do you mean?"

"I mean, madam, that the boys were accompanied by the Bard."

"The Bard? I can assure you I have not met the man. There was an older boy with the younger ones, but he left immediately. I was too intent on getting the boys inside to take any notice." Quick snippets of Mrs. Forsyth and Reverend Bayley's high praise of the man rushed through her mind. "I do wish I had known. I would have so liked to have met him, thanked him for his work with the boys."

"I can help you meet the Bard, Miss Sarah. He be such a kindly man," one of the boys piped up.

Edmund cuffed the unfortunate boy across the ears. "Enough, you impertinent fool! You have no right to speak without being spoken to first!"

"Begging your pardon, sir." The boy touched his forelock to Edmund, as he apologetically backed away. "Humble apologies, Miss."

"Edmund!" Sarah was so shocked at Edmund's actions she could scarcely speak.

"Have I displeased you in some way, wife?" Edmund asked with sarcasm not lost on Sarah.

"The poor boy you just hit was only trying to help, Edmund. He did not deserve your wrath, did he?"

Edmund glared at her. "Standing up for the poor mistreated convict once again, Sarah. You should, in future, think very well before speaking up for them. Given half a chance they would murder us in our beds."

"That may be so, Edmund, but I still cannot believe how you treated that poor boy. I declare this island seems to be changing you."

Concerned about Edmund's reactions toward the boys she started to gather up the boys like a mother hen protecting its chicks. She directed Mr. Fletcher to take them into the next room. Moving over to the sideboard, Sarah poured her husband a cup of tea, hoping it might settle his temper. In a gesture of reconciliation she handed it to him.

"Leave me be, woman!" The cup smashed to the floor, hot tea splashing Edmund's boots. He jumped out of the way.

Startled, but in control, Sarah squatted down and began to pick up the pieces.

Edmund stared at the broken cup for a moment and then fell to his knees in front of his wife. He tenderly placed his hand over hers. "Please forgive me, Sarah, I am not myself, what I have seen today, what I have heard..." His voice faded off.

Sarah stroked his brow. "It is all over now, Edmund, you are here with me. You can stop thinking about it."

There was a long pause before Edmund answered. Sarah looked into her husband's eyes, expecting to see remorse, but she saw only hate. Confused, she stood up carefully and placed the pieces of broken crockery on the sideboard.

"That is just it, Sarah, it is not all over," Edmund said. "I am required for duty this evening. Some of the convicts have escaped into the bush."

"Tonight Edmund, but tonight is our wedding night. Have the other officers forgotten already." Secretly, though, she found herself to be relieved that he would not be sharing her bed that night.

"I am sorry, my dear. It has been a very tiring day. Please believe me, Sarah, I did not mean to hurt you. You are my life."

Not wanting Edmund to guess at her reluctance in sharing the wedding bed, she said soothingly. "It is all forgotten." She took his huge hands in hers. "We will have the rest of our lives together. I am sure I can part with you this one night."

"Yes, just this one night." He sighed. "I will let Mr. Fletcher know that I am taking you to Judge Forsyth's home. You will be safer there."

"As you wish, Edmund." She picked up her wedding bonnet and skirted around him so as to miss his embrace.

She saw longing and desire burning in his eyes now. She lowered hers and turned away. *I do not know which is worse, his anger or his love.*

"She still loves him!" Edmund spat the words with contempt as he left the Forsyth's home. "She thinks I don't know but her eyes and her kiss told me all I need."

He strode toward the military barracks mumbling under his breath. *Sarah does not realise it, but her actions today sealed your fate, Michael Hanlan. This island is too small for both of us. I will have to be on my guard at all times. I can never leave her side. Thank God, she did not recognise you this day.*

As Edmund returned the salutes of tired and bloodied soldiers making their way back into the safety of the barracks, the fallout of Michael's words suddenly dawned. If Michael was ever allowed to tell all he knew about him, his own past indiscretions would sully the proud standing of the regiment, not to mention the ramifications for himself. Under no circumstances could he allow him to utter one word of the truth.

"Devil's breath, Hanlan, you've given me no choice!"

In desperate need of a drink he stormed into the military mess, but stopped short as he entered the room. Discarded plates with half-eaten meals and half-empty glasses littered the tables, remnants of the wedding breakfast, not yet cleared away. Edmund stood for a moment and stared, wondering how things could have changed so much in such a short time. He consoled himself with the knowledge that only he knew the Bard's true identity, so Sarah would never learn the extent of his betrayal. But how close had it been? The very thought made him shudder.

His attention moved to the uncut wedding cake, delicately decorated in yellow and green, his own beloved Eleventh's colours. All doubts disappeared then. He was sure that what he intended to do was right. *I'm doing this for Sarah and the regiment,* he told himself. *It would not do her reputation any favours to be tainted by the close acquaintance of a convicted criminal.*

There was no other way. Picking up a half empty rum bottle he drained its contents and looked around for a full bottle. Finding one he held onto it tightly and strode out into the evening shadows.

Edmund knocked with brute force on the heavy wooden door of the commissariat store.

A pimple faced young corporal cautiously opened the door when Edmund identified himself.

"Sorry sir, I was told to open the door to no-one but seeing as it is you I'm sure it will be all right."

"Of course it's all right," yelled Edmund. "Now shut that door behind me and guard it. I won't be long. I know exactly what I need." Edmund grabbed a sack and filled it with the stores he required. "Right, well done corporal, keep up the good work. There is no need to speak of my visit to anyone. Is that understood?"

"Yes, sir!" The corporal gave a quick salute.

The sun was low in the sky when he left the commissariat store. Golden rays of the setting sun forced their way through the thick clouds. Edmund's stomach churned as he followed their trail. One ray fell directly on the gallows giving it a ghostly appearance, yet another lit the hospital, accentuating every stone and barred window, as though it was being touched by the very Hand of God. He shuddered, suddenly feeling the burden of his choices on his mortal soul. Thoughts of hell and damnation stopped him in his tracks for but a fleeting moment. He assured himself, as he stepped forward again.

Even God, as my Judge, will see this as more an act of love than an act of vengeance.

Striding forward, he calmly acknowledged each sentry as they barred his way with their muskets and demanded his business. He simply told them that he had business near the hospital, which for all intents and purposes was absolutely true. It surprised Edmund that considering the situation none questioned the sack that he carried over his shoulder, but then the sentries were corporals and he was a lieutenant.

Once clear of all the guards, he crept behind the hospital and past the surgeon's quarters. Peering around to make sure he was not being observed, he disappeared into the forest of pines. Eventually he recognised the hollow pine tree he had been looking for, not too far from the back of the hospital.

He congratulated himself at the ease with which his plan was taking shape. Taking off his military uniform, he stretched, his muscles rippling, as he enjoyed the momentary freedom of his nakedness. Opening the sack he turned it upside down and shook it. A pair of yellow trousers, a shirt and a cap fell to the ground, the clothes of a convicted man.

Amazing what you can get from the commissariat store when you are the one in charge, he chuckled.

The smile soon left his face. Even in the fading light he could see that they looked remarkably clean. Too clean, Edmund realised, for his masquerade to be believed. He turned them into the ground with the heel of his foot. Minutes later, satisfied that they were dirty enough, he began to dress. The clothes were itchy and uncomfortable, unlike any he had worn before. Scratching, he noticed his white skin glistened pale in the final light of the setting sun.

"Devil's breath!" he swore, staring at his bare feet against the ground. "I'll never pass for a convict."

Taking up large lumps of dirt, he rubbed them into his nakedness, concentrating on his feet, his toenails, his hands, his fingernails, and finally his face. Looking at his hands, he was happy with the result and hoped that his face had taken on the same greying shadows. A dark curl fell across his forehead as he looked down. *My hair!* He swore. Picking up more dirt he matted it into his locks. Taking a deep breath he adjusted the convict clothing.

"My God," he cried, "this should have been me."

Tormented by confused emotions he began to shake uncontrollably, suddenly unsure of where he was, of what he was doing. His hand fell upon the discarded bottle of rum and he drank greedily of its contents. Sitting down and gaining control of himself, he yelled once again, this time with more determination and resolve, "No, it is not me, never will be me! He is the only one who knows, he is the only one who can tell." He lifted the bottle once more to his lips. "After this night's work he will never be able to tell!"

He folded his uniform with great care and then put it into the sack. Digging a deep hole at the base of the pine, he buried it, marking the place with a pile of stones so that he could retrieve it later.

All there was to do now was sit and wait for the settlement bell to ring at midnight. He would take advantage of the change of guard to slip into the hospital and do the deed. "Even now I can feel my hands around your scrawny neck, Michael Hanlan." He laced his fingers together, tightly, cruelly. "Just like a rabbit but slowly, slowly squeezing the life out of you, squeezing you out of Sarah's life. My Sarah's life!" His knuckles went white with brute force.

He drained the rum bottle, the contents warming him. Nestling into the back of the pine's hollow trunk to wait, sleep eventually overtook him.

As he slept, a severe storm brewed overhead. Lightning split the sky, thunder rumbled and cold winds blew in squalls. The majestic pines swayed violently in the storm's wrath. Pine cones began to break loose and rattle down through the branches.

The sound broke into Edmund's sleep. In a drunken haze he rubbed his eyes, trying to discern where he was. The rattling sound grew closer, louder. He scrambled to his feet in fear. *The watchman's rattle! I have to get away but where to hide? There, behind that tombstone.*

He raced toward a large rock and squatted behind it. *They will run right past me and catch Hanlan instead. He deserves to be caught. He has my Sarah's heart.*

The shouting grew louder. Massive shadows overwhelmed him.

"Over 'ere!" The shadows became men.

The flickering flame of a lighted torch held close to his face blinded him for but a moment.

"What a prize, the ringleader, Edward Lawton!"

"Don't let 'im escape!"

The ground rumbled as heavy boots ran across it. The flash of gun fire sparked close to Edmund. He began to run, blindly.

He heard no more as the world collapsed into pain and darkness around him.

Chapter Thirty-Three

Michael woke startled at the sound of his own raspy breathing. He could sense someone near him. "Thornton!" He jolted. Excruciating pain pulsed through his body.

"Steady there, Bard. Any movement will only break open the wounds once more. Now, stay still while I try to cool your back. I have bought some banana leaves. I have been told that they will help soothe your cuts."

A sense of relief surged through Michael as his vision cleared and he found himself looking into a familiar face.

"Reverend?"

The minister wiped a cooling wet rag across the back of Michael's neck. Michael's gaze darted feverishly to and fro as he tried to make out where he was, why he was there, why his back burned.

"You are in the hospital Bard. They brought you here after…"

Michael could only nod, nausea washing over him. He winced with every wipe of the cloth. He could feel every touch of the minister's fingers as he tried to pull mangled skin together. Memory of the day before came flooding back, agonising memories of each lash as it sliced across his bare back. More agonising, however, were the memories of his friend's betrayal.

"I have been sitting with you most of the night. You have been drifting between life and death for most of that time. Can you tell me what happened, man? One minute you are safe with us, and the next, the boys and I are forced to witness such a bloody spectacle. It was thought you were dying."

"I am dying, dying inside," Michael mumbled. Visions of Sarah in her wedding gown floated before his eyes. Michael grabbed at the minister's arm in his delirium. "He went and married my..."

"Who, Bard, who did what?"

Michael turned and stared at the stonewalls, tears pouring down his cheeks.. *When I saw her, my world turned upside down. Damn it! I was so sure she was safe at home in England, waiting for me. To find her here and in his arms!* He sobbed freely. "All hope is lost," he cried aloud, not caring who heard.

"Hope is never lost, my son. There is always some answer to your prayers. Pray with me."

With stabbing pain, Michael turned his head back toward the minister, and listened as the man began to pray. *Prayers will not help me now,* Michael thought. *Only I can help me now. I must get a message to Sarah somehow before it's too late.* He looked toward the doorway, half expecting to see Edmund there. *I must act now. Thornton must know I am here. By now he must know that I am not dead.*

He raked his fevered mind for an answer; his gaze darted nervously back and forth before resting on an empty cot beside him, blankets still covered in blood.

Reverend Bayley looked up from his prayers and followed Michael's gaze. "Perkins," he said sadly. "Another innocent betrayed by yesterday's bloody retribution. Poor man was not as lucky as you, Bard. The lash proved too much for his weak body. But you Bard, you have the constitution of an ox. You have shown that often these past months."

Unwittingly the minister had given him the answer to his prayers. His pulse began to race. He could feel his heart thumping on the thin straw mattress beneath him. "I am afraid that I am not as strong as an ox this time, Reverend. Truly, I feel my life ebbing away as I lie here."

"Do not speak so, Bard. You have much to live for. Think of your boys."

"May I be so bold as to ask you a favour, Reverend?"

The reverend nodded.

"The judge's wife, Mrs. Forsyth, she wrote a letter for me some time ago."

"I remember."

"Do you think she would write me another?"

"We do not need to worry Mrs. Forsyth, Bard. If you wish to have a letter written I will go immediately and get paper and pens from the dispensary." Reverend Bayley started to rise from his chair.

Michael grabbed frantically at the man's robes, trying to stop him leaving. He remembered Mrs. Forsyth as a kindly lady. Surely he could persuade her to take a message to his Sarah. It was his only chance, his only hope.

"Pray, have pity on a poor dying man, Reverend. I mean no offence, sir." Thinking quickly he went on. "Please, in your generosity, let the last face I look upon in this world be one so like my own dear mother's."

The minister was silent for some time. "I can ask, Bard. But I am not sure if she will come, not after the consequences of the last time."

Michael would not be defeated now. "I am sure you can persuade her," he said. Fear that Edmund would get to him first made him shake uncontrollably, made him sound desperate. He kissed the man's robes. "Ask her to come with all haste."

Chapter Thirty-Four

Sarah lifted the damask curtain in the judge's parlour a little and peeped out into the street. She could still see armed soldiers marching up and down Military Road, stabbing their bayonets into shrubs and trees. She glanced over toward Mrs. Forsyth. "I heard Judge Forsyth leave early this morning. I hope all is well?"

"Yes, the judge received word that they had captured the ring leader of yesterday's revolt. Perhaps your husband even helped capture him. That would indeed be a feather in his cap."

Sarah blushed at the mention of her husband. "I suppose that means that Edmund might not be back this morning." She hoped she had disguised the sense of relief she felt. She sat down and poured herself a cup of tea, then offered to pour one for Mrs. Forsyth, who shook her head.

"I hope the boys were able to get back to their barracks safely. I tried to convince Reverend Bayley that I should be allowed to accompany them but he would have none of it."

"Quite right, too. A lady, a newly wed lady at that, has no right to be traipsing after convicts on such a day. You were very lucky that you were not murdered in their midst. Your dear aunt would never forgive me if I was to write her of your impending marriage and in the very next letter I write of your murder. What ever would she think of me? No, Lieutenant Thornton was right to bring you back here to the judge's house as soon as that infernal alarm bell sounded the all clear. Now drink your tea, my dear, it will keep your mind from all that has happened."

Margaret Forsyth buttered herself a warm scone. "What a day yesterday was, what a day! I do declare have you ever known a day of such extreme contrasts?" Not waiting for an answer she continued. "You were indeed a beautiful bride, my dear. Everyone was commenting most favourably. Even, I believe, some of the gentlemen. And Lieutenant Thornton, he looked so fine in his regimentals. Oh, and the guard of honour." She rattled on. "And to think that it was all ruined. To separate a happy couple on their wedding day, their wedding day of all days, it is unforgivable. I cannot even begin to imagine how you must be feeling Mrs. Thornton."

"Mrs. Thornton, oh, Mrs. Forsyth, it sounds so formal. Please will you not continue to call me Sarah?"

"My dear, you are Mrs. Thornton now, a married woman."

"I am still your Sarah, am I not?"

"Of course, my dear, you will always be my Sarah. But now you are also the lieutenant's wife."

"Yes, everything has changed now, I suppose," Sarah said almost to herself. "I had imagined it all to be so very different."

"Different how?" her guardian enquired.

Sarah lifted the curtain again and stared outside again, thinking, *A different groom, for one thing*. She sighed, then turning back to Mrs. Forsyth, she said, "Truthfully, Mrs. Forsyth, I am not sure how I should be feeling."

At that moment, both women stopped what they were doing at the sound of the front gate clicking. Reverend Bayley called out to let the ladies know that it was only him. With relief, Sarah stood up and opened the front door. Matthews, as usual was nowhere to be seen, so she welcomed the minister herself and showed him into the parlour. "Would you care to join us for breakfast, Reverend?"

"Most kind of you to offer, Mrs. Thornton."

Sarah reddened.

"Good morning, Reverend." Margaret Forsyth indicated an empty chair. "Please sit down."

"Thank you, Mrs. Forsyth. I have eaten very little since, since, my goodness, yesterday's wedding breakfast. I suddenly feel famished." He buttered himself a scone, then took a large bite and chewed it thoughtfully. "The prison is all excitement this morning with the capture of the ringleader. However, ladies, that is not the reason for my visit. I have sadder news. About the Bard."

Sarah and Mrs. Forsyth braced themselves.

"Unfortunately, it seems that after he left us yesterday, Mrs. Thornton, he was mistaken as one of the convicts from the revolt. How I wish I could have been at his trial, spoken up for him, saved him so much suffering. I did not get there in time." he said. "Suffice to say, the Bard now lies dying in the hospital."

"Oh, good grief. Poor man. How can we help?"

"Actually Mrs. Forsyth, he begged me to find you and ask if you would kindly consent to write another letter."

"Oh dear, I am not sure, Reverend. Do you recall what happened then? I am not sure that I can go through that again."

"I understand your concerns, Mrs. Forsyth, but for a dying man, might you not reconsider?"

"I will do it," Sarah said. "I would like to thank the man for his care of the boys, especially Billy. If what you say is true, Reverend, I may not have much time."

Reverend Bayley raised his eyebrows as he looked towards Mrs. Forsyth.

"Well, I suppose it would be all right, Reverend, if you can assure me of her safety."

"I will accompany her myself, ma'am."

Margaret Forsyth walked across to the bureau and opened the top drawer. Taking out some folded sheets of paper she handed them to Sarah. "This is the Bard's first letter, Sarah. He became so upset after we finished it he forbade me to post it. Perhaps now, considering the circumstances, he might allow me to. Now go and get your coat and bonnet, my dear."

As Sarah went out into the hall, the minister stood up to follow her. "You know, Mrs. Forsyth, before I left him the poor man asked for last rites. He whispered his name to me, Michael Hanlan."

"Michael Hanlan, you say?" Margaret Forsyth repeated. "It is strange, but I feel sure I have heard that name before. No matter, I cannot place it for the moment. At least now, if the poor man does dies, we can engrave his headstone with his true identity."

Sarah dropped her bonnet. *What name did he say? Michael Hanlan? It cannot be. My aching heart is now causing me to hear things now. He is dead. Edmund told me he is dead.*

At that moment two soldiers came hurrying up the path to the door. Upon opening it, one of them addressed her. "Excuse me, ma'am, we are looking for the minister, Reverend Bayley. We were told he might be here."

The reverend made his presence known. "We are to escort you immediately to the convicts' barracks, sir."

"I see. I believe I will only require one of you to accompany me. Mrs. Thornton needs to get to the hospital as soon as possible. One of you can escort her."

"As you wish, sir, but we must go now."

The minister scribbled a note and handed it to Sarah. "Give this to the guard at the door of the hospital. He should not hesitate to let you in on my authority."

Sarah nodded, picked up her bonnet and tied the ribbon under her chin. She kissed Mrs. Forsyth on the cheek and took the letter from the hall table where the lady had left it.

Following the soldier down the garden path, Sarah was surprised to see her three young parakeets flying on their own and settling on the gate post, as if to bid her farewell. One then fluttered so close she could hear its wings as they touched the letter she was holding.

She examined the parchment closely. *What if I did hear the name correctly? What if it is my Michael?*

But still the doubts lingered and the hopes persisted. *One look at his letter will tell me. I will not read the contents, so I will not be breaking any of the man's confidences. But I need to know for sure.*

Careful not to draw the attention of her escort, she opened the letter. Her heart missed a beat. It was indeed addressed to a

Sarah. Still she hesitated, unable to look at the end of the letter. She feared all would be dashed when she looked at the last page. With apprehension she lifted the top pages and scanned the last.

Abruptly, she stopped, stunned, shaken. There in front of her were the words she had hardly dared to hope to read again. She could still clearly hear his voice as he teased her with them.

Lavenders blue dilly, dilly,
Lavenders green.
When I am king, dilly, dilly,
You shall be queen.

Her relief was flooded with guilt. How had her heart been so easily deceived into believing he was dead? She knew, then, that it was her heart that had died that day, not her Michael. And now with a simple stroke of a pen her heart was overwhelmed with love and renewed hope, resurrecting her spirit.

"Are you all right, ma'am?" The private in front of her had also stopped.

Sarah looked up at him, dazed. "Oh, yes, just a little out of breath. You walk on and I will catch up to you very soon."

"It is best that we walk together, ma'am, although order has been restored we cannot be sure that all the escaped convicts have been caught. Would you care to sit a moment, catch your breath?"

Michael, my Michael, dying. Her heart raced.

"Sit? No, indeed not, private. We must get on or we may be too late." She hurried past the stunned soldier.

With great apprehension Sarah took the soldier's extended hand and accepted his offer of help up the steep, stone stairs leading to the hospital. She stood, fidgeting, a couple of stairs from the top, as the soldier handed the note from Reverend Bayley to the guard barring their entry into the building.

The guard looked the note over. "Ummph," he said. "Hey, I hear they caught Lawton, the ringleader."

"Yeah, that's what I hear. I was sent to get the minister over to the trial, but instead he sent me here with Mrs. Thornton." Sarah's escort pointed a pudgy finger.

"Should be some trial, from what I hear. Can't understand it though. I hear he was caught right nearby. I would have thought the sod would have disappeared into the pines. Lots of hiding places out there."

Sarah listened with impatience. *Whoever this damn Lawton is, he deserves everything that is coming to him. My Michael is dying in there because of him.*

She wanted to yell at the guard, *Let me past, I have to see him. He is dying!* But she kept silent, biting her lip to hold her tongue as she waited.

The guard glared at the note. Sarah let out a sigh of relief as he eventually unbolted the heavy door. But her relief was short lived, however, as he disappeared inside, bolting the door again behind him. The soldier, who had accompanied Sarah, turned towards her and shrugged.

Sarah stared at the door, willing it to open. After what seemed an interminable time, the door creaked open again. The guard reappeared and, sounding very self-important, he announced, "The surgeon will see you in the dispensary. This way, ma'am, if you please."

On impulse, Sarah began to straighten her skirts, push her hair back under her bonnet and fan her flushed face with her hand. Oppressive heat and the vile smells of sickness and death assaulted her senses as she stepped through the doorway. Her mind raced. Where was he? Was she too late? Would she know him? Had he changed much? *Will he know me?*

The surgeon greeted her at the dispensary door. "Do come in, Mrs. Thornton." He stepped aside to let her pass, indicating to the soldier to wait outside. Pulling out a chair from behind his desk, he offered it to Sarah and then sat in another. "I must say, I am surprised to see you Mrs. Thornton, today of all days. I would have thought that your husband would be demanding of your attentions today."

Startled, she looked up at the surgeon, realising that she had not thought of Edmund. Struggling with her conscience, she chose her words carefully. "Lieutenant Thornton has not yet returned from his duty last evening."

Sarah could hear the surgeon muttering under his breath, something about wedding night, sacred institution. But she chose to ignore the insinuations, folding her gloved hands tensely in her lap.

"We were expecting Mrs. Forsyth, ma'am, and Reverend Bayley. Totally against regulations, you know." He reread the minister's note.

Sarah began to grow frantic that the blasted man was not going to let her see her Michael.

"Mrs. Forsyth is unwell, or, I assure you, she would have come herself." She felt justified in the little lie. It was, Michael, after all she was here to see. "She and the minister were concerned for the Bard's welfare, so asked if I would be willing to come in her stead."

"Sad state of affairs, indeed. I, too, hold the Bard in high regard. His good work with the boys is unquestionable. If the minister had requested such a consideration for any other man, I would not have entertained the idea."

As casually as she could manage, she replied, "I, too, have heard of the Bard's good deeds, sir, but have not, as yet, had the good fortune to meet him. Surely a man such as this deserves considerations that others might not."

"You are very convincing, Mrs. Thornton. But I must warn you. This island changes men, good men. I cannot guarantee the Bard's actions after yesterday. I blame myself, you know. I could not stomach the afternoon's punishment list, so I sent my assistant. It seems he enjoys the sight of blood and men's torment."

Sarah cringed at the thought. Her Michael flogged. It was too much to endure. She had to see him, see him now.

"Begging your pardon, Mrs. Thornton. I quite forgot to whom I was speaking. Pray forgive my outburst."

She replied as graciously as she could, "Forgiven, sir. From what I have heard of the Bard, I am sure he bears you no ill will."

"Be that so." He wiped his forehead with a piece of linen cloth. Standing up, he motioned to a hospital orderly who was walking past. "Take this chair to the ward where the Bard is." He indicated the chair he had just vacated. "Mind you place it near the door, far from his bed." He looked directly into Sarah's eyes as if to emphasise his next words. "My experience has been that men, who have received the same punishment as was metered out to the Bard yesterday, display violent tendencies, even towards those who are only trying to help. Now, where is that soldier who accompanied you?"

Taking a nibbed pen, ink and paper from his own desk he handed them to the soldier. "Mrs. Thornton, you will find a small desk just inside the door of the ward which should be adequate for your purposes."

As she followed the surgeon into the dank hallway, her trepidation grew. The man she thought was dead, the man she mourned, the man she loved, was but a few short steps away. Taking a deep, unsteady breath as they reached the room, she peered around the doorway.

The room was dim and musty. The only light was coming from a small window high in the stone wall. It lit the face of the man lying on his stomach in the bed, his head turned toward the door. She forced herself to look past his broken body and concentrate only on his face, his unchanged face. He lay there so still. From this distance she could not even discern if he was breathing. Was she too late?

Relief surged through her when she saw him move, ever so slightly, but he did move. She wanted to run to him, take him in her arms, comfort him. His nearness made her senses spin. She faltered in her step.

"It is too much for you, ma'am." The surgeon watched Sarah with concern. "I was worried it would be. Do you require smelling salts?"

She gave the surgeon a reassuring smile. Taking deep breaths, she tried to settle her racing pulse. She sat down behind the small desk in the corner of the room, nervously rearranging the pen, ink and paper before speaking.

"Good morning, Bard. I am ever so pleased to be finally meeting you." Sarah spoke softly, hoping he would understand that she could not let the surgeon know that they knew each other. To her disappointment, it seemed his body recoiled at the sound of her voice and he turned his head towards the wall, as though in disgust.

"Did you not hear the lady, Bard?" The surgeon flicked the man's legs. "This kind lady has come to write your letter. You did ask for it, did you not?"

Sarah interrupted. "Perhaps he is disappointed that I am not Mrs. Forsyth."

"Yes, perhaps that is what is ailing him. I must leave you now in the care of this private. I have other patients to attend."

"Please, sir. Could I move a little closer?" Sarah asked. Her body ached to feel Michael's touch. "The man seems so weak. I am sure he will be of no threat to me."

"No, I must insist, ma'am, that you remain sitting in that chair for your own safety. You must keep in mind that he is, after all, a convicted felon."

As he was leaving the room he whispered to the private, pointing towards her and then to his musket. With the soldier's nod of agreement the surgeon assessed the room once more and, apparently, finding it to his satisfaction, he turned and left.

Michael groaned as he struggled to turn his head back toward Sarah, his face was contorted with pain. "Could we begin the letter writing Miss? There is not much time."

His panic-stricken eyes stared right past her. Such was their intensity that she too, looked behind her, sure that she would see someone standing there. There was no-one but the soldier, leaning on his musket, staring disinterestedly, down the corridor.

255

"Yes, yes, of course, let us begin." She selected a piece of paper and laid it neatly in front of her, filled her pen with ink and held it poised to begin. "Now to whom should I address this letter?" Trying to concentrate on an illusion of detached interest in taking the letter, she hoped her voice sounded composed.

"I would like you to address it to 'My darling Sarah'." The familiar mischievous smile lit up his face.

"Go on," she whispered.

"Although we are very far apart, every night I hold you close in my dreams. I think of you safe at home in England." He paused a moment. "I know it has been two years since we were last in each other's arms but know this." He looked deep into Sarah's eyes. "I still love you as much now as I did then, if not more, if that could be possible."

"I am sure she loves you too, Bard. I am sure she must love you with all her heart." She could not help but let her gaze wander over Michael's semi-covered body. The muscles in his mangled back rippled and contracted as he breathed, struggling to mask his pain. Beads of sweat lined his forehead and matted his hair. She longed to reach out and tend his brow, to assure him that everything would be all right. It was excruciating to be so close to him but separated by the watchful gaze of the soldier.

The Bard continued. "Every waking moment I am thinking of you. Just trying to survive, doing anything and everything possible to stay alive until my sentence is over and we can once again be together."

A suffocating sensation tightened Sarah's throat. "I am sure she has done everything in her power to try to find you."

"Be that as it may, she does not know what I have endured, all in the hope of being with her again. I would like you to write the following: Alas, my love, I know we have been apart a long time. I would not blame you if you had forgotten me and married another." He stared at her wedding ring.

Blushing, Sarah felt his stare burn her hand and hid the offending ring under the desk. "I am sure, Bard, that she would not have married, if she had known you were alive. If indeed, she has given her affections to another, perhaps that other told her you were dead and was there to comfort her as she mourned the loss of her one true love. I do know that I can promise you that she will never find happiness or true love with anyone other than her first and only love."

All at once hysterical yelling reverberated throughout the hospital. Sarah's guard grabbed one of the convict orderlies as he raced past. "What in God's name has happened?"

"One of the convicts has a knife against the throat of the assistant surgeon. He's threatening to kill him. I've got to get help," the man panted, panic stricken.

The soldier stood at the doorway, uncertain of how to proceed. The cries grew more urgent.

Making his decision, he grabbed Sarah by the arm. "Please, Mrs. Thornton. I need you to come with me back to the dispensary, now! You will be safe in there until I return." The soldier pulled Sarah, protesting, from the room.

Sarah paced the dispensary, listening to the sounds coming down the corridor. She cautiously opened the door and peered out. From where she stood she could see the open door of Michael's room. She was so close she could almost hear him breathing. Her heart ached to be with him, hold him, protect him, love him.

Before she allowed her doubting mind to stop her, she again found herself staring down at the man she loved with all her heart.

"You came back!" He winked and all Sarah's defences melted. "Perhaps we could finish my letter? I always finish my letters to my love with a nursery rhyme. She knows it well." His blue eyes never left hers for a moment as he recited:

> *"Lavenders blue dilly, dilly*
> *Lavenders green*
> *When I am king dilly, dilly*
> *You shall be my queen."*

Sarah could not help but be drawn into the heart rending tenderness of his gaze. She let herself become lost in their warmth, remembering the first time that they had shared the rhyme. "You have forgotten the last two verses." Her voice faltered.

"Roses are red dilly, dilly
Violets are blue
Because you love me dilly, dilly
I will love you.

Let the birds sing dilly, dilly
And the lambs play
We shall be safe dilly, dilly
Out of harm's way."

She fell to her knees beside him, their faces so close she could feel his warm breath on her cheek. "I will keep you safe always," she mouthed.

"Sarah, you're here, I can't believe it," he whispered into her hair.

"Shh!" She put her finger to his lips.

His body trembled as she stroked his cheek, and felt his stubbled jaw wet with tears. She knew the ache of love and longing that burdened his heart, for it was mirrored in her own. As she pushed back his hair from his fevered brow their eyes met. The depth of his love was evident and she knew then that her guilt was unfounded and that her love was pure; as pure as the day that she had first gazed into the depths of those blue eyes. Ever so gently, their lips touched.

"Mrs. Thornton." The surgeon entered the room, flicking through papers. "It has become necessary for me to ask you to leave. You will have to finish the letter later."

He looked up and stopped. "Mrs. Thornton. Ma'am. You are a married woman!"

Chapter Thirty-Five

Edmund touched a hand to his swollen face and winced. He tried to coax his eyes open. What on earth had happened? His head was spinning and it hurt to breathe. Vague recollections of being dragged through the pines danced at the edge of his consciousness. He seemed to remember raised excited voices. But nothing was making any sense. Forcing his eyes open he found himself in virtual darkness. He could feel cold dampness surging through his body, only then did he realise that he was sitting on a rough stone floor. His befuddled mind tried to piece together what had happened. He tried to raise himself to his knees. His legs felt heavy and he could hear the sound of clanking chains very close to him.

Gaining his feet with much difficulty, he reached out and felt along the stone wall for any sign of familiar surroundings, led only by a sliver of light emanating from somewhere beneath him. His fingers scraped against a cumbersome wooden door to which he desperately pressed his ear. He could make out the muffled voices of two men laying bets on how long Edward Lawton would swing on the gibbet.

Panic gripped him. Instantly he comprehended the horror of his plight. *My God, they think I am Edward Lawton!* He lunged for the door but the weight of the ball and chain fettered about his ankles pinioned him to the ground. He slumped to his knees, hitting his head on the stone wall.

Exhausted and in a haze of pain, Edmund sat where he had fallen. There was another sound. He realised he was not alone in this tiny, dank cell. The sound of weeping came from one of the corners. As his eyes fought to adjust to the dim light he could see a young lad huddled against the far wall, rocking back and forth, weeping. "I didn't do it, I didn't do it."

Disturbing memories of the face and voice of another young convict, of Michael, began to haunt him, awakening his conscience. *"I didn't tell, Edmund. I kept my word, I didn't tell."*

Remorse and guilt engulfed Edmund, his stomach turned. *Devil's breath! He didn't tell. Michael kept his word, kept my secret even though it cost him everything.*

He struggled to his feet and shuffled clumsily toward the corner of the cell opposite the boy. He cast his eyes around the damp, claustrophobic space and realised that he was now living Michael's nightmare, but unlike Michael, his was of his own making. Michael had waited in the hope that Edmund would come to his aid, but there was no such hope here for Edmund.

He held his shaking hands up in front of his face, recalling that it wasn't so long ago that he had considered using these very hands to end Michael's days.

His head throbbed. Blood trickled down his cheek from the opened wound on his temple. He pulled and yanked at his clothes, trying feverishly to relieve the scratching and itching that was swarming across his body.

It was then he remembered dressing in a convict's coarse garb. How on earth could he ever explain why he was dressed like this? How could he explain his willingness to sneak into the hospital to kill an innocent man? Hot tears began to run down his cheeks. This was not the behaviour of an officer and a British gentleman. He had sworn an oath to uphold the values of the regiment. He had made it his responsibility to make sure all the soldiers in his command understood that upholding the honour of the regiment was of paramount importance. His own motto, the one he strove to live by, now teased the edges of his confused consciousness: *The needs of the regiment far outweigh the needs of the individual.*

He had forgotten his own teachings. He had lowered his standard to the level of a convict, to the level of Edward Lawton.

No, Edmund realised, he had fallen even lower. Lawton had tried to do away with those who had oppressed him, while he himself had felt no compunction at the idea of killing his best friend for his own personal gain.

He had betrayed everything he held dear. He had dishonoured his regiment, his family, but mostly Sarah and Michael. He could see nothing to live for now. He could never redeem himself to his Sarah or to his regiment.

The man standing in the dock was almost unrecognisable, his clothes and hair matted by blood and mud, his eye blackened and swollen. Judge Forsyth stared at him, trying to see some sign of remorse.

This was a very different man to the one that has appeared before him so many times. He was usually such a defiant man, so outspoken. But today he looked like a man broken, bereft of feelings, a man lost.

The judge reverently placed the square of black cloth over his white wig. A hushed silence fell over the packed police court, waiting for him to pronounce judgement.

Clearing his throat, Judge Forsyth spoke in a loud, commanding voice. "Prisoner in the dock, the convict known as Edward Lawton, you are convicted of inciting mutiny, murder and escaping from custody. You will be taken from this place back to your cell from whence, later this day, you will be taken to the place of execution where you shall be hung by the neck until dead. God have mercy on your soul."

Judgement had been made and his fate sealed, although if Edmund was honest with himself, he had sealed his own fate the instant he conspired against Michael. In his attempts to show Sarah the depth of his love, this would be the only honourable deed he had done, for if he truly loved her, he should set her free. Edmund determined to set things right. He could not undo the suffering he had forced Michael to endure but he could now be the man he had led Sarah to believe he was, strong, brave and honest. Yes, his fate was decided, but it was his own decision to put an end to the suffering of his friends and to put things to right.

There was a sharp knock at the cell door. The peephole creaked open and Reverend Bayley's face appeared. "I have come to help you make your peace with your maker, my son."

Edmund stood back in the darkest corner of the cell and tried to make his voice sound coarser, more like that of a hardened criminal than an English Officer. "I not be worthy to be in yo'r 'oly presence, sir."

"The Lord listens to all who are truly repentant, my son."

Edmund thought for a moment, not wanting to risk the chance of recognition but still in fear for his mortal soul. "Pr'aps, sir, we could pray through the closed door?"

"If that is what you wish, my son, I will not argue with a condemned man."

Edmund breathed a sigh of relief as he heard what he supposed was a chair being dragged up to the cell door.

Edmund found solace in the minister's monotone voice, as the man recited prayers and read passages from the scriptures. He let the voice wash over him, finding spiritual peace in the rhythm of the prayers, all the while becoming more resolved in his decision.

He heard the minister stand. Presuming that the man was about to leave, Edmund urged him to stay a moment longer.

"Of course, my son, I will be with you for as long as you need."

"Beggin' your pard'n, Reveren'. In me last moments on this 'ere earth, pen and paper would help ease me soul."

"Ah, so you are able to write, a worthy accomplishment indeed. If you feel that the written word will help prepare you for what is to come, then pen and paper will be yours at once."

Edmund requested that the peephole be left open to let in more light so that he could write. Balancing the paper and ink on the wooden board that Reverend Bayley had supplied as his desk, Edmund awkwardly tried to write, tried to write what was in his heart, tried to make amends for the past.

Tears smudged the ink as he wrote, his heart wrenching apart. Regaining control, he reread the spidery scrawl, hoping that Judge Forsyth would be able to decipher it, hoping he would be forgiven. Satisfied, he sealed it with the red wax left for him.

Banging on the door of his cell, he called to the turnkey. Edmund could see the man's bloodshot eye staring at him through the door's peephole. "I have a letter for Judge Forsyth." Edmund waited as the door was shoved open only a crack. He pushed the letter through. "Make sure he gets it after I have left this world, not before, mind. He will know what to do."

The sky was a brilliant blue, flecked with drifts of clouds. The air was filled with the pungent smell of pine and the taste of salt spray.

Dressed in white, his hands pinioned behind his back, Edmund shuffled between the two warders toward the blacksmith's forge. As the smithy removed his fetters, Edmund calmly watched the hangman's preparations, as he had on so many previous occasions. The man generously greased the rope hanging from the high beam, checking it was knotted correctly, and that the length had been accurately measured to account for Edmund's huge frame.

Reverend Bayley met him at the forge. Edmund noticed that he never looked up from his prayer book. He had done this final walk many times before.

Now at peace with his decision Edmund took those last steps toward the gallows, keeping his head bowed low, deep in prayer. His dark curls shadowing his still swollen face to all onlookers. No-one disturbed the condemned man during his last discourse with his maker.

Only, as he took his first step up to the gallows stairs, did his resolve start to falter. He looked back in vain, searching for Sarah, to *see* her one last time, to gaze into her clear blue eyes, to see her smile, to inhale her scent of lavender. She had for a time, made him the most fortunate of men.

He stumbled onto the platform, now trembling, whilst the hangman adjusted the heavy noose around his neck.

The magistrate took his place beside the condemned man and held up his hand for silence. Clearing his throat he began to read from a heavy journal, the long list of crimes and infringements attributed to Edward Lawton.

The voice faded into the background of Edmund's tortured mind. *Sarah, she's waiting for me, she doesn't know this has happened. We could start again. I will change for her. I have changed.* He started to breathe faster, his nervous eyes searching for an escape.

He looked down then, and saw his regiment resplendent in their uniforms, boots blackened and buckles shining in the sun. Remorse again filled his thoughts. What right did he have to tarnish his beloved Eleventh? He became conscious that he was actually proud to be the living epitome of all the Regiment's beliefs and principles, a man willing to give his own life so as not to blacken its reputation. He allowed himself to feel self-righteous in his decision.

Then he felt the rope pull slightly around his neck as he leant forward. Fear gutted him. His mind raced as he scanned the assembled regiment, looking for some sign of recognition, some sign of compassion, but his eyes only met the hollow faces of men forced to watch yet another convict get their comeuppance.

The voice of the magistrate continued to drone on.

Edmund looked around in panic. There was still Judge Forsyth. He knew nothing of Edmund's past and would believe him still to be the honourable man he had known.

As Edmund searched the crowd frantically for the judge he saw Sarah.

His heart leapt. She was so close, standing on the landing at the top of the hospital stairs. It seemed to him that their eyes met for the briefest of moments. But, it was in that brief moment that Edmund finally understood it was not enough merely to love someone. How could he deliberately subject Sarah to a life filled with lies and deceit? No, she deserved better than him. His love for her, and his desire to amend his betrayal, strengthened his resolve. This was his time to be the man she deserved. This was his chance to grant her freedom from his lies.

A hood was lowered over his head, blocking out his last sight of Sarah. But it was of no matter. Her image was imprinted in his memory. He stood straighter then. He stood prouder.

Sarah, Sarah my love.

The gallows' floor gave way beneath him.

Epilogue

Judge Forsyth watched the surgeon check for any signs of life. The man checked for a pulse, he put his ear to the unfortunate man's chest, listening for even the faintest beat of his heart. Finally he held a mirror to the dead man's lips to checking for any mist to appear upon it.

So engrossed was he in watching, that he was startled as a man, breathing heavily, ran up beside him. "Excuse me, sir. The convict, Lawton, asked me to give you this after he was gone. He stressed I was not to give it to you before."

Puzzled, Judge Forsyth took the letter. He broke the seal and began to read.

> *Dear Sir,*
> *I write this as my last will and testament…*

He was just about to re-fold it so that he could read it later when the style of writing caught his eye. Curious, he glanced over the page at the signature:

> *Edmund Thornton, Lieutenant, Her Majesty's Eleventh Regiment of Foot*

"Oh my God!"

"Excuse me, Judge Forsyth," the surgeon interrupted the judge's reading, trying to hand him a parchment. "They are waiting to take the body. Could you please counter sign the death certificate?"

Judge Forsyth looked right through him and yelled at the men who were beginning to lift the body onto the cart. "Stop at once! Put that body down immediately! Gently mind you."

The men looked from the judge to the surgeon for guidance. The surgeon gave an impatient shrug but motioned for them to lower the body down again.

Judge Forsyth began to read.

I, of course, bequeath all my worldly goods to my dear wife, Sarah.

I cannot express in words how happy she made me feel the day she consented to be my wife. I was indeed the most fortunate of men.

But now I must confess to the skulduggery I undertook to win her heart.

Her betrothed, Michael Hanlan, the man I told you was dead, is actually alive and here on this island. He is now known as the Bard.

"Good God," he mumbled, reading on:

It is true we were the very best of friends back home in England. Even then I loved Sarah passionately, sir. But she had eyes for no other man than Mr. Hanlan. I have always known this.

It is I who am solely responsible for Mr. Hanlan's sentence and transportation. I swear it was only meant to be a prank. Drunk, and on a dare, we entered a Romanish Church. When I noticed the silver salver I saw it as the answer to my gambling debts. Mr. Hanlan, to his credit, tried to persuade me to leave it, but I took no notice. I can state with certainty that Mr. Hanlan was only an innocent bystander to my crime.

When we heard the night watchman's rattle, we both ran. I panicked when Mr. Hanlan was captured so dropped the salver behind a gravestone and ran for my life.

Mr. Hanlan believed he owed me a debt of honour because I had saved his young sister from drowning. To my shame I let him take full blame.

I loved Sarah then, as I love her now. I saw Michael's downfall as a way to get him out of Sarah's life. I used him ill. I never envisioned meeting either of them on this island of felons.

It was I, who should have been transported and Mr. Hanlan should have been free to marry his Sarah.

In a jealous rage, I convinced two overseers of the most questionable nature, to spy on the Bard for me and report even the most minor infringement.

You, sir, were most surprised at the change in the Bard. Know now that it was not of the Bard's doing but of my own.

The judge took a moment to pause and think back to the many harsh punishments he had been forced to declare on the Bard, punishments that were not deserved. He could not help but feel a little gratified that he had been right all along about the man, but at the same time he became angry that he had not acted on his own feelings and saved the man from so much pain.

Finding his place he continued to read:

Please be assured, sir, that you did not condemn an innocent man to death this day.

Completely bereft of sanity, I was going to kill Mr. Hanlan – murder probably the best friend I have ever known for my own gratification.

And now sir, I go to my Creator in peace, in the hope I will be forgiven for all the wrong I have done.

I have been justly tried and condemned. I truly believe that this was the most honourable way to make amends to my dear wife Sarah and to my dear friend Michael.

Please tell Sarah I have never loved another. Do not allow her to grieve for me. She and Mr. Hanlan deserve to be together. I implore you, sir. Please do what you can to help him, to help them both.

Judge Forsyth re-read the signature, still trying to fully comprehend what he had read.

He was pensive as he walked over to the body and tentatively lifted the blanket now covering it.

Reeling in the shock of seeing what he now knew to be true, he stumbled backwards. The surgeon rushed over, trying to understand the judge's strange behaviour.

"Get Lieutenant Saunders! Now!" Judge Forsyth barked.

As ordered, Richard Saunders was soon at the judge's side. "You wanted to see me, sir?"

Once again, the judge lifted the blanket. "Were we not at this man's wedding only yesterday?"

Saunders turned and retched.

Judge Forsyth reverently replaced the blanket and said as calmly as he could, "Please, lieutenant, I charge you to send my deepest condolences to Mrs. Thornton and inform her that she is now a widow."

Newspaper clippings found in a diary belonging to Mrs. Margaret Forsyth – deceased April 16th, 1862

Tasmanian Mercury – February 1849
    Shipping arrivals Hobart
    Incoming passengers from Norfolk Island
    Cabin passengers – Judge and Mrs. John Forsyth, Mrs. Edmund Thornton.
    Thirty-three prisoners of the crown in hold.

Tasmanian Mercury – December 1849
    Permission is hereby granted for Mrs. Sarah Thornton, widow, free, to marry indentured servant to Judge Forsyth, Michael Hanlan.

Tasmanian Mercury – March 1850
    His Excellency the Governor directs it to be notified that Her Majesty has been pleased to grant an Absolute Pardon to Michael Hanlan.

Tasmanian Mercury – June 1851
    Shipping departures to London
    Cabin passengers – Judge and Mrs. John Forsyth, Mr. and Mrs. Michael Hanlan esquire, their son, Edmund Thornton Hanlan, and their adopted son, Billy Scott Hanlan.

Author's Note

This novel is a result of an amateur historian's fascination with the history of Norfolk Island, particularly the convict era of the second settlement (1825-1855).

The story is not meant to depict any one event of the second settlement period or any persons who actually lived during that period but rather a mixed tapestry of events.

I hope the purists of history will forgive me and that my story might encourage more people to explore the history of this wonderful small island in the middle of the Pacific Ocean.

JdM
July 2012

About the Author

Winning a place in the inaugural Queensland Redland City Council Writers' competition in 2008 gave Josie de Moor the opportunity to complete her debut novel *Heart of a Beast* under the guidance of author Louise Cusack, writer of romantic fantasy.

A fascination of Australian History was instilled in her at an early age at school. She began researching her own family story in 1979 and has helped many other family historians to discover their roots through her volunteer work at the Queensland Genealogical Society. It is not uncommon to find her traipsing through cemeteries looking for "lost relatives".

South Australian history, her home state, was her first love and then Australia's convict past became an all-consuming passion. She has surrounded herself with an extensive personal library of diaries and works written at the time by people who lived through what we now know as history. Norfolk Island and its second convict settlement captivated her. Dragging her long suffering husband, Robin, on four visits to the island (so far) she has researched extensively every facet of that period.

She lives in Brisbane with her husband and is surrounded by her own extended family of three children and four grandchildren.